LOVING
IN THE
WAR YEARS

Praise for the first edition of
Loving in the War Years

An important book of the purest perception, courage, intensity, power. Innovative, heartachingly beautiful at times, deeply honest—it can act as a change-making book.

—Tillie Olsen, author, Tell Me a Riddle

From childhood in California to the tenements of New York, Moraga records with shocking honesty her search for identity, questioning each step which leads her into the arms of Malinche, her violated-legendary mother, her contemporary sister-lover.

—Rudolfo A. Anaya, author, Bless Me, Ultima

Una realidad que se desnuda ante la luz para sacarse las espinas de fuego negro—lyrical, evocative and well-calibrated pieces—searching through layers of experience common to all Chicanas—finding the very source of freedom—voice and action.

—Lucha Corpi, author, Black Widow's Wardrobe

As a poet, Moraga brings to her nonfiction essays images so hard, honest, and disturbing that her political analysis is breathtakingly personal and immediate.

—San Francisco Chronicle

A beautiful tribute to the cultures that have sustained Moraga, a book that is insightful and relentlessly tough.

—Sojourner, The Women's Forum

Moraga boldly examines the meaning of being Chicana and lesbian in the United States today.

—Women's Review of Books

Moraga draws from her love of her mother's home, the sense of community among Chicana women, the smell of candles in church, and the spiritual need to respect something beyond herself to create a portrait of beauty, anger, and independence.

—Holly Smith, 500 Great Books by Women

LOVING IN THE WAR YEARS

Cherríe L. Moraga

LO QUE NUNCA PASÓ POR SUS LABIOS

Expanded Edition
South End Press Classics Series
SOUTH END PRESS
Cambridge, Massachusetts

Cover design by Ellen P. Shapiro
Cover and inside photographs by Hulleah J. Tsinhnahjinnie
Page design and production by Terry J. Allen
Printed in Canada

Library of Congress Cataloging-in-Publication Data

Moraga, Cherríe.
Loving in the war years : lo que nunca pasó por sus labios / by Cherríe Moraga. 2nd ed.
p. cm. (South End Press classics series ; vol. 6)
Includes bibliographical references.
ISBN 0-89608-627-5 (hard cover) — ISBN 0-89608-626-7 (pbk.)
ISBN 978-0-89608-626-5
I. Mexican American women — Literary collections. 2. Feminism — Literary collections.
I. Title. II. South End Press classics ; . 6.

PS3563.O753 L6 2000
818'.5409dc21

00-057344

South End Press, 7 Brookline Street #1, Cambridge, MA 02139-4146
www.southendpress.org
10 09 08   4 5

CONTENTS

DEDICATION

Para mi familia de "scratch" . . .
and all the rest of the tribe.

AGRADECIMIENTOS

Gracias to all the women who helped me in the writing of this book throughout its many incarnations, most especially: Gloria Anzaldúa, Elly Bulkin, Jan Clausen, Myrtha Chabrán, Amber Hollibaugh, Deborah Geneva Leoni, Minnie Bruce Pratt, Mirtha Quintanales, and Barbara Smith.

MAS AGRADECIMIENTOS

In the completion of this new edition of *Loving in the War Years*, I wish to thank the following cadre of conspirators: Ricardo A. Bracho, for his fine critical mind's eye and for keeping me intellectually "al corriente;" Irma Mayorga for her invaluable research and passion para el detallito; Hulleah J. Tsinhnahjinnie for the generous use of her photographic images; and Celia Herrera Rodríguez for moving my mind through the heart and providing all that home-based support. Also, to Loie Hayes of South End Press for many years of service to radical literature.

Amar Durante Los Años de Guerra

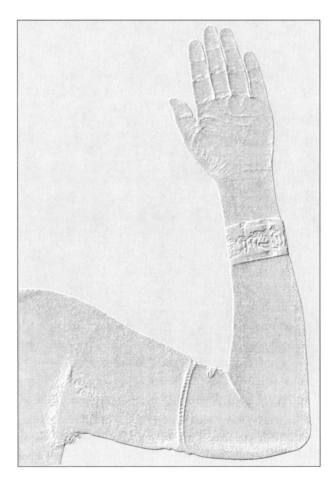

LOOKING BACK

FOREWORD TO THE SECOND EDITION

As my Beloved starts the ceremonial fire, we turn in the moon's direction to watch its near-fullness crest over the darkening hills. In the Aztec tradition, the moon is a warrior-sister dismembered by the male god of war and exiled into the darkness of the night. Is this not you, hermanaguerrera, la Coyolxauhqui returned, that woman of the earth, broken into pieces, that moon-diosa rising up from behind those juniper-blue tejano hills?

Written at the memorial of artist-activist
Marsha Gómez (1951-1998).

In 1977 when I wrote the first poems of what later would become part of *Loving in the War Years*, I had never heard of Coyolxauhqui, severed into pieces in the war against her brother, but I knew her brokeness.* I had felt the breast of my lesbian desire amputated from the warrior loins of my cultura. What I had imagined would protect me—the armored helmet of my feminism—provided no shield against the neogringo theft of tongue and tierra. She, like me, was a woman betrayed by her brother. She was an ancient Xicanawarrior deported into darkness. I, a young Xicanadyke, writing in exile.

Without knowing, I looked for Coyolxauhqui in these dark wartime writings of twenty years ago, the dim reflection of my own pale moon-face lighting my way. *I am not the first,* I kept telling myself, *I am not the only one to walk this road.* But it felt so at the time, the danger of putting the words "lesbian" and "Chicana" together on the same page, within the same line. The danger of walking in the body of she who put them together. The month that *Loving* was to be released, I escaped to the

---

* The icon of the moon goddess Coyolxauhqui is a huge stone disk, which contains the figure of a mutilated warrior-woman wearing traditional Aztec regalia. The circular figure seems to be in motion, her parts rolling around and about, one on top of the other, as described in the Aztec myth. Accordingly, Coyolxauhqui was cut into pieces by her brother (the sun god, Huitzilopotchli) and her body parts hurled down the mountainside of Coatepec, where the battle between the moon and sun took place. For further discussion on the myth, see "Looking for the Insatiable Woman" in this volume.

anonymity of México, somehow thinking the distance would shield me from a more profound banishment waiting to happen. Still, I thought only of return, someday, to my Califas, where I could be all my fragmented parts at once: the re-membered Coyolxauhqui taking up permanent residence in Aztlán.

Twenty years later, I can say . . . I am returned. Neither Aztec goddess nor completely whole, but well accustomed to the darkness. In looking back at the writer I was a generation ago, I am not ashamed. Of the voice. Of the writing. I see this same young poet in the writings of my daughter-students, how they forge the shape of their coloredwomanhood through the bodies of their mothers and their mothers' histories: the deaths, the suicides, the betrayals, the silences. Twenty years ago, my intimate reflections on my mother served as the focal point of my meditations on "familia," which have gradually evolved, through the 90s, into broader reflections on Xicanos and Xicanas as "tribe" and "nation."* The final section of this new edition, "A Flor de labios" speaks to this evolution, drawing from seedling ideas I first germinated in *Loving in the War Years*.

> [T]he foundation [of our families] is the *earth beneath the floorboards of our homes.* We must split wood, dig bare-fisted into the packed dirt to find out what we really have to hold in our hands as ground.
>
> —*A Long Line of Vendidas*

Earth. Dirt. Ground. Land.

And what are these essays, these stories and poems, other than just shovel, hoe and pickax "digging up the dirt" in an attempt to uncover a buried Xicana/o history, both personal *and* political. I am ever-grateful to feminism for teaching me this, that *political* oppression is always experienced *personally* by someone. This feminist tenet, *the personal is political,* has provided me the poet's permission to use my own life as evidence of what I believe to be true about *us* and *them.* Us and them: that binary that binds us in its ever-shifting shapes of body and thought.

So, I begin here again: a new introduction to writings which are both old and new, once or twice read and never read. I begin again in a new

---

* *The Last Generation* examines these themes at length; published by South End Press ten years after *Loving in the War Years*.

millennium, which means little to me except that I know my life is significantly more than half over. As a child, I had anticipated this "coming of age," regularly counting the years ahead to configure how old I'd be at the turn of the century. Now I barely believe in *their* calendar, how they count backward to invent a history in Christ's birth, and Columbus, and Cortéz's arrival into the translucent turquoise waters of a misnomered América. How they count forward to invent a "nation" since the declaration of independence of whitesons from whitefathers.

So, some things have changed. An evolution of thought, I'd like to believe. I'd like to believe that the voice of a forty-seven-year-old veterana Chicana lesbian writer, recorded in this foreword and in the final section of this book, juxtaposed with an emerging Chicana writer twenty years earlier, might provide some insights for each of us about our own evolving history and política. Yes, some things have changed. Between the first and second edition of *Loving*, the USSR was dissolved, the Sandinista Revolution was dismantled, AIDS was "discovered" and took on pandemic proportions. Audre Lorde died, Cesar Chávez died, Toni Cade Bambara died, my abuelita passed on to the spirit world and mis queridos padres grow to fear disability and death in their weakening bodies and advancing years. Affirmative action and bilingual education were outlawed in California, and cancer has clustered throughout the central agricultural valley of California and along the poisoned perimeter (the border) of Aztlán.

When I compiled the first edition of *Loving in the War Years*, I did so without the aid of a computer; twenty years later, the computer has invaded the lives of most middleclass citizens of "developed" countries. Thanks to a global internet, the computer is the fastest-growing site of amerikan investment of time and money. It is where Amerika shops, dates, reads, writes, makes pornography, and makes profit. It is where middleclasswhitekids can be college dropouts and become millionaires overnight. The computer is also where getting this book to press took about a quarter of the time it would have twenty years ago. It is where I have found innumerable resources on prison rights, human rights abuse, Chicanaindígena organizing, public protests against latino-loathing legislation, y mas y mas y mas informacíon, at times more than one small being can handle.

Twenty years. A litany of change, political and personal. Twenty years ago, I was not a mother, only a daughter. Still, I can state, unequivocally, as I did in the first edition of *Loving*, "It is the daughters who are my audience." And any son who will listen. Now, in fact, I have a son of seven-years, who I hope *is* listening. I also have a whole family of queer and blood relations I couldn't have dreamed possible at twenty-seven. (Is this the road to Coyolxauhqui's re-memberment?)

Since the first publication of *Loving*, I have also become a playwright, my transition into dramatic writing, the direct result of *Loving*'s completion. I tell my writing students who fear they will always be confined to autobiography, "When *Loving* was done and out of my hands, I felt an enormous emotional burden being lifted from me. I had finally told my own story, for better or for worse, and felt free of it, free for other voices, other stories to enter me." I have been writing drama professionally for over fifteen years now. It is my fictionalized voice made possible through the autobiographical musings of my nonfiction writings. Theater has also become, for me, a new and oftentimes embattled forum for cultural criticism. In the meantime, I have made a living mostly as a teacher and lecturer, traveling to conferences and colleges around the country, where I have witnessed in just one generation the deradicalization of many ethnic and feminist studies programs.

Twenty years later and this a bit of the biography of my life, my times.

. . . . .

When they discovered El Templo Mayor beneath the walls of this city, they had not realized that it was She who discovered them. Nothing remains buried forever. Not even memory, especially not memory.

—*Giving Up the Ghost*

Maybe what I like best about writing is that it always knows better than you where you're going, if you let it. This is what also makes writing so dangerous, that it can reveal to you what you didn't know you knew. I wrote the lines above, a year after *Loving in the War Years'* publication. I was describing how Mexican workers, repairing underground electrical lines in the central Zócalo in Mexico City, had inadvertently unearthed what would later be revealed as the ruins of El Templo Mayor, the last of the major Aztec temples. Without thinking, I referred to the temple as "She." What I learned later is that the first evidence of the Templo that workers "discovered" under the "walls of (that) city" was the giant, 3.25 meters in diameter, stone disk sculpture of Coyolxauhqui, the dismembered moon goddess. From her, all the rest of the Templo would be eventually unearthed, where it stands resurrected today.

I had called the templo "She." And without my knowing it, She, Coyolxauhqui, was speaking to me. Me, her distant mixed-blood pocha relative, living in the northern land of her ancestors. Maybe these are just delusions of my own self-importance. But another thing I learned from feminism is that such self-indulgence is critical to the writing process. Because without indulging our fears, our fantasies, our fury, how then are we to land upon truth? And, from that time forward, I decided maybe I could remember (know) more than what the small biography of my life determined. Maybe I could re-member Coyolxauhqui at least in this writing, this teaching, this praying, this home.

So, that gives me hope. That as artists we might have something to contribute between and beyond what we are allowed to live here in this americanprison of forgetfulness, durante los años de guerra.

oakaztlán, califas,
8 de junio 2000

INTRODUCCIÓN
TO THE FIRST EDITION

SUEÑO

My lover and I are in a prison camp together.
We are in love in wartime.
A young soldier working as a guard has befriended us.
We ask him honestly—the truth—"are we going to die?"
He answers, "yes, it's almost certain." I contemplate escaping. Ask him to help us. He
blanches. "That is impossible," he says. I regret asking him, fearing recriminations.

I see the forest through the fence on my right. I think, the place between the trees, I could
burrow through there, toward freedom? Two of us would surely be spotted. One of us has
a slim chance. I think of leaving my lover, imprisoned. But immediately I understand that
we must, at all costs, remain with each other. Even unto death. That it is our being togeth-
er that makes the pain, even our dying, human.

Loving in the war years.

1

Este libro covers a span of seven years of writing. The first poems were
written in 1976 when I was still in Los Angeles, living out my lesbianism
as a lie on my job and a secret to my family. The two main essays of the
book, "La Güera" and "A Long Line of Vendidas," were completed in
1979 and 1983, respectively.* Now I write the final introduction here in
Brooklyn, New York, "out-to-the-world" it feels to me to be in print.

Tonight the summer heat takes on the flavor it had when I first moved into
this room, makes me tired by the thought of all this moving and working.
How slow and hard change is to come. How although this book has taken
me from Los Angeles, north to Berkeley, across the Bay to San Francisco,
across the country to Boston and Brooklyn, south to México and back again
to Califas, sigo siendo la hija de mi mamá. My mother's daughter.

---

* The selections are not arranged chronologically by dates written; rather, I have tried to create an emotional/political chronology.

My mother's daughter who at ten years old knew she was queer. Queer to believe that God cared so much about me, he intended to see me burn in hell; that unlike other children, I was not to get by with a clean slate. I was born into this world with complications. I had been chosen, marked to prove my salvation. Todavía soy bien católica—filled with guilt, passion and incense and the inherent Mexican faith that there is meaning to nuestro sufrimiento en el mundo.

The first time I went to the Mexican basilica where el retrato de La Virgen de Guadalupe hovers over a gilded altar, I was shocked to see that below it ran a moving escalator. The escalator was not one that brought people up to the image that we might reverently kiss her feet; but rather it moved people along from side to side and through as quickly as possible. A moving sidewalk built to keep the traffic going. In spite of the irreverence imposed by such technology, the most devout of the Mexican women—las pobres, few much older than I—clung to the ends of the handrailing of the moving floor, crossing themselves, gesturing besos al retrato, their hips banging up against the railing over and over again as it tried to force them off and away. They stayed. In spite of the machine. They had come to spend their time with La Virgen.

I left the church in tears, knowing how for so many years I had closed my heart to the passionate pull of such faith that promised no end to the pain. I grew white. Fought to free myself from my culture's claim on me. It seemed I had to step outside my familia to see what we as a people were doing suffering. This is my politics. This is my writing. For as much as the two have eventually brought me back to my familia, there is no fooling myself that it is my education, my "consciousness" that separated me from them, that forced me to leave home. This is what has made me the outsider so many Chicanos, very near to me in circumstance, fear.

I am a child. I watch my mamá, mis tías en una procesión cada día llegando a la puerta de mi abuela. Needing her, never doing enough for her. I remember lying on my bed midday. The sun streaming through the long window, thin sheer curtains. Next door I can hear them all. Se están peleando. Mi abuela giving the cold shoulder, not giving in. Each daughter vying for a place with her. The cruel gossip. Las mentiras. My mother trying to hold onto the truth, her version of the story, su integridad.

I put my head back on the pillow and count the years this has been going on. The competition for her favor. My grandmother's control of them. I count my mother's steps as I hear her click high-heeled angry down the gravel driveway, through the fence, up the back steps. She's coming in. Estará llorando. Otra vez. I tell my sister reading a book next to me, "How many years, JoAnn? It can't be this way for us too when we grow up."

Mi abuelita se muere muy lentamente. Están cerrados los ojos, y su boca está callada. El hospital le da comida por las venas. No habla ella. No canta como cantaba. She does not squeeze my mother's hand tight in her fight against la sombra de su propia muerte. She does not squeeze the life out of her. Ya no. Está durmiendo mi abuela, esperando a La Muerte.

And what goes with her? My claim to an internal dialogue where el gringo does not penetrate? Su memoria de noventa y seis años going back to a time where "nuestra cultura" was not the subject of debate. *I write this book because we are losing ourselves to the gavacho. I mourn my brother in this.*

Sueño: 5 de enero 1983
My grandmother appears outside la iglesia. Standing in front as she used to do after la misa. I am so surprised that she is well enough to go out again, be dressed, be in the world. I am elated to see her, to know I get to have the feel of her again in my life. She is, however, in great pain. She shows me her leg, which has been operated on. The wound is like a huge crater in her calf—crusted, open, a gaping hole. I feel her pain so critically.

Sueño: 7 de enero 1983
En el sueño trataba de sacar yo una foto de mi abuela y de mi mamá. Mientras una mujer me esperaba en la cama. The pull and tug present themselves en mis sueños. Deseo para las mujeres, anhelo para la familia. I want to take the photo of my grandmother because I know she is dying. I want one last picture. The woman keeps calling me to her bed. She wants me. I keep postponing her.

Después soñé con mi hermano. El ha regresado a la familia, not begging forgiveness, but acknowledging his transgressions against la familia. Somos unidos.

x/CHERRÍE L. MORAGA

2

Can you go home? Do your parents know? Have they read your work? These are the questions I am most often asked by Chicanos, especially students. It's as if they are hungry to know if it's possible to have both—your own life and the life of the familia. I explain to them that sadly, this is a book my family will never see. And yet, how I wish I could share this book with them. How I wish I could show them how much I have taken them to heart, even my father's silence. What he didn't say working inside me as passionately as my mother wept it.

It is difficult for me to separate in my mind whether it is my writing or my lesbianism which has made me an outsider to my family. The obvious answer is both. For my lesbianism first brought me into writing. My first poems were love poems. That's the source—*el amor, el deseo*—that brought me into politics, that taught me my first major lesson about writing: it is the measure of my life. I cannot write what I am not willing to live up to. Is it for this reason I so often fear my own writing, fear that it will jump up and push me off some precipice?

Women daily change my work. How can it be that I have always hungered for, and feared, falling in love as much as I do writing from my heart? Each changes you forever. For me, sex has always been part of the question of freedom, the freedom to want passionately. To live it out in the body of the poem, in the body of the flesh. So that when I feel the stirrings of creativity, it is a fresh inhale of new life, life I want to breathe back into my work, into my woman. And I long to be a lover like youth.

I watch my changes in the women I love.

JOURNAL ENTRY: 2 DE JULIO 1982

It takes the greatest of effort even to put pen to paper—so much weighing on me. It's as if I am bankrupt of feeling, but that's not really so. My lover comes into my room, sees me face flat on the bed, gathers me into her arms. I say I am depressed and she reminds me of how I tell her so often how depression is not a feeling. Depression covers a feeling that doesn't have a chance to come out. Keeping it down. Keeping the writing back.

So often throughout my work on this book I felt I could not write because I have a movement on my shoulder, a lover on my shoulder, a family over my shoulder. On some level you have to be willing to lose it all to write—to risk telling the truth that no one may want to hear, even you. Not that, in fact, you must lose, only que el riesgo siempre radica en el acto de escribir, amenazándote. In relation to my family, I realize now that even as my writing functioned to separate me from them (I cannot share my work with them), it has freed me to love them from places in myself that had before been mired in unexpressed pain. Writing has ultimately brought me back to them. They don't need this book. They have me.

The issue of being a "movement writer" is altogether different. Sometimes I feel my back will break from the pressure I feel to speak for others. A friend told me once how it was no wonder I had called the first book I co-edited (with Gloria Anzaldúa) *This Bridge Called My Back. You have chronic back trouble,* she says. Funny, I had never considered this most obvious connection, all along my back giving me constant pain. And the spot that hurts the most is the muscle that controls the movement of my fingers and hands while typing. I feel it now straining at my desk.

Riding on the train with another friend, I ramble on about the difficulty of finishing this book, feeling like I am being asked by all sides to be a "representative" of the race, the sex, the sexuality—or at all costs to avoid that. "You don't speak for me! For the community!" My friend smiles kindly, almost amused, at me across the aisle among the sea of grey suits and ties. We are on the commuter train and no one would give up their single seat for us to sit together. We speak in secret code. Nos hablamos español.

"Ah, Chavalita," she says to me. "Tú necesitas viajar para que veas lo que en verdad es la comunidad. There's really no such thing as community among políticos. Community is simply the way people live a life together. And they're doing it all over the world. The only way to write for la comunidad is to write so completely from your heart what is your own personal truth. This is what touches people."

Some days I feel my writing wants to break itself open. Speak in a language that maybe no "readership" can follow. What does it mean that the Chicana writer, if she truly follows her own voice, may depict a world so specific, so privately ours, so full of "foreign" language to the anglo reader, there will be no publisher for it. The people who can understand it, don't/won't/can't read it. How can I be a writer in this? I have been translating my experience out of fear of an aloneness too great to bear. I have learned analysis as a mode to communicate what I feel the experience itself already speaks for. The combining of poetry and essays in this book is the compromise I make in the effort to be understood. In Spanish, "compromiso" means obligation or commitment And I guess, in fact, I write as I do because I am committed to communicating with both sides of myself.

I am the daughter of a Chicana and an anglo. I think most days I am an embarassment to both groups. I sometimes hate the white in me so viciously that I long to forget the obligation my skin has imposed upon my life. To speak two tongues, one of privilege, one of oppression. I must. But I will not double-talk and I refuse to let *anybody's* movement determine for me what is safe and fair to say.

3

The completion of this book finds me in the heart of change. So there is no definitive statement to make here in this introduction that will prepare you for the ever-evolving story of my life. For that is all this collection really is/can be—my story of change. But for whom have I tried so steadfastly to communicate? Whom have I worried over in this writing? Who is my audience?

Todavía soy la hija de mi mamá. Keep thinking, *it's the daughters.* It's the daughters who remain loyal to the mother, although this loyalty is not always reciprocated. To be free means on some level to release that painful devotion when it begins to punish us. Stop the chain of events. La procesión de mujeres, sufriendo. Dolores my grandmother, Dolores her daughter, Dolores her daughter's daughter. Free the daughter to love her own daughter. It is the daughters who are my audience.

I write this on the deathbed of my abuela. We have made one last procession to her: my mother, my sister, her daughter and I. My grandmother's eyes are open today. I hold the bone of her skull in the palm of my hand. It is a light bird-weight.

I whisper into her better ear. "¿Abuelita? ¿Me reconoce? Soy Cherríe, grandma. Acabo de llegar de Nueva York."

"¡Ay, Chorizo!"* She recognizes me. "Mi'jita!" Pulling my head into the deep bowl of her thin neck, she kisses me. "Mi chorizito! Tengo hambre! ¡Quiero Chorizo! ¡Tengo tanta hambre!" She kids as she used to and as always I give her the fleshy part of my arm for her to mimick taking a bite from it.

"¿Dónde está tu mamá?" she wants to know.

"Aquí estoy, mamá." My mother grabs her hand.

"Elvira. ¿Y La JoAnn, está aquí también?"

"Sí, grandma, aquí stoy y Erin," my sister says lifting her daughter up to give my abuela a kiss.

"Hi, little grandma," Erin says softly.

"¡Ay, mi chulita!" She wraps her thin veined hands around Erin's cheeks, then gnashes her teeth together, shaking her head, pretending like she wants to eat her up. It seems to me that my abuelita has never been so full of life.

I am holding the moment. La línea de las mujeres, la raíz de nuestra familia. Mi mamá tiene tanto orgullo en este momento. She has taught us well to value these simple signs of love.

I write this on the deathbed of mi abuela. On the table of a new life spread out for us to eat from.

La muerte de mi abuela. Y yo nunca le hablé en la lengua que entendiera.

Brooklyn, New York,
1983

*A Mexican sausage. The nickname my grandmother has for me.

THE VOICES OF THE FALLERS

Because Jay Freeman was imprisoned at the age of nineteen for more than twenty years because she murdered the son of her lesbian lover by throwing him off a cliff. And, because, at the age of nineteen, my high school friend Charlotte, also a lesbian, fell from a cliff and died.

for M.

You were born queer with the dream
of flying
from an attic with a trap
door opening
to a girl who could
handle a white horse
with wings   riding her
away   opening
to a girl who could
save a woman
on a white horse
riding her
away.

I was born queer with the dream
of falling
the small sack of my body
dropping
off a ledge
suddenly.
                    Listen.
                    Can you hear my mouth crack
                    open   the sound
                    of my lips bending
                    back against the force
                    of the fall?

Listen.
Put your ear deep
down
through the   opening
of my throat and
listen.

. . . . .

The nun said
"Young lady
you have a chip
on your shoulder
that's going to get you
in plenty of trouble
some day."

The queer
flicks off
the chip
with the nonchalance
with the grace
with the cool
brush of lint
from a 200-dollar
three-piece

the chip tumbling
off
her shoulder

her   shoulder first
tumbling
off
the cliff   the legs

following
over
her head   the chip

spinning onto the classroom floor
(silently imagined)
her body's
dead

silent

collision
with the sand.

> *I'm falling*
> *can't you see*
> *I'm*
> *falling?*

. . . . .

DARE ME
DARE ME
DARE ME
to push this kid off
the cliff   DARE
ME
Some queer
mother I am
who would kill her kid
to save her own neck
from cracking
on the way
down

You bet your ass I am
if push comes to shove
the kid goes
queer

> *I'm falling*
> *can't you see*
> *I'm falling?*

. . . . .

It was not an accident

I knew then sitting in the row next to her she would not survive she could not survive this way this unprotected defiance her shoulders pushing up against me grabbing me by the collar up against the locker "motherfucker you mess with my girlfriend?"

her pale face twitching
cover it up
cover it up
I wished she would
cover it up
for both our sakes
she would not
survive this way
pushing
people
around.

. . . . .

When I fell
from the cliff   she tells me
it was the purest move
I ever made she tells me
she thought of me
as a kind of consolation
surviving
just as she made
the move
to fall
just as her shoulders split
the air.

Do you know what it feels like finally
to be up

against nothing?
Oh it's like flying, Cherríe
I'm flying

> *I'm falling*
> *can't you see*
> *I'm*
> *falling?*

. . . . .

She confesses to me—

I held the boy's body between my hands
for a moment it was like
making love
the bones of my fingers resting
between the bones of his ribcage
I held him there
I guess we both felt   safe
for a split   second
but then he grew
stiff and then he resisted
so I pushed
up against him
I pushed until the wall
of his body vanished
into the air so thick
it was due to eat both of us up
sooner or later.

> *I'm falling*
> *can't you see*
> *I'm*
> *falling?*
> *Momma, I tell you*

I'm falling
right
now

. . . . .

In this child
killer
I could have
buried the dead
memory of Charlotte
falling   once
and for all
I could have
ended there   holding
the silence
but it is
this end
I fear.

        Waking
to the danger
of falling
again
            falling
in love
the dream.

WHAT KIND OF LOVER
HAVE YOU MADE ME MOTHER?

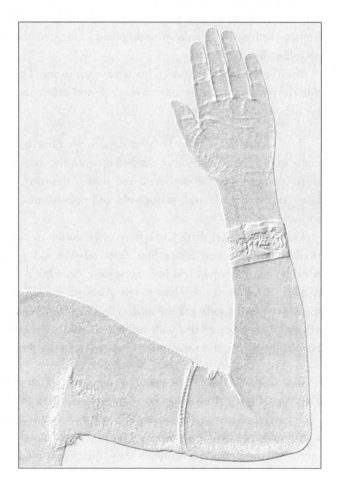

IT IS YOU, MY SISTER,
WHO MUST BE PROTECTED

1

Maybe you'll understand this. My mother was not the queer one, but my father.

Something got beat out of that man. I don't know what. I don't have any stories of him to speak of, only a memory as tame and uneventful as his movement through the house. You *do* remember the man with skin white as a baby's and that is how we thought of him—a battered child. Yeah, something hit him down so deep and so for sure, there seems to be no calling him back now.

But it is this queer I run from. This white man in me. This man settling into the pockets of a woman's vicious pride and conviction to make a life for herself and her children.

The year he was left to his own devices, we came back to find our home in shambles. My mother climbed up onto the stool in the kitchen, stuck her head into the cupboard, and started throwing onto the floor boxes and boxes of cereal, seasons-old and opened, now crawling with ants and roaches.

Do you remember that? And how so often during those days my mom would interrogate dad, asking him about religion and god and *didn't he believe anything.* He would nod back nervously. "Sure honey sure I believe," he'd say. "I just don't know how to talk about it." And I'd stare across the top of my glass of milk and the small yellow kitchen table, and as far back as I could imagine into that wide rolling forehead, I saw nothing stirring. For the life of me, there was no god happening in that head of his.

It is this queer I run from. A pain that turns us to quiet surrender. No. Surrender is too active a term. There was no fight. Resignation.

I'm afraid of ever being that stuck. Stuck back in a story of myself as a six-year-old blond-haired boy, very quiet. I guess he was probably very quiet, even then, watching his father leave. When dad told me the story of his father's return, the restaurant visit sixteen years later, the three hours together after a lifetime of abandonment, I asked him, "Were you angry with him, Dad? How did you feel?"

"I was very nervous," he answered sighing. That's all I could get out of the man, how nervous he was.

I thought of the old man now sleeping in his grave somewhere in Canada, blameless as an English saint. In our children's imagination, he was so unlike the other one, the dark one, who died a young and defiant death. We had seen that grandfather's grave with our own eyes, touched with our own hands the dry and broken earth which held the stone. Sister, do you remember during those visits to Tijuana how you and I would stand so reverently at the sides of the tombstone, our eyes following my mother carrying water in small coffee cans back and forth in silent ritual to wash the face of the grave? Then grandma would brush it off carefully with the crumpled kleenexes she drew from her purse, until the letters of his name, *Esteban*, shown through as vividly as the man they chose to remember at that moment.

This is the portrait of a father whose memory you could live with, kicking and screaming. But the saint? I vaguely recall only one picture of my dad's dad in a double-breasted grey suit. He was standing alone. Palm trees in the background. Hat dipped.

After dad had finished the story, I sat with him watching his face slowly curl up into a squint, his eyes fluttering to a close. You know the expression—where the vertical crease along the side of his forehead deepens into a kind of scar. I realized then that he was going fast—to the place past and beyond the pain where he had laid his face in the lap of a woman and, like a boy begging, promised never to ask for much, if only she would keep him there, safe.

I wanted to shake the old man from his grave! Bring him back to life for a reckoning! But it's hard, I'm sure you feel this too, to sustain any passion, really, for my father.

> *Daddy, you did not beat me, but every blow I took*
> *from the hand of my mother came from a caress*
> *you could not give her.*

The hole burning through her belly had nothing to do
with my lack of loving. I loved her through and through,
alive and in the flesh.

(We women settle for dead men with cold or absent touches.
We carry the weight of your deaths, and yet we bore you
as the first life you knew.

You have your father to thank, father, for his leaving you.
Not your mother nor mine who fed you all the days of your life.

2

The only time I ever saw my father cry, sober, was about six months after
his mother's death. Do you remember? We must've been only about five
and six and we had gone to see a movie, a famous one. I don't recall its
name, but I vaguely remember that a woman dies at the end in a hospital
bed. And my dad, later, driving the family home, suddenly out of nowhere
begins to cry. I don't, at first, understand that he is crying, only that he is
making these strange blurting noises, his head falling down onto his chest.
Then I hear my mom in the front seat snap, "Pull over! Pull over!" As if
she were talking to a child. And my dad does. Draping his arms over the
steering wheel, he starts bawling like a baby.

There seemed to be no tears. I don't remember seeing any. I only knew
that I had never seen a person, a grown man, look so out of his body.
Lost. Awkward. Trying to reach for a cry so much deeper than the one he
was hitting on.

3

My mother tells me that it is you, my sister, who must be protected, that
this will hurt you too much. But I can understand these things. I am
worldly and full of knowledge when something goes queer.

Splitting a beer between us, she says, "Cecilia, mi'jita, your father, he
has no feeling left in him." I think, *this is no news.* "It's in a certain place in
his body," she explains. The absence.

She asks me, have I noticed how he's "so soft, not very manly?"

"Yeah, mamá, I've noticed," I say too eagerly, hungry for the first time to speak of my father with some kind of compassion. A real feeling.

"I think he's different like you, ¿entiendes? Pero, no digas nada a tu hermana."

"No, mamá," I say, "but daddy does seem to love men. It's true. You know how he always gets so excited with any ol' new friend he makes at work. Like a kid. How he goes overboard when my brother or cousins are around. Not like the way he is around women, just part of the scenery." I regret these last words, seeing her face flinch.

I bite my tongue down hard, holding it. I must not say too much. I must not know too much. But I am so excited, thinking of the possibility of my father awakened to the touch. Imagining my father feeling *something* deep and profound and alive.

Alive.

She knows the difference, she says, she knows what it's like to have a "real" man touch her. "If it hadn't been for Baker, the first one," she says, "maybe I wouldn't of known, maybe it wouldn't of mattered, but . . . forty years, mi'jita, forty years."

Grabbing my hand across the table, "Honey, I know what it's like to be touched by a man who wants a woman. I don't feel this with your father," squeezing me. "¿Entiendes?"

The room falls silent then as if the walls, themselves, begged for a moment to swallow back the secret that had just leaked out. And it takes every muscle in me not to leave my chair, not to climb through the silence, not to clamber toward her, not to touch her the way I know she wants to be touched.

"Yeah, Mamá, I understand."

Pulling her hand back, she pours the last few drops left in the bottle into my glass. "Talk to your father," she says. "He listens to you. Don't let him know you know. Tiene vergüenza."

4

The ride back to the airport.

I am driving his car. Feeling more man than my father. The car is entrusted to me to handle. I am on a mission. I am man enough to handle the situation, having a sex-talk with my father. But I can't say anything decent to the man; I'm not supposed to know. I must only be a son to him, supportive, encouraging, reliable—stroking and coaxing the subject.

How to advise a man and keep his manliness intact?

"Daddy?"

"Uh-huh?"

"Sometimes when you've gotten hurt, you know, and . . . "

"Uh-huh."

" . . . you . . . you can't let yourself feel it . . . "

"Uh-huh . . . ," nodding.

" . . . like you feel. . . . "

"Uh-huh."

" . . . dead all over."

"Uh-huh . . . ," nodding. "Uh-huh," nodding.

"It can catch up with you . . . "

"Uh-huh . . . sure, honey. Uh-huh."

" . . . and you start . . . "

"Uh-huh."

" . . . forgetting how . . . "

"Uh-huh . . . ," nodding.

" . . . to feel."

"Uh-huh." Bobbing.

"You need to let your feelings out more . . . "

"Uh-huh."

" . . . Dad."

"Sure, honey." Nodding.

Bobbing.

Beating.

"I see . . . "
a
dead

" . . . what you mean."

horse.

"Mom's worried about you, Dad," wrapping the conversation up as I wrap around the last interchange.
"Yep. I'll sure try to be better to your mother," he says.

At the airport, we have a drink together. Right there on the shoulders of my sensitivity. If I were a man, I could be one bastard of a sensitive guy. Since I am a woman, people—men and women alike—drink from me. I am the eternal well of pathos.

When is someone going to make love to me, unequivocally? Me. I am worried about me, mother sister brother father. All of you. Boarding the plane, I want to say, *Daddy, I am worried about me.*

From my window, I can see him now behind the grill of the airport fence. He'll go home thinking we had a good conversation, scratching at something. It tingles of *something* alive, breathing still. A small pale man waiting like a father, *like . . .*

The plane begins to roll

beating a dead horse, I think

When is someone going to make love to *me,* unequivocally?

LA DULCE CULPA

What kind of lover have you made me, mother
who drew me into bed with you at six/at sixteen
oh, even at sixty-six you do still
lifting up the blanket with one arm
lining out the space for my body with the other

      as if our bodies still beat
      inside the same skin
      as if you never noticed
      when they cut me
      out
      from you.

What kind of lover have you made me, mother
who took belts to wipe this memory from me

      the memory of your passion
      dark & starving, spilling
      out of rooms, driving
      into my skin, cracking
      & cussing in spanish

      the thick dark *f* sounds
      hard *c*'s splitting
      the air like blows

      you would *get a rise out of me*
      you knew it in our blood
      the vision   of my rebellion

What kind of lover have you made me, mother
who put your passion on a plate for me

nearly digestible. Still trying to swallow
the fact that we lived most of our lives
with the death of a man
whose touch ran
across the surface of your skin
never landing nightly
where you begged it
to fall

>to hold your desire
>in the palm of his hand

>for you to rest there
>for you to continue.

What kind of lover have you made me, mother
so in love

with what is left

unrequited.

. . . . .

What is left

Mamá
I use you
like the belt
pressed inside your grip
seething for contact

I take
what I know
from you and want
to whip this world
into shape.

The damage
has defined me
as the space you provide
for me in your bed

. . . . .

I was not to raise an arm against you

But today
I promise you
I *will* fight back

Strip the belt from your hands

and take you

into
my arms.

LIKE FAMILY
LOVING ON THE RUN

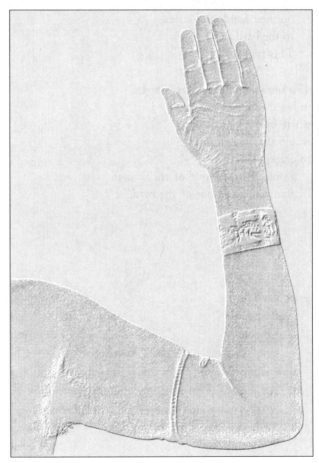

THE PILGRIMAGE

She saw women
maybe the first time
when they had streamed in long broken
single file
out from her mother's tongue—

    "En México, las mujeres crawl
    on their hands and knees
    to the basilica door.
    This proves their faith."

The brown knotted knees were hers
in her dreaming, she wondered
where in the journey
would the dusty knees begin
to crack,
    would the red blood of the women
    stain the grey bone of the road.

LATER, SHE MET JOYCE

1

Later, she met Joyce
and after they had been friends for a whole
school year, formed their own
girls' gang with code words & rhymes
that played itself coolly
on *this* side of trouble
they got separated by the summer.

> Joyce, without a phone
> and so far away
> into the bordering
> town.

But just once, they rendezvoused
on the front porch of a pair
of old white folks, friends of the family.
"Come see me," Joyce whispered
over the telephone line. "I'm
only a few blocks away."

And without expecting to, Cecilia climbed
right up those steps and straight into Joyce's
arms and she would never forget the shape
of the girl's chest, a good one
and a half year's older and
how her own small chest & cheek
sunk into it.

It spread through her body
the cool breath and release
of a tightness she didn't know
she had held back, waiting

for the summer's end.
Waiting to look
into Joyce's round-like-an-olive
face and see it, full of tears, too.
It was the first time for both of them.

And Cecilia thought, *so this is love.*

2

Later, she met Joyce
who didn't come back
to cath-lic school
it being too hard she guessed
(there *was* no telephone)
in a big winter coat
after mass one sunday
looking more like a momma
than her childhood friend.
Rounder than Cecilia had ever seen her
hair teased high off her head.

    "Hi," Cecilia said.
    "Eh, ésa, 'ow you doing? Whadchu say, man?"

Joyce moved back and forth, her suedes
toeing the ground, talking that talk
that Cecilia's momma called
a difernt claz o'people
that had something to do with your tongue
going thick on you, wearing
shiny clothes and never getting
to college.
Seems in other people's eyes
Joyce was a fat half-breed
that flunked close-to-twice

in other people's eyes
in other people's eyes.

In Joyce's eyes that morning
Cecilia looked for a sign,

C'mon Joyce   be kidding   please
you remember me   you remember
me   you remember
please

and thought she detected
some trace there between the two thick lines
of turquoise, of the brown eyes that cried
over missing her.

Missing Joyce turned
pachuca on her, walking away
talking about the "guyz"
she would like to have
ride her low
through the valley floor.

3

Later that year,
Cecilia was picked
by the smart
white
girls
for president.

AN OPEN INVITATION TO A MEAL

I am
you tell me
a piece of cake.

I wonder about your eating habits
which make me dessert
instead of staple
a delicacy, like some chocolate mousse
teasing your taste buds, melting
in your mouth—stopping there.

There's nothing pretty about me.

I am brown and grainy and can stick to the ribs
a food source that won't run out on you
through the toughest winter.

Come, sit down.
Give up that sweet tooth
and we'll put it in a jar
to remind us of the polite
society that can afford
such things.

Right now, it's beginning to snow.

Come, sit down.
The day is getting shorter
and it's beginning
to snow.

Yes, here.

Sit down.

Here.

YOU UPSET THE WHOLE SYSTEM OF THIS PLACE

for Julie

I've been inside all day.

you enter sleek, wet from winter rain. hot heaving chest. hot breath. the still heatered air of this house melts around your shoulders as you pass through it, dripping down along your thighs to bare calloused feet. you upset the whole system of this place.

approaching, your footsteps are solid and silent.

I, wrapped in bedclothes, billows of quilts and pillows. I rock to the rhythmic sound of my own breathing inside my head. stuffed mucus. my small chest, a battleground. it is fragile and bony. a cough that scrapes it dry each time. an ache like a rash beneath my ribs.

all that keeps you from me is this guatemalan drape which lines my bed like a mosquito net, only one simple striped panel. you wave it aside with a backhand motion. you move into the bed with me, not afraid of catching cold. the thick warm dough of your hands pours into the hollow parts of me.

"I've been trying not to cry for you all day," I say. You stroke my mouth closed.

"I need you now, I have this terrible cold."

without reply, you go into the green kitchen and pull out the remains of a gallon of cider. I imagine you crushing the nutmeg into the liquid while it warms over the low flame, squeezing in lemon, imitating me.

you return, mug in hand. you are dry now, your hair straggly. I drink the
hot cider and you stay and roll with me until dinnertime. you ease me a
half an hour into the night.

"Are you coming back?"

"Yes," you answer, "when you're better."

then I lean into your cheek, breathing in with my mouth.

I follow your footsteps exiting through the hardwood hallway, down a
step, across the carpet, out the door and down the many red wet steps into
the neon night that swallows you up.

LOVING ON THE RUN

for women who travel in packs of one

1

I found you on a street corner
hangin out with a bunch of boys
lean brown boys
you too lean
into them
talkin your girl-head off
with your glasses
like some wizard
sayin
"I know what that feels like."

I found you there
you guys hangin out
like family to each other
talkin about women
you sayin
how they make your hips roll
without thinkin
those pale green
hips of yours
deep and oiled
like a woman

they don't catch on
about you bein one
for all your talk about women/likin them
they don't catch the difference
for all your talk about
your common enemy
you operatin on a street sense

so keen that it can spot danger
before he makes it around the corner
before he scarcely notices you
as a woman
they marvel at this

they don't catch on
them seein your words
like the body of a dark brother
you sayin
"I know what that feels like"
being shitted on
and they believin you
about your allied place on the block
about the war goin on
they believin you
because you know
you got
no reason
to lie to them

2
I found you among blarin stereos
while walkin thru the neighborhood
there you were
kicked back on some porch
actin like family
like you belonged
callin to me
hangin over the railing
wavin
coaxin me to your steps
gettin me to sit there
you strokin my head
slow and soft, sayin
"you are soooo sweet"
drawin out the "so"

like a long drink
like a deep moan
comin out from inside
you like a deep sigh
of lovin

lovin
like your brothers
lovin hard-won
lovin gotten in snatches
in collisions
in *very* desperate situations
lovin which sometimes squatted
rested
took a vacation
would not get up off its ass
to meet a woman
face on
lovin on the run

3
collecting me
into your thin arms
you are woman to me
and brother to them
in the same breath
you marvel at this
seeing yourself
for the first time
in the body of this sister
like family
like you belong
you moving up against this woman
like you this streetfighter
like you whom
you've taken in
under your bruised wing

your shoulderblade bent
on bearing alone

seeing yourself
for the *first* time
in the body of her boyhood
her passion to survive
female and *un*compromising

taking all this under your wing
letting it wrestle there
into your skin
             changing you

LOVING IN THE WAR YEARS

Loving you is like living
in the war years.
I *do* think of Bogart & Bergman
not clear who's who
but still singin a long smoky
mood into the piano bar
drinks straight up
the last bottle in the house
while bombs split
outside, a broken
world.

A world war going on
but you and I still insisting
in each our own heads
still thinkin how
if I could only make some contact
with that woman across the keyboard
we size each other up
    yes . . .

Loving you has this kind of desperation
to it, like do or die, I
having eyed you from the first
time you made the decision to move
from your stool
to live dangerously.

All on the hunch
that in our exchange of photos
of old girlfriends, names

of cities and memories
back in the states
the fronts we've manned
out here on the continent
all this on the hunch
that *this* time there'll be
no need for resistance.

Loving in the war years
calls for this kind of risking
without a home to call our own
I've got to take you as you come
to me, each time like a stranger
all over again. Not knowing
what deaths you saw today
I've got to take you
as you come, battle bruised
refusing our enemy, fear.

We're all we've got. You and I

maintaining
this war time morality
where being queer
and female
is as warrior
as we can get.

THE SLOW DANCE

Thinking of Elena, Susan—watching them dance together. The images return to me, hold me, stir me, prompt me to want *something*.

Elena moving Susan around the floor, so in control of the knowledge: how to handle this woman, while I fumble around them. When Elena and I kissed, just once, I forgot and let too much want show, closing my eyes, all the eyes around me seeing me close my eyes. I am a girl wanting so much to kiss a woman. She sees this too, cutting the kiss short.

But not with Susan, Susan's arm around Elena's neck. Elena's body all leaning into the center of her pelvis. This is *the way she enters a room*, leaning into the body of a woman. The two of them, like grown-ups, like women. The women I silently longed for. Still, I remember after years of wanting and getting and loving, still I remember the desire to be that *in sync* with another woman's body.

And I move women around the floor, too—women I think enamored with me. My mother's words rising up from inside me, "A *real* man, when he dances with you, you'll know he's a *real* man by how he holds you in the back." I think, *yes*, someone who can guide you around a dance floor. And so, I do, moving these women kindly, surely, even superior. *I can handle these women. They want this.* And I do too.

Thinking of my father, how so timidly he used to take my mother onto the small square of carpet we reserved for dancing, pulling back the chairs. She really leading the step, he learning to cooperate so it *looked* like a male lead. I noticed his hand, how it lingered awkwardly about my mother's small back, his thin fingers never really getting a hold on her.

I remember this as I take a woman in my arms, my hand moving up under her shoulder blade, speaking to her from there. It is from *this* spot, the dance is directed. From *this* place, I tenderly, with each fingertip, move her.

I am my mother's lover. The partner she's been waiting for. I can handle whatever you got hidden. I can provide for you.

But when I put this provider up against the likes of Elena, *I* am the one following/falling into her. Like Susan, taken up in the arms of this woman. *I want this.*

Catching the music shift; the beat softens, slows down. I search for Elena through the bodies, the faces. *I am ready for you now.* I want age. Knowledge. *Your body that still, after years, withholds and surrenders—keeps me there, waiting, wishing.* I push through the bodies, looking for her. Willing. Willing to feel *this time* what disrupts in me. Girl. Woman. Child. Boy. Willing to embody what I will in the space of her arms. Looking for Elena, I'm willing, wanting.

And I find you dancing with this other woman. My body both hers and yours in the flash of a glance.

I can handle this.

I am used to being an observer.
I am used to not getting what I want.
I am used to imagining what it must be like.

FEAR, A LOVE POEM

1

If fear is two girls awakening in the same room
after a lifetime of sleeping together
she saying, *I dreamed it was the end of the world*
sister, it was the end   you knowing this in your sleep
her terror seeping through skin into your dreams, holding her
sensing something moving too fast

> as with a lover,
> dressing and dreaming
> in the same room.

If fear is awakening in the same room
feeling something moving too fast
the body next to you awake   the back ignoring
your dream which breaks *her* sleep, too   you
waiting for the embrace to be returned   you
waiting to be met in the nightmare
by a sister, by a lover—

If fear is wishing there were some disease to call it
saying, I AM GOING CRAZY   always for lack
of a better word   always because we have no words
to say we need
attention, early on.

If fear is this, these things
then I am neither alone, nor crazy
but a child, for fear of doom, driven
to look   into the darkest
part
of the eye—

> the part of the eye
> that is not eye   at all
> but hole.

At thirteen, I had the courage
to stare that hole down   Face up
to it alone in the mirror.
I can't claim the same simple courage
now, moving away from the mirror
into the faces of other
women   to *your* face which dares
to answer mine. That it is

in
this
hole
round, common and black
where we recognize each other.
That in looking to the hole
the iris, with all its shades
of contrast and persuasion,
blurs peripheral
and I am left, standing
with your face
in my hands
like a mirror. This clear
recognition I fear
to see our hunger bold-faced like this
sometimes turning the sockets in your head
stone cold, *sometimes*
enveloping your eyes with a liquid
so pure and full
of longing I feel
it could clean out the most miserable parts
of myself   melt down
a lifetime of turned backs.

2

I know now, with you
no one's turning her back.
I may roll over and over

in my mind, toss back and forth
from shoulder to shoulder the weight
of a child in me, battered wanting walking
through the streets   armored and ready
to kill   a body
wrestling now with the touch of your surrender
but I won't turn my back.

You reach for me in bed.
It is 4 am
your arm stretching
across a valley of killings I fear
no one can survive.
                all this in one night, again?

You reach for me in bed.
Look at me, you say, turning
my chin into your hand
what do *you see?*

It is
my face, wanting
and refusing everything.

And at that moment
for a moment, I want
to take that slender hand
and place it between my breasts
my hand holding it there.
I want to feel
your touch *outside*
my body, on the *surface*
of my skin.

I want to know, *for sure,*
where you leave off
and I begin.

PESADILLA

There came the day when Cecilia began to think about color.

Not the color of trees or painted billboards or the magnificent spreads of color laid down upon the hundreds of Victorians that lined the streets of her hometown city. She began to think about skin color. And the thought took hold of her and would not give; would not let loose. So that every person—man, woman and child—had its particular grade of shade. And that fact meant all the difference in the world.

Soon her body began to change with this way of seeing. She felt her skin, like a casing, a beige bag into which the guts of her life were poured. And inside it, she swam through her day. Upstream. Downtown. Underground. Always, the shell of this skin, leading her around. So that nothing seemed fair to her anymore: the war, the rent, the prices, the weather. And it spoiled her time.

Then one day, color moved in with her. Or, at least, that was how she thought of it when the going was the roughest between her and her love. That was how she thought of it after the animal had come and left. Splattered himself all around their new apartment or really the old apartment they had broken their backs to make livable.

. . . . .

After brushing their way out the front door, leaving the last coat of varnish on the hardwood floor to dry, Cecilia and Deborah had for the first time in weeks given themselves the afternoon off and headed for the city. They returned in the early evening, exhausted from the heat, and the crowds, and the noise of the subways and slowly began the long trek up to their sixth-floor apartment. Why couldn't we have found an apartment with an elevator in the building, Cecilia thought each time she found herself at the bottom of the stairs, arms full of packages, staring up at the long journey ahead of her.

But no, this was the apartment they had wanted—the one they believed their love could rescue from its previous incarnation.

The woman who lived there before them was said to have had five dogs and five children crowded into the one-bedroom apartment. Each time Juanito came by from across the hall to spy on them at work, he had a different version to tell of "La Loca" who had lived there before them. "She was evicted," he would announce, almost proudly, with all the authority an eight-year-old can muster, puffing out his bare brown chest. "She was so dirty, you could smell it down to the basement!"

The signs of filth, yes, still remained. But that Cecilia and Deborah believed they could remove under coats of paint and plaster. The parts of broken toys found in the corners of cupboards, children's crayola markings on the wall, torn pieces of teenage magazines stuck up with dust-covered strips of scotch tape—all indicated too many people in too small a space. *¿Quién sabe la pena que sufría esa mujer?* Cecilia thought.

It was the woman's rage, however, that could not be washed out of the apartment walls. There was no obliterating from Cecilia's mind the smell and sight of the dog food she had found stuffed into the mouth of the bathroom sink—red and raw in its anger. As Cecilia scraped it out—"La mierda del mundo. ¡Qué coma mierda!"—she tried not to believe that all this was the bad omen she suddenly felt rising hot and thick in her throat.

Finally, making it up to the sixth-floor landing, the two women dropped their bags, exhausted, and Cecilia drew her keys out from her purse. But before she could turn the key in the lock, the door easily gave way. She quickly tried to convince herself that yes, she had been negligent. The last to leave. The first to forget in her fatigue to secure the lock. But she knew different. Entering the apartment, her heart pounding, Cecilia led the way down the long hallway—a dark labyrinth to the pesadilla that awaited them. At the end of it, she could see their bedroom, the light burning. A tornado had hit it!

No, this was not the result of some faceless natural disaster. This was a live and breathing thing. An animal. An animal had broken in. And the women broke down. What kind of beast, they cried, would do this? His parts drawn all over their freshly painted walls for them to see and suck and that's what he told them there on the wall.

SUCK MY DICK   YOU HOLE

He had wanted money and finding no such thing, but a picture of a woman who could have been a sister or a lover or a momma and no sign of man around, he wrote:

I'M BLACK YOU MOTHERFUCKER BITCH
YOU BUTCH

And Cecilia knew if he had had the time and sense enough he would have even written her lover's name out there upon the bedroom wall. He wanted Dee, too. Even in his hatred, he wanted Cecilia's lover. Everybody, it seemed, had something to say about Deborah's place on the planet.

Seeing his scratches on the wall, both women knew they were very close to giving it up altogether. Cecilia closing up the thought just as it broke open inside her. Closing in on Deborah, she brought the woman into her arms and they fell against the wall, crying. The animal's scrawl disappearing behind them. It was the first time in their life together that Cecilia wondered if she were up to the task of such loving.

It had scarcely been a week since they had carried down their five flights of stairs the last torn-up suitcase of the animal's debris. They needed the rest, the relief from the city and found it in the home of friends by the Hudson, drinking iced seltzer with lime in the bake of the sun. The violation, a million miles away from the one hour's drive out of town.

Dee grew blacker as she slept on the deck. And when Cecilia rose to refill her glass it took the greatest rigidity of spine not to bend down and kiss the wet and glistening neck of the woman stretched out before her, sound asleep.

Cecilia wanted her. She was afraid to want her.

Closing the sliding glass door behind her, the house hit Cecilia with a cool that she had nearly forgotten in the heavy humidity of the city. Even the city park could not provide this quality of coolness—cement blocks hovering around it on all fours. This was the kind of coolness that only grew from a ground now hollowed out by tunnels and steaming underground trains. *Berkeley.* It reminded her of the hills of Berkeley. The blend of drying jasmine and eucalyptus hot-whipped into a cloudless sky, the scent carrying itself out to the bay.

In Brooklyn, she still found it hard to believe she lived by the water. The tops of neighboring ships were to her merely another line of differently shaped structures rising up from the stiff water-floor. The real mother ocean was three thousand miles behind her.

The kitchen was flooded with sunlight and houseplants—those that hung and those that seemed to grow right out from under the linoleum floor. Cecilia found herself breathing more deeply than she had in months. She felt calmer somehow. A feeling she had left somewhere, she thought, back in California.

But what? . . . What exactly was it?
The smell?
The light? She held the bottle to pour. *Yes, both these things, but . . .* "Salud." She mimed a toast in the air, pushing back the thought coming at her, her heart speeding up.
It was . . . white.
It was whiteness and . . . safety.

Old lovers who carried their whiteness like freedom/and breath/and light. Their shoulders, always straight-backed and sweetly oiled for color. In their faces, the luxury of trust.

It was whiteness and money.

In this way, she had learned to be a lesbian. Not that any of her friends actually had cash on hand. In fact, she was the one among them who came from the least, but who always seemed to have the most—the one who always managed to find something "steady." But there was the ambience of money: the trips cross-country, the constant career changes, the pure cotton clothing and yes, the sunshine. In her memory, it was never dark, except at night when it was always quiet and nearly suburban.

But the feeling she remembered most, the feeling that she could not shake, was of some other presence living amongst those women. Some white man somewhere—their names always monosyllabic: Tom, Dick, Jack. Like boys, flat-topped and tough, cropping up in a photograph, a telephone call, a letter, who, in the crunch, would be their ticket.

Nobody would have said that then (or even thought of it that way). Cecilia certainly wouldn't have. But she could see it now, now that they were gone—the man's threatening and benevolent presence living with them all. They were his daughters after all, these white lesbian lovers, these middle-class "college girls," as long as they remained without a man.

Blood is blood.

It was that night that Deborah had her attack (or "fit" as Deborah used to say, mocking some 1930s sci-fi version of epileptics or schizophrenics). It was the first time Cecilia had ever witnessed one in Dee, although for years Dee had spoken of them, sometimes beneath a rush of tears.

Standing on her knees in bed, she would go through the motions once again of the man coming down on her with the back of his hand. The hand enlarging as it advanced—broad and blacker than she's ever seen it.

"That's when my fits began," she'd say, then suddenly, "Blahblahblah—blahblah! Po' lil cullud girl, me!" He was the second and last man her mother kicked out.

"My babies come first." Both their mommas could have been found saying the same thing, wrists bent back into hipbones. That's what had brought them together—the dark, definite women of their childhood.

But that night, there were no science-fiction parodies. Waking to Deborah's absence in the bed, Cecilia quickly got up and, entering the bathroom, found her lover thrown back against the tank of the toilet. Mouth open, unconscious. It was not how Cecilia had imagined it. No tongue-gagging. No gutteral sounds, no jerking movements. No joke.

Gathering the dead weight into her arms, Cecilia brought the heavy head to her chest, holding it there. The weight like a hot rock against her breast-bone—the same shape of the fear now forming inside her heart. And then, as if she had rehearsed the role, she began to rock the body. And the more she rocked, the more the motion slowly began to dissolve the stone inside her chest and allowed, finally, for her tears to come. She rocked. She cried. "Oh Deborah, baby, wake up!" She cried, "¡Por favor, despiértate! ¡Chula, por favor!" She rocked. Until at last, she felt the head stiffen and pull away.

"Get my pills," Deborah moaned.

Cecilia rushed back into the bedroom and began rummaging around in Deborah's bag, frantically trying to find the pills, finally dumping the entire contents onto the floor. There on her knees she felt something turn in her. She felt her heart like a steel clamp inside her chest, twisting what was only moments ago a living beating fear into a slow cool numbing between her breasts.

Her loving couldn't change a thing.

Cecilia remembered the first time she had ever felt this same sensation of "coldness." Her memory rushing back in flashes to the picture of a woman, her mother, elbows dug into the kitchen table, yellow, the pho-tograph curled into her hand, yellow too, tears streaming down her cheeks.

Again. A river returned. A river whose pull always before that moment had swept Cecilia off her chair and into her mother's arms. But on that particular day, Cecilia stepped outside the circle of pain her mother drew like hot liquid from the girl's body, the mother's tears commingling with her own, like communion.

The eleven-year-old Cecilia didn't understand why her feelings were changing, only that they had to change. *Change or die,* she thought. And suddenly she grew stiff and fixed in her chair, hands pressed between her knees, riveted against the tide of rage and regret she knew her mother's memories would call forth. Old wounds still oozing with the blood of sinners in wartime.

"I forgive," her mother would announce. "But I never forget." And mustering up what courage she could, the girl first whispered to herself, then shouted out loud, "You gotta change, Mamá! You gotta let it go!"

When she didn't change. When Cecilia had prayed and pleaded, practiced and preached every form of childish support she could think of, she left the woman. It was years later, but she took a walk right out of that kitchen and family-way of passing on daughter-to-daughter misery. Her momma cursing after her, "You're just like the rest of 'em. You don't know how to love."

"Honey? Are you coming?"
"Yeah, right away, baby."

Cecilia grabbed the pills and returned to the bathroom to find Deborah now with eyes open and blinking alive. But Cecilia couldn't rid herself of the feeling in her chest. It was as if a different woman had stepped back into the room and Cecilia now stood somewhere else, outside the room, watching this other one nurse her lover back to health. In silence, giving Deborah the pills. In silence, moving her back to bed. In silence, watching her fall into a deep and exhausted sleep.

Lying awake in bed, the sunlight now cracking through the window, Cecilia thought of the times when as a child she always lived her nights like days while the rest of the house slept. Never soundly sleeping like the woman now curled under her arm. Getting up six and seven times a night, locking and re-locking the doors. Praying in whispers the same prayers over and over and over again, nodding into sleep, resisting. Resisting the pictures the dreams would bring. The women, wanting. The men, like flaming devils, swollen with desire.

Locking and re-locking the doors. Keeping the fearful out, while it wrestles inside without restraint. During those hours before dawn, *anything is* possible—the darkness giving permission for the spirit to shake itself loose in Deborah. Cecilia wanted Dee. She was afraid to want her. Afraid to feel another woman's body. Like family.

When she discovered the first woman wouldn't change, it had sort of wrapped things up for the rest of them. Still she'd go through the changes of asking for changes como su abuelita during the english mass mouthing spanish a million miles an hour, kissing the crucifix of the rosary wrapped 'round her neck at each and every "amen." Nothing to disturb her order of things. No matter what was said or done in english, she knew the spanish by heart. In her heart, which long ago forgot the clear young reason for the kissings, the vicious beating of the breast, the bending to someone else's will.

What frightened Cecilia so was to feel this gradual reawakening in her bones. Since the break-in, her hands had merely skimmed her lover's flesh, never reaching in. Cecilia pressed her nose into Dee's hair. The sun, almost full now through the window, had warmed the fibers into a cushion of heat which promised rest, continuance. In the intake of breath, there was more familiarity, more loss of resistance, more sense of landing *somewhere* than any naming she had tried to do with words inside her head. Words were nothing to the smell.

. . . . .

Pesadilla.

There is a man on the fire escape. He is crouched just below the window sill. I could barely catch the curve of his back descending, but I have seen the movement. I know it is the animal, returned.

The figure suddenly rises to attack. . .

DEBORAH!!

The dark woman looking in through the glass is as frightened as I am. She is weeping. I will not let her in.

PASSAGE

on the edge of the war near the bonfire
we taste knowledge[1]

There is a very old wound in me
between my legs
where I have bled, not to birth
pueblos or revolutionary
concepts or simple
sucking children

> but a memory
> of some ancient
> betrayal.

So that when you touch me
and I long to freeze, not feel
what hungry longing I used to know
nor taste in you a want
I fear will burn
my fingers to their roots
> *it's out of my control.*

Your mouth opens, I long for dryness.
The desert untouched.
Sands swept without sweat.
Aztlán.[2]

Pero, es un sueño. This safety
of the desert.
My country was not like that.
> Neither was yours.
We have always bled
with our veins
and legs
open
to forces
beyond our control.

VIEW OF THREE BRIDGES

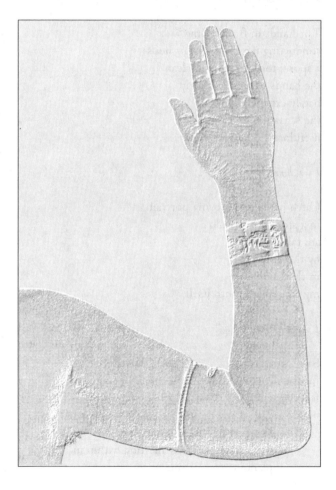

RAW EXPERIENCE

1

There is this motor inside me
propelling me
forward

I watch myself for clues.

The hands in front of me
conducting me through this house
a spoon too soon wiped clean
the hands sweeping it away
barely experiencing
the sensation of fullness
usefulness

I watch myself for clues.

Catch my face, a moving portrait
in a storefront window
am taken aback
by the drop
in cheekline
my face sinking into itself

I watch myself for clues.

Say "extricate"
for the first time in my life
feel the sound
bulldoze out of my mouth
        I earned that word somewhere
        the syllables secretly meeting within me
        planning to blast me open.

There *is* this motor inside me
propelling me
forward.

I watch myself for clues,
trying to catch up
inhabit my body
again.

2

On the highest point of a hill
sitting, there is
the view of three bridges

each one with a special feature
a color
an island
a view of the red rock

Each with a particular destination
coming and going.

I watch them for clues

their secrets
about making connections
about getting
someplace.

LA GÜERA

It requires something more than personal experience to gain a philosophy or point of view from any specific event. It is the quality of our response to the event and our capacity to enter into the lives of others that help us to make their lives and experiences our own.

—Emma Goldman[1]

I am the very well-educated daughter of a woman who, by the standards in this country, would be considered largely illiterate. My mother was born in Santa Paula, Southern California, at a time when much of the coast and neighboring central valley was still farmland. Nearly thirty-five years later, in 1948, she was the only daughter of six to marry an anglo, my father.

I remember all of my mother's stories, probably much better than she realizes. She is a fine storyteller, recalling every event of her life with the vividness of the present, noting each detail right down to the cut and color of her dress. I remember stories of her being pulled out of school at the ages of five, seven, nine and eleven to work in the fields, along with her brothers and sisters; stories of her father drinking away whatever small profit she was able to make for the family; of her going the long way home to avoid meeting him on the street, staggering toward the same destination. I remember stories of my mother lying about her age in order to get a job as a hat-check girl at Agua Caliente Racetrack in Tijuana. At fourteen, she was the main support of the family. I can still see her walking home alone at 3 a.m., only to turn all of her salary and tips over to her mother, who was pregnant again.

The stories continue through the war years and on: walnut-cracking factories, the Voit Rubber factory, and then the electronics boom. I remember my mother doing piecework for the plant in our neighborhood. In the late evening, she would sit in front of the TV set, wrapping copper wires into the backs of circuit boards, talking about "keeping up with the younger girls." By that time she was already in her mid-fifties.

Meanwhile, I was college-prep in school. After classes, I would go with my mother to fill out job applications for her, or write checks for her at the supermarket. We would have the scenario all worked out ahead of time. My mother would sign the check before we'd get to the store. Then, as we'd approach the checkstand, she would say—within earshot of the cashier—"oh honey, you go 'head and make out the check," as if she couldn't be bothered with such an insignificant detail. No one asked any questions.

I was educated, and wore it with a keen sense of pride and satisfaction, my head propped up with the knowledge, from my mother, that my life would be easier than hers. I was educated; but more than this, I was "la güera"—fair-skinned. Born with the features of my Chicana mother, but the skin of my Anglo father, I had it made.

No one ever quite told me this (that light was right), but I knew that being light was something valued in my family, who were all Chicano, with the exception of my father. In fact, everything about my upbringing, at least what occurred on a conscious level, attempted to bleach me of what color I did have. Although my mother was fluent in Spanish, I was never taught much of it at home. I picked up what I did learn from school and from overheard snatches of conversation among my relatives and mother. She often called other lower-income Mexicans "braceros," or "wet-backs," referring to herself and her family as "a different class of people." And yet, the real story was that my family, too, had been poor (some still are) and farmworkers. My mother can remember this in her blood as if it were yesterday. But this is something she would like to forget (and rightfully), for to her, on a basic economic level, being Chicana meant being "less." It was through my mother's desire to protect her children from poverty and illiteracy that we became "anglocized"; the more effectively we could pass in the white world, the better guaranteed our future.

From all of this, I experience, daily, a huge disparity between what I was born into and what I was to grow up to become. Because, as Goldman suggests, these stories my mother told me crept under my "güera" skin. I had no choice but to enter into the life of my mother. *I had no choice.* I took her life into my heart, but managed to keep a lid on it as long as I feigned being the happy, upwardly mobile heterosexual.

When I finally lifted the lid to my lesbianism, a profound connection with my mother reawakened in me. It wasn't until I acknowledged and confronted my own lesbianism in the flesh that my heartfelt identification with and empathy for my mother's oppression—due to being poor, uneducated and Chicana—was realized. My lesbianism is the avenue through which I have learned the most about silence and oppression, and it continues to be the most tactile reminder to me that we are not free human beings.

You see, one follows the other. I had known for years that I was a lesbian, had felt it in my bones, had ached with the knowledge, gone crazed with the knowledge, wallowed in the silence of it. Silence *is* like starvation. Don't be fooled. It's nothing short of that, and felt most sharply when one has had a full belly most of her life. When we are not physically starving, we have the luxury to realize psychic and emotional starvation. It is from this starvation that other starvations can be recognized—if one is willing to take the risk of making the connection—if one is willing to be responsible to the result of the connection. For me, the connection is an inevitable one.

What I am saying is that the joys of looking like a white girl ain't so great since I realized I could be beaten on the street for being a dyke. If my sister's being beaten because she's Black, it's pretty much the same principle. We're both getting beaten any way you look at it. The connection is blatant; and in the case of my own family, the difference in the privileges attached to looking white instead of brown are merely a generation apart.

In this country, lesbianism is a poverty—as is being brown, as is being a woman, as is being just plain poor. The danger lies in ranking the oppressions. *The danger lies in failing to acknowledge the specificity of the oppression.* The danger lies in attempting to deal with oppression purely from a theoretical base. Without an emotional, heartfelt grappling with the source of our own oppression, without naming the enemy within ourselves and outside of us, no authentic, nonhierarchical connection among oppressed groups can take place. When the going gets rough, will we abandon our so-called comrades in a flurry of racist/heterosexist/what-have-you panic? To whose camp, then, should the lesbian of color retreat? Her very presence violates the ranking and abstraction of oppression. Do we merely live hand to mouth? Do we merely struggle with the "ism" that's sitting on top of our heads? The answer is: yes, I think first we do; and we must do so thoroughly and deeply. But to fail to move out from there will only isolate us in our own oppression—will only insulate, rather than radicalize us.

To illustrate: a gay white male friend of mine once confided to me that he continued to feel that, on some level, I didn't trust him because he was male; that he felt, really, if it ever came down to a "battle of the sexes," I might kill him. I admitted that I might very well. He wanted to under-stand the source of my distrust. I responded, "You're not a woman. Be a woman for a day. Imagine being a woman." He confessed that the thought terrified him because, to him, being a woman meant being raped by men. He *had* felt raped by men; he wanted to forget what that meant. What grew from that discussion was the realization that in order for him to cre-ate an authentic alliance with me, he must deal with the primary source of his own sense of oppression. He must, first, emotionally come to terms with what it feels like to be a victim. If he—or anyone—were to truly do this, it would be impossible to discount the oppression of oth-ers, except by again forgetting how we have been hurt.

And yet, oppressed groups are forgetting all the time. There are instances of this in the rising Black middle class, and certainly an obvious trend of such "capitalist-unconsciousness" among white gay men. Because to remember may mean giving up whatever privileges we have managed to squeeze out of this society by virtue of our gender, race, class, or sexuality.

Within the women's movement, the connections among women of dif-ferent backgrounds and sexual orientations have been fragile, at best. I think this phenomenon is indicative of our failure to seriously address some very frightening questions: How have I internalized my own oppres-sion? How have I oppressed? Instead, we have let rhetoric do the job of poetry. Even the word "oppression" has lost its power. We need a new language, better words that can more closely describe women's fear of, and resistance to, one another, words that will not always come out sounding like dogma.

What prompted me in the first place to work on an anthology by radical women of color[2] was a deep sense that I had a valuable insight to contribute, by virtue of my birthright and my background. And yet, I don't really understand first-hand what it feels like being shitted on for being brown. I understand much more about the joys of it. Being Chicana and having family are synonymous for me. What I know about loving, singing, crying, telling stories, speaking with my heart and hands, even having a sense of my own soul comes from the love of my mother, aunts, cousins . . .

But at the age of twenty-seven, it is frightening to acknowledge that I have internalized a racism and classism, where the object of oppression is not only someone *outside* my skin, but the someone *inside* my skin. In fact, to a large degree, the real battle with such oppression, for all of us, begins under the skin. I have had to confront the fact that much of what I value about being Chicana, about my family, has been subverted by anglo culture and my own cooperation with it. This realization did not occur to me overnight. For example, it wasn't until long after my graduation from the private college I'd attended in Los Angeles that I realized the major reason for my total alienation from, and fear of, my classmates was rooted in class and culture.

Three years after graduation, in an apple orchard in Sonoma, a friend of mine (who comes from an Italian Irish workingclass family) says to me, "Cherríe, no wonder you felt like such a nut in school. Most of the people there were white and rich." It was true. All along I had felt the difference, but not until I had put the words "class" and "race" to the experience did my feelings make any sense. For years, I had berated myself for not being as "free" as my classmates. I completely bought that they simply had more guts than I did to rebel against their parents and run around the country hitchhiking, reading books and studying "art." They had enough privilege to be atheists, for chrissake. There was no one around filling in the disparity for me between their parents, who were Hollywood filmmakers, and my parents, who wouldn't know the name of a filmmaker if their lives depended on it; and precisely because their lives didn't depend on it; they couldn't be bothered. But I knew nothing about "privilege" then. White was right. Period. I could pass. If I got educated enough, there would never be no telling.

Three years after that, I had a similar revelation. In a letter to Black feminist, Barbara Smith (whom I had not yet met), I wrote:

I went to a concert where Ntosake Shange was reading. There, everything exploded for me. She was speaking in a language that I knew, in the deepest parts of me, existed, and that I ignored in my own feminist studies and even in my own writing. What Ntosake caught in me is the realization that in my development as a poet, I have, in many ways, denied the voice of my own brown mother, the brown in me. I have acclimated to the sound of a white language which, as my father represents it, does not speak to the emotions in my poems, emotions which stem from the love of my mother.

The reading was agitating. Made me uncomfortable. Threw me into a week-long terror of how deeply I was affected. I felt that I had to start all over again, that I turned only to the perceptions of white middle-class women to speak for me and all women. I am shocked by my own ignorance.

Sitting in that Oakland auditorium chair was the first time I had realized to the core of me that for years I had disowned the language I knew best. I had ignored the words and rhythms that were the closest to me: the sounds of my mother and aunts gossiping—half in English, half in Spanish—while drinking cerveza in the kitchen. And the hands—I had cut off the hands in my poems. But not in conversation; still the hands could not be kept down. Still they insisted on moving.

The reading had forced me to remember that I knew things from my roots. But to remember puts me up against what I don't know. Shange's reading agitated me because she spoke with power about a world that is both alien and common to me: "the capacity to enter into the lives of others." But you can't just take the goods and run. I knew that then, sitting in the Oakland auditorium (as I know in my poetry), that the only thing worth writing about is what seems to be unknown and, therefore, fearful.

The "unknown" is often depicted in racist literature as the "darkness" within a person. Similarly, sexist writers will refer to fear in the form of the vagina, calling it "the orifice of death." In contrast, it is a pleasure to read works such as Maxine Hong Kingston's *Woman Warrior,* where fear and alienation are depicted as "the white ghosts." And yet, the bulk of literature in this country reinforces the myth that what is dark and female is evil. Consequently, each of us—whether dark, female, or both—has in some way *internalized* this oppressive imagery. What the oppressor often succeeds in doing is simply *externalizing* his fears, projecting them into the bodies of women, Asians, gays, disabled folks, whoever seems most "other."

call me
roach and presumptuous
nightmare on your white pillow
your itch to destroy
the indestructible
part of yourself
—*Audre Lorde*[3]

But it is not really difference the oppressor fears so much as similarity. He fears he will discover in himself the same aches, the same longings as those of the people he has shit on. He fears the immobilization threatened by his own incipient guilt. He fears he will have to change his life once he has seen himself in the bodies of the people he has called different. He fears the hatred, anger and vengeance of those he has hurt.

This is the oppressor's nightmare, but it is not exclusive to him. We women have a similar nightmare, for each of us in some way has been both the oppressed and the oppressor. We are afraid to look at how we have failed each other. We are afraid to see how we have taken the values of our oppressor into our hearts and turned them against ourselves and one another. We are afraid to admit how deeply *the man's* words have been ingrained in us.

To assess the damage is a dangerous act. I think of how, even as a feminist lesbian, I have so wanted to ignore my own homophobia, my own hatred of myself for being queer. I have not wanted to admit that my deepest personal sense of myself has not quite "caught up" with my "woman-identified" politics. I have been afraid to criticize lesbian writers who choose to "skip over" these issues in the name of feminism. In 1979, we talk of "old gay" and "butch and femme" roles as if they were ancient history. We toss them aside as merely patriarchal notions. And yet, the truth of the matter is that I have sometimes taken society's fear and hatred of lesbians to bed with me. I have sometimes hated my lover for loving me. I have sometimes felt "not woman enough" for her. I have sometimes felt "not man enough." For a lesbian trying to survive in a heterosexist society, there is no easy way around these emotions. Similarly, in a white-dominated world, there is little getting around racism and our own internalization of it. It's always there, embodied in someone we least expect to rub up against. When we do rub up against this person, *there* then is the challenge. *There* then is the opportunity to look at the nightmare within us. But we usually shrink from such a challenge.

Time and time again, I have observed that the usual response among white women's groups when the "racism issue" comes up is to deny the difference. I have heard comments like, "Well, we're open to *all* women; why don't they (women of color) come? You can only do so much . . . " But there is seldom any analysis of how the very nature and structure of the group itself may be founded on racist or classist assumptions. More important, so often the women seem to feel no loss, no lack, no absence when women of color are not involved; therefore, there is little desire to change the situation. This has hurt me deeply. I have come to believe that the only reason women of a privileged class will dare to look at *how* it is that *they* oppress, is when they've come to know the meaning of their own oppression. And understand that the oppression of others hurts them personally.

The other side of the story is that women of color and white working-class women often shrink from challenging white middle-class women. It is much easier to rank oppressions and set up a hierarchy than to take responsibility for changing our own lives. We have failed to demand that white women, particularly those who claim to be speaking for all women, be accountable for their racism.

The dialogue has simply not gone deep enough.

In conclusion, I have had to look critically at my claim to color, at a time when, among white feminist ranks, it is a "politically correct" (and sometimes peripherally advantageous) assertion to make. I must acknowledge the fact that, physically, I have had a *choice* about making that claim, in contrast to women who have not had such a choice and have been abused for their color. I must reckon with the fact that for most of my life, by virtue of the very fact that I am white-looking, I identified with and aspired toward white values, and that I rode the wave of that Southern California privilege as far as conscience would let me.

Well, now I feel both bleached and beached. I feel angry about this—about the years when I refused to recognize privilege, both when it worked against me and when I worked it, ignorantly, at the expense of others. These are not settled issues. This is why this work feels so risky to me. It continues to be discovery. It has brought me into contact with women who invariably know a hell of a lot more than I do about racism, as experienced in the flesh, as revealed in the flesh of their writing.

I think: *what is my responsibility to my roots: both white and brown, Spanish-speaking and English?* I am a woman with a foot in both worlds. I refuse the split. I feel the necessity for dialogue. Sometimes I feel it urgently.

But one voice is not enough, nor are two, although this is where dialogue begins. It is essential that feminists confront their fear of and resistance to each other, because without this, there *will* be no bread on the table. Simply, we will not survive. If we could make this connection in our heart of hearts, that if we are serious about a revolution—better, if we seriously believe there should be joy in our lives (real joy, not just "good times")—then we need one another. We women need each other. Because my/your solitary, self-asserting "go-for-the-throat-of-fear" power is not enough. The real power, as you and I well know, is collective. I can't afford to be afraid of you, nor you of me. If it takes head-on collisions, let's do it. This polite timidity is killing us.

As Lorde suggests in the passage I cited earlier, it is looking to the nightmare that the dream is found. There, the survivor emerges to insist on a future, a vision, yes, born out of what is dark and female. The feminist movement must be a movement of such survivors, a movement with a future.

Berkeley, California,
September 1979

FOR THE COLOR OF MY MOTHER

I am a white girl gone brown to the blood color of my mother speaking to her through the
unnamed part of the mouth the wide-arched muzzle of brown women

at two
my upper lip split open
clear to the tip of my nose
it spilled forth a cry that would not yield
that traveled down six floors of hospital
where doctors wound me into white bandages
only the screaming mouth exposed

the gash sewn back into a snarl
would last for years

I am a white girl gone brown to the blood color of my mother speaking for her

at five, *her* mouth
pressed into a seam
a fine blue child's line drawn across her face
her mouth, pressed into mouthing english
mouthing yes yes yes
mouthing stoop lift carry
(sweating wet sighs into the field
her red bandanna comes loose from under the huge brimmed hat moving
across her upper lip)

at fourteen, her mouth
painted, the ends drawn up
the mole in the corner colored in darker larger mouthing yes
she praying no no no
lips pursed and moving

at forty-five, her mouth
bleeding into her stomach
the hole gaping growing redder
deepening with my father's pallor
finally stitched shut from hip to breastbone
    an inverted V
    Vera
    Elvira

I am a white girl gone brown to the blood color of my mother speaking for her

. . . . .

as it should be,
dark women come to me
                    sitting in circles
I pass thru their hands
the head of my mother
painted in clay colors

                    touching each carved feature swollen eyes and mouth

they understand the explosion, the splitting
open   contained within the fixed expression

they cradle her silence
                    nodding to me

IT'S THE POVERTY

for Kim

You say to me,
"Take a drive with me
up the coast, babe
and bring your typewriter."

All the way down the coast
you and she stopped at motels
your typewriters tucked under your free arm
dodging the rain fast to the shelter
of metal awnings, red and white
I imagine them—you two
snorting brandy in those vinyl rooms
propping your each machine onto an end table.

. . . . .

This story becomes you.
A fiction I invent with my ears
evoking heroism in the first
description of the weather.

I say
my typewriter sticks in the wet.
I have been using the same ribbon
over and over and over again.
Yes, we both agree I could use
a new ribbon. But it's the poverty
the poverty of my imagination, we agree.
I lack imagination you say.

No. I lack language.

The language to clarify
my resistance to the literate.
Words are a war to me.
They threaten my family.

To gain the word to describe the loss,
I risk losing everything.
I may create a monster,
the word's length and body
swelling up colorful and thrilling
looming over my *mother*, characterized.
Her voice in the distance
unintelligible   illiterate.

These are the monster's words.

. . . . .

Understand.
My family is poor.
Poor. I can't afford
a new ribbon. The risk
of this one
is enough
to keep me moving
through it, accountable.
The repetition, like my mother's stories retold,
each time reveals more particulars
gains more familiarity.
You can't get me in your car so fast.

. . . . .

You tell me how you've learned
to write while you drive
how I can leave my droning machine behind
for all
you care.

I say, not-so-fast
not
so
fast. The drone
a chant to my ears
a common blend of histories
repeatedly inarticulate.

Not so fast.
I am poorer than you.
In my experience, fictions
are for hearing about,
not living.

WHAT DOES IT TAKE?

for Sally Gearhart upon the death of Harvey Milk

1

The martyrs they give us
have all been men
my friend, she traces her life
through them   a series of assassinations
but not one, not
one making her bleed.

This is not the death of my mother
but my father
the kind one/the provider
pressed into newsprint
in honest good will.

If they took *you*
I would take to the streets scream, BLOODY MURDER.

But the deaths of our mothers
are never that public
they have happened before
and we were not informed.
Women do not coagulate into one
hero's death; we bleed
out of many pores, so constant
that it has come to be seen
as the way things are.

2

Waiting
my mother's dying
was not eventful.
Expecting it
I put a hole in my arm
no TNT blast
but a slow excavation
my nails, in silent opposition
digging down to the raw part
inside the elbow.

If they took *you*
I would take to the streets
scream, BLOODY MURDER.

What does it take to move me?
your death
that I have ignored
in the deaths of other women?

Isn't the *possibility*
of your dying
enough?

SALVATION, JESUS, AND SUFFER

Last night at work, a woman younger than me with rosary beads and a scapular wrapped 'round her neck came floating into the restaurant, acting like she was gonna have a fit or something crazy—her eyelids blinking a hundred miles an hour, her eyeballs rolling up into her head, only the whites showing.

It was sunday-rush and she stood there in the middle of the floor, telling everybody they should all leave immediately because *Jesus was coming*. And what was funny is that everybody stopped eating, their forks hanging in the air in front of their open mouths, and listened. Just for a second, but for that second, she had their complete attention.

As a nut, people noticed her. She'd be nobody if she weren't a crazy woman.

I hate religion, I said to Jeanne the hostess who kept trying to get the crazy woman to sit down, shut up and eat some soup. I hate that she has all those words about salvation and jesus and suffer to pull off this scene with. Confusing the point.

The woman left and came back at least seven times before she finally left for good. Nobody wanted to throw her out—to where? But every time she came in again, my stomach would get all tied up in knots and I kept getting these hits of myself at about eleven years old, shaking my body up and down trying to rattle the "impure thoughts" outta it.

She and I, we're the same woman, but nobody notices me like that.

ANATOMY LESSON

A black woman and a small beige one talk about their bodies.
About putting a piece of their anatomy in their pockets
upon entering any given room.

When entering a room full of soldiers who fear hearts,
you put your heart in your back pocket,
the black woman explains. It is important, not to intimidate.
The soldiers wear guns, *not* in their back pockets.

You let the heart fester there. You let the heart seethe.
You let the impatience of the heart build and build
until the power of the heart hidden begins to be felt in the room.
Until the absence of the heart begins to take on the shape
of a presence.
Until the soldiers look at you and begin to beg you
to open up your heart to them, so anxious are they to see
what it is they fear they fear.

Do not be seduced.

Do not forget for a minute that the soldiers wear guns.
Hang onto your heart.
Ask them first what they'll give up to see it.
Tell them that they can begin with their arms.

Only then will *you* begin to negotiate.

IT GOT HER OVER

1

To touch
her skin felt thick
like hide, not
like flesh
and blood
when an arm is raised
the blue veins shine
rivers running under-
ground with shadow
depth, and tone.

No, *her* skin
had turned on her
in the light of things.
In the light of Black
women and children
beaten/hanged/raped
strangled
murdered in Boston
Atlanta
in California where redneck
hunters coming home
with empty white hands
go off to fill 'em
with Black Man.

Her skin had turned
in the light of these things.
Stuck to her now
like a flat immovable paste
spread grey over a life.

Still,
    it got her over
in laundromats
when machines ate her change
swallowed whole her dollar bill
when cops stopped to check what the problem was
Remember
I could be your daughter she used
looking up from the place on the sand
where two women were spread out, defiant
where he read, *the white one*
must be protected   that time
saving them both.

It got her over
when the bill was late
when she only wanted to browse not buy
when hunger forced them
off the highway and into grills
called "Red's" and "Friendly's"
coffee shops packed suburban
white on white, eyes shifting
to them   and away
to them   and away
and back again
then shifted into safety
lock inside their heads.

2

She had never been ashamed of her face.

Her lust, yes
Her bad grammar, yes
Even her unforgiving ways
but never, her face
recently taken to blushing
    as if the blood wanted
    to swallow
        the flesh.

Bleed through
        guilt by association
        complicity to the crime.
Bleed through
        Born to lead.
        Born to love.
        Born to live.
Bleed through

and flood the joint
with a hatred so severe

people went white
with shock
and dying.

   . . . . .

No, she had *never*
been ashamed of her face
not like this
        grabbing her own two cheeks
her fingers pressed together
as if to hold between them
the thin depth of color.

See this face?
        Wearing it like an accident
of birth.
        It was
a scar sealing up
a woman, now darkened
by desire.

See this face?

Where do you take this hate
to lunch?

How
to get over
this one.

WINTER OF OPPRESSION, 1982

The cold in my chest comes
from having to decide

while the ice builds up on *this* side
of my new-york-apt.-bldg.-living window,
whose death
has been marked
upon the collective forehead
of this continent, this
shattering globe
the most indelibly.

Indelible. A catholic word
I learned
when I learned
that there were catholics and there
were not.
      But somehow
we did not count the Jews
among the have-nots, only protestants
with their cold & bloodless god
with no candles/no incense/no bloody
sacrifice or spirits
lurking.

Protestantism. The white people's
religion.

  . . . . .

First time I remember
seeing pictures of the Holocaust

was in the tenth grade and the moving pictures
were already there in my mind
somehow *before* they showed me
what I already understood
that these people were killed
for the spirit-blood
that runs through them.

They were like us in this.
Ethnic people with long last names
with vowels at the end or the wrong
type of consonants
combined   a colored kind of white people.

But let me tell you
first time I saw an actual
picture glossy photo of a lynching
I was already grown & active
& living & loving Jewish.
Black. White. Puerto
Rican.

And the image blasted
my consciousness
split it wide   I
had never thought   seen
heard   of such a thing
never even imagined the look
of the man   the weight
dead hanging swinging heavy
the fact   of the white people
cold bloodless
looking on   It

had never occurred to me
I tell you   I
the nuns failed to mention

this could happen, too
how could such a thing happen?

because somehow dark real dark
was not quite real
people killed
but some
thing not
taken to heart
in the same way it feels
to see white shaved/starved
burned/buried
the boned bodies stacked & bulldozed
into huge craters made by men
and machines
and at fifteen I counted 22
bodies only in the far left-hand
corner of the movie screen
& I kept running
through my mind
and I'm only one
count one
it could be me
it could be me
I'm nothing
to this cruelty.

. . . . .

Somehow tonight,
is it the particular coldness
where my lover sleeps with a scarf
to keep it out
that causes me to toss
and turn the events of the last weeks
the last years of my life
around in my sleep?

Is it the same white coldness
that forces my back up
against the wall—*choose.*
choose.

I cannot
choose nor forget

how simple
to fall back
upon rehearsed racial memory.

I work to remember
what I never dreamed possible

what my consciousness could never
contrive.

Whoever I am

I must believe
I am not
and will never be
the only
one
who suffers.

THE ROAD TO RECOVERY

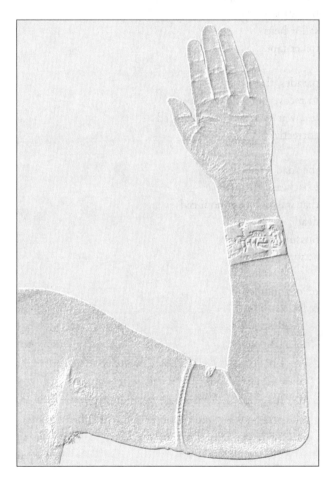

MINDS & HEARTS

the road to recovering
what was lost
in the war
that never pronounced itself

left no visible signs
no ration cards
sailor boys
ticker tape

parades, the road
to recovering what was lost
in a war that never pronounced
correctly

the road to recovering
what was lost in a war
that was never pronounced
dead
missing in
action, prisoner

of our minds
& hearts

NO BORN-AGAIN CHILDREN

"Somebody in my family just died!
Now are you gonna stay dead or pull a lazarus?"

Woman, if I could simply rise up
from this bed of doubt, miraculous and beaming,
I would.
    if I could,
    I would.

. . . . .

You told me that when your brother saw the train coming
he didn't move. He was   transfixed somehow
intensely curious   a boy of twelve with a body of pure
speed and a death wish
he's ready to dump   into the nearest river
or body that can swallow
it.

    He opened you up, pink and hungry, too
    but for the tenderness in his fingers talking
    you into, coaxing you into
    turning cold and quiet into you.

And taking the orange into your five-year-old fist
the boy coming at you again, you flung it out the window.

He stopped dead cold in his tracks.

. . . . .

I don't know why your brother died. I don't know why.
Was it the face of the orange, alive and bright, spinning
before his eyes? The vision of a girl

pushing life through the hole of doom that bore you both?
It *was* a suicide, woman. A suicide we both refuse
daily with all our good brains and tenderness. Still,
you can see me in him, can't you? Riveted onto that track
putting my cheek up against the size of a locomotive
just to see what it's like
just to taste how close it'll get before—

stone still & trembling
I split   off   that rail.

But I am not your brother. I will not die on you
no matter how you dare me
to reenact that tragedy
            like your momma dragging you down
            to the railroad tracks
            still hot from his suicide

        another child dead.

No, I will not die on you and yet, death keeps us
watching. We look to each other for miracles
to wipe out a memory full of dead men and dying
women, but we can't   save each other
from what we learned
to fear.

We can't.

There are no miracles.
No Lazarus.
No born-again children.

Only an orange flung out of a window
like a life line that bears repeating
again and again
until we're both
convinced.

NOVEMBER AGAIN

she called it, *the black pearl* of my conviction
the security of knowing
at least our fear is unchangeable.

at the beach in november, there is a woman
with a thin silk robe draped around her bare shoulders
the rest of her bare, too, and a child coming after her.

naked on the beach and flaunting it, waving the silk
robe up around her head, leaping over its skirt, dancing.
the child humming to himself, like accompaniment.

three times, I imagine myself coming up to her,
taking her by the wrist, explaining to her
how she should cover up, not expose herself so,
not joyfully like this.

passing the woman, I find a thin stone on the shore.
I lick the sand and salt clean from it, then rub it
dry and dull on the thigh of my pants.

leaving the beach, I place it in my pocket.

YOU CALL IT, "AMPUTATION"

Macalister's boy took one of the fish and cut a square out of its side to bait his hook with. The mutilated body (it was alive still) was thrown back into the sea.
— Virginia Woolf, *To the Lighthouse*

You call it
"am pu tation"

but even after the cut
they say the toes still itch
the body remembers the knee,
                    gracefully bending

she reaches down to find her leg gone
the shape under the blanket dropping off
suddenly, irregularly

it is a shock, Woolf says
that by putting into words
we make it whole

still, I feel
the mutilated body
swimming in side stroke
pumping twice as hard
for the lack
of body, pushing
through your words
which hold no water
for me.

FOR AMBER

when her friend Yve died of a stroke

I want to catch it while it's still fresh
and living in you, this talking like
you don't know what's gonna come outta your mouth
next. I watch the bodies pour
right out between those red lips of yours
and without thinking, they're changing me
without trying, they're transforming
before my eyes.

I told you once
that you were like my grandmother
the white one, the gypsy
all dolled up
in a white cadillac convertible
with Big Fins—she red deep
behind the wheel, her bleached blonde
flying. At stop lights she'd be there
just waiting for some sucker
to pull up, thinking she was
a gal of twenty. She'd turn
and flash him a seventy-year-old
smile, and press pedal.

Oh honey, this is you
in all your freeway glory,
the glamour of your ways.

And without stopping
last night you talked about the places
in *you thinking of your body*

that are lost to you, how we locate
that damage in our different parts
like a dead foot, you said, how we run
inventory—checking on which show
promise of revival
and which don't.

. . . . .

What I didn't tell you
was how my grandmother stopped
all of a sudden
turned baby, all of a sudden
speechless
my momma giving her baths
in the tub, while I played nearby
her bare white skin slipping
down off those cold shoulders
piling up around her hips and knees,
slowing her down.

My grandma turned baby
and by the toilet I'd sit with her
she picking out designs in the linoleum
saying this one looks like a man
in a tub, scrubbing his back
with a brush,

and it did.

HEADING EAST

We are driving this car on determination, alone.

The miles seem to repair us
convince us that we are getting somewhere
that we won't have another breakdown

we end up leaking into somebody's movie
trapped in a ghost town   shaniko, oregon   pouring rain

we dive under the car
                              expose its underside, our fingers
feeling into the machine for its sore spot

"I've got it," I scream
"I know where the hole is," our eyes fire each other's

thinking we have conquered the unknown
we patch up the lacerated hose with black tape.

. . . . .

In this town of livery stable, turned museum
we roll out our bags onto the floor
of an abandoned caboose.

    we are *in* somebody's movie

Two women stranded in a ghost town.
They are headed east.
They think they'll make it.

MODERN-DAY HERO

I would not have stopped, but there was the love that I wasn't getting from you which I had to put somewhere. Setting down the two six-packs of beer onto the sidewalk, lifting up the head of the woman lying next to them.

A modern-day hero. If it takes heroism to win you back, then I guess that's what it takes. Kay and I lift the woman into my car. "There, honey, you'll be fine," I hear Kay say for all of us, to each other. "There, honey, we got you. . . . Yes, hold onto your purse."

That was how I found her, clutching her purse into her belly. Every other part of her limp, but her hands tight around her purse. And there was a man with her—drunk like her—trying to get something out of her. Move her. Leave her. Take her purse. I don't know. All I know is that he's standing and she's face down with a mouth full of cement.

The police cars arrive. Some white man comes charging out of his house. "I called the police," he shouts, glad for himself. I could have throttled the guy, waving his hands over his head like a crazy person. *More men to contend with.*

The three of us—the woman, Kay and I—are getting quickly out-numbered. Two cars have pulled up with four cops inside. They pile out. There's only one brown one in the lot, but he's the one that says, looking at me, "Can you ladies get her home all right?" "Yes," I answer. And we do.

As the cop cars pull away and we pull the woman into my car, I can't get you clearly out of my mind. All along wondering how you could see me here, managing these men to save a woman. Lifting this woman up that long flight of stairs, home.

THE WARBRIDE

The minute we got back from Monterey Beach, sat down to table with two taquitos apiece laid out in front of us, I knew our relationship was on the road to recovery. The waitress, built like Tía Vicky—stocky, stick-legs, make-up & busy efficiency—convinced me.

Who can survive the Pacific Ocean? When not bordered by 24th Street Mission District storefronts. When not L.A. Venice Beach pre-redevelopment. When not simple like two sisters who knew the sun's setting into the water as the course of a day—no big deal, no romance, floating in a big black tube beyond the waves. Still counting on the fact that a mother would surely live forever—like a life forever wakening in the kitchen, cooking.

Who can survive the pacific ocean? Not in california. I know the beaches too well to fool you into thinking they are anything but fatal. It's not the water, exactly; it's what drives people to its edge. ROMANCE. SEX. MOMENTS OF QUIET CONTEMPLATION. STEAK & LOBSTER & cliffside mansions owned by hollywood producers clinging to the canyon walls, praying *this* winter's mud will go around them.

"That rock is old," a friend said, "brittle and bitter. It was never meant to hold . . . ," slipping away. But the beaches are about serious living, as if there were actually some huge neon splitting the orange atmosphere overhead as you barrel down highway one, warning: *Danger. Pacific Ocean Ahead. Check Your Life for Meaning.*

It's about taking stock. Makes sense now, in retrospect, how I would find my eyes so fixated on those stockpiles of weapons the army used to store in big cement tombs on their beachfront property just outside Monterey. When I was a warbride, my boyfriend's job was to keep guard there, smoking joints. I wishing there was some *real* Vietnam he could object to, conscientiously. But I'd spread my legs for him anyway in seaside Motel 6's to relieve his misery that he was not out shooting shots & the shit with his dog and his buddies. And what else would I be doing anyway, if not spreading my thighs?

With you, it's supposed to be different and I guess it is when the beat of your hand against my bone/isn't worked against the beat of the water flooding memory/against the walls of my heart beating fast/against the flash of boys beating off, inside me.

LO QUE NUNCA PASÓ POR SUS LABIOS

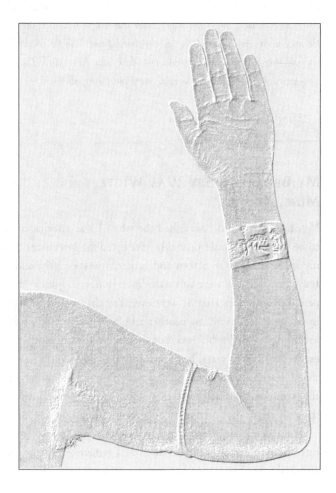

A LONG LINE OF VENDIDAS

para Gloria Anzaldúa, in gratitude

Sueño: 15 de julio 1982

During the long difficult night that sent my lover and I to separate beds, I dreamed of church and chocha. I put it this way because that is how it came to me. The suffering and the thick musty mysticism of the catholic church fused with the sensation of entering the vagina—like that of a colored woman's—dark, rica, full-bodied. The heavy sensation of complexity. A journey I must unravel, work out for myself.

   I long to enter you like a temple.

My Brother's Sex Was White. Mine, Brown

If somebody would have asked me when I was a teenager what it means to be Chicana, I would probably have listed the grievances done me. When my sister and I were fifteen and fourteen, respectively, and my brother a few years older, we were still waiting on him. . . . . I write "were" as if now, nearly two decades later, it were over. But that would be a lie. To this day in my mother's home, my brother and father are waited on by the women, including me. I do this now out of respect for my mother and her wishes. In those early years, however, it was mainly in relation to my brother that I resented providing such service. For unlike my father, who sometimes worked as much as seventy hours a week to feed my face every day, the only thing that earned by brother my servitude was his maleness.

   It was Saturday afternoon. My brother, then seventeen years old, came into the house with a pile of friends. I remember Fernie, the two Steves and Roberto. They were hot, sweaty and exhausted from an afternoon's basketball and plopped themselves down in the front room, my brother demanding, "Girls, bring us something to drink."

"Get it yourself, pig," I thought, but held those words from ever forming inside my mouth. My brother had the disgusting habit on these occasions of collapsing my sister JoAnn's and my name when referring to us as a unit: his sisters. "Cher'ann," he would say, "we're really thirsty." I'm sure it took everything in his power *not* to snap his fingers. But my mother was out in the yard working and to refuse him would have brought her into the house with a scene before these boys' eyes that would have made it impossible for us to show our faces at school the following Monday. We had been through that before.

When my mother had been our age, more than forty years earlier, she had waited on her brothers and their friends. And it was no mere lemonade. They'd come in from work or a day's drinking. And las mujeres, often just in from the fields themselves, would already be in the kitchen making tortillas, warming frijoles or pigs' feet, albóndigas soup, what-have-you. And the men would get a clean white tablecloth and a spread of food laid out before their eyes and not a word of resentment from the women.

The men watched the women—my aunts and mother moving with the grace and speed of girls who were cooking before they could barely see over the top of the stove. Elvira, my mother, knew she was being watched by the men and loved it. Her slim hips moved patiently beneath the apron. Her deep thick-lidded eyes never caught theirs as she was swept back into the kitchen by my abuelita's call of "Elvirita," her brown hands deepening in color as they dropped back into the pan of flour.

I suppose my mother imagined that Joe's friends watched us like that, too. But we knew different. We were not blonde or particularly long-legged or "available" because we were "Joe's sisters." This meant no boy could "make" us, which meant no boy would bother asking us out. Roberto, the Guatemalan, was the only one among my brother's friends who seemed at all sensitive to how awkward JoAnn and I felt in our role. He would smile at us nervously, taking the lemonade, feeling embarrassed being waited on by people he considered peers. He knew the anglo girls they visited would never have succumbed to such a task. Roberto was the only recompense.

As I stopped to satisfy their yearning throats, "jock itch" was all that came to my mind. Their cocks became animated in my head, for that was all that seemed to arbitrarily set us apart from each other and put me in the position of the servant and they, the served. I wanted to machine-gun them all down, but swallowed that fantasy as I swallowed making the boy's bed every day, cleaning his room each week, shining his shoes and ironing his shirts before dates with girls, some of whom *I* had crushes on. I would "lend" him the money I had earned house-cleaning for twelve hours so he could blow it on one night with a girl because he seldom had enough money because he seldom had a job because there was always some kind of ball practice to go to. And as I pressed the bills into his hand, the car honking outside in the driveway, his double-date waiting, I knew I would never see that money again.

Years later, after I began to make political the fact of my being Chicana, I remember my brother saying to me, "*I've* never felt 'culturally deprived'," which I guess is the term "white" people use to describe people of color being denied access to *their culture*. At the time, I wasn't exactly sure what he meant, but I remember in re-telling the story to my sister, she responded, "Of course, he didn't. He grew up male in our house. He got the best of both worlds." And yes, I can see that truth now. *Male in a man's world. Light-skinned in a white world. Why change?*

The pull to identify with the oppressor was never as great in me as it was in my brother. For unlike him, I could never have *become* the white man, only the white man's *woman*.

The first time I began to recognize clearly my alliances on the basis of race and sex was when my mother was in the hospital, extremely ill. I was eight years old. During my mother's stay in the hospital, my tía Eva took my sister and me into her care; my brother stayed with my abuela; and my father stayed by himself in our home. During this time, my father came to visit me and my sister only once. (I don't know if he ever visited my brother.) The strange thing was, I didn't really miss his visits, although I sometimes fantasized some imaginary father, dark and benevolent, who might come and remind us that we still *were* a family.

I have always had a talent for seeing things I don't particularly want to see and the one day my father did come to visit us with his wife/our mother physically dying in a hospital some ten miles away, I saw that he couldn't love us—not in the way we so desperately needed. I saw that he didn't know how and he came into my tía's house like a large lumbering child—awkward and embarrassed out of his league—trying to *play* a parent when he needed our mother back as much as we did just to keep him eating and protected. I hated and pitied him that day. I knew how he was letting us all down, visiting my mother daily, like a dead man, unable to say, "The children, honey, I held them. They love you. They think of you," giving my mother *something.*

Years later, my mother spoke of his visits to the hospital. How from behind the bars of her bed and through the tubes in her nose, she watched this timid man come and go daily, going through the motions of being a husband. "I knew I had to live," she told us. "I knew he could never take care of you children."

In contrast to the seeming lack of feeling I held for my father, my longings for my mother and fear of her dying were the most passionate feelings that had ever lived inside my young heart.

We are riding the elevator. My sister and I pressed up against one wall, holding hands. After months of separation, we are going to visit mi mamá in the hospital. My tía tells me, "Whatever you do, no llores, Cherríe. It's too hard on your mother when you cry." I nod, taking long deep breaths, trying to control my quivering lip.

As we travel up floor by floor, all I can think about is not crying, breathing, holding my breath. "¿Me prometes?" she asks. I nod again, afraid to speak fearing my voice will crack into tears. My sister's nervous hand around mine, sweating too. We are going to see my mami, mamá, after so long. She didn't die after all. She didn't die.

The elevator doors open. We walk down the corridor, my heart pounding. My eyes are darting in and out of each room as we pass them, fearing/anticipating my mami's face. Then as we turn around the corner into a kind of lobby, I hear my tía say to an older woman, just skin and bones—an Indian, I think—straight black-and-grey hair pulled back, I hear my tía say, "Elvira."

I don't recognize her. This is not the woman I knew, so round and made-up with her hair always a wavy jet black! I stay back until she opens her arms to me—this strange and familiar woman—her voice hoarse, "¡Ay mi'jita!" Instinctively, I run into her arms, still holding back my insides. "Don't cry. Don't cry," I remember. "Whatever you do, no llores." But my *tía* had not warned me about the smell, the unmistakable smell of the woman, *mi mamá, el olor de aceite y jabón* and comfort and home. "*Mi mamá.*" And when I catch the smell I am lost in tears, deep long tears that come when you have held your breath for centuries.

There was something I knew at that eight-year-old moment that I vowed never to forget—the smell of a woman who is life and home to me at once. The woman in whose arms I am uplifted, sustained. Since then, it is as if I have spent the rest of my years driven by this scent toward la mujer.

> *when her india makes love*
> *it is with the greatest reverence*
> *to color, texture, smell*
>
> *by now she knew the scent of earth*
> *could call it up*
> *even between the cracks*
> *in sidewalks*
> *steaming dry*
> *from midday summer*
> *rain*

With this knowledge so deeply emblazed upon my heart, how then was I supposed to turn away from La Madre, La Chicana? If I were to build my womanhood on this self-evident truth, it is the love of the Chicana, the love of myself as a Chicana I had to embrace, no white man. Maybe this ultimately was the cutting difference between my brother and me. To be a woman fully necessitated my claiming the race of my mother. My brother's sex was white. Mine, brown.

Like a White Sheep I Followed

SUEÑO: 3 DE JULIO

I am having my face made up, especially my eyes, by a very beautiful Chicana. The make-up artist changes me entirely for only five dollars. I think this is a very low price for how deep and dark she makes me look.

When I was growing up, I looked forward to the days when my skin would toast to match my cousins', their skin turning pure black in the creases. I never could quite catch up, but my skin did turn smooth like theirs, oily brown—like my mamá's, holding depth, density, the possibility of infinite provision. Mi abuela raised the darkest cousins herself, she never loving us the way she molded and managed them.

To write as a Chicana feminist lesbian, I am afraid of being mistaken, of being made an outsider again, having to fight the kids at school to get them to believe Teresita and I were cousins. "You don't *look* like cousins!" I feel at times I am trying to bulldoze my way back into a people who forced me to leave them in the first place, who taught me to take my whiteness and run with it. Run with it. Who want nothing to do with me, the likes of me, the white of me—in them.

When was I forced to choose? When Vivian Molina after two years of the deepest, richest friendship, two years of me helping her through "new math," helping her not flunk once more—once was enough—and her so big already, fat and dark-skinned. When Vivian left me flat, I didn't know what happened, except I knew she was beginning to smell like a woman and once, just before our split-up, the neighbor-kid talked of Vivian growing hair "down there." I didn't get it, except I knew that none of these changes were settling right in Vivian. And I was small and thin, still, and light-skinned and I loved Vivian which didn't seem to matter in the way teachers were wondering if Vivian was going to make it through the year. So, one day that year Vivian came to school and never spoke to me again. Nothing happened between us. I swear nothing happened.

I would call her and plead, "Vivian, what did I do?" "Vivian, ¿por qué?" I would have asked in Spanish had I been taught. "¿Qué pasó? No entiendo ¿Qué pasó?" But she never let on, except once when she nearly started to cry near the water fountain in the school corridor when I asked her for the last time and her eyes met mine finally and she said, I think or I'd like to remember, "I'm sorry." And even if she didn't say that, exactly, I know she said something that told me we were in different leagues now. And it couldn't be helped. It was out of our control. Something she, a year and a half older and much darker, knew before I knew, and like a white sheep I followed the path paved for me.

Rocky Hernández was brilliant and tough. Got mostly A's in school, like Carmen Luna, who was her second cousin in the same grade. They were both wizards, but Rocky was sharper and mean in her sharpness. "Antagonistic," the nuns would say, and she'd prove it in her handwriting which slanted way off to the left which I admired greatly, which the nuns found "incorrigible." When it came time for the Catholic high school entrance exams, we learned in May what track we would be in for the coming freshman year. To my amazement, I got into the "A" group—college prep. To my equal amazement, Rocky and her cousin were tracked into the "C" group—business and general education, where they teach you home economics and typing. Rocky could talk and write and compute circles around me, which didn't seem to compute on our entrance exams. After we got into high school, the Irish and Italian girls became my friends. And Rocky and I seldom, if ever, spoke.

The bitter irony is that my Mexican mother, not my anglo father, fixed me on the singular idea of getting an education, while my grade school and high school years continued to persuade me, and my Mexican classmates, that academic learning was the privilege of gringos in this country. "Without an education, you're nothing," my mother would say. "Look at me. If only I could write better, I could get a different kind of job, I wouldn't have to do the kind of work I do." She was constantly criticizing this or that younger aunt or uncle or in-law who had what she did not—basic reading and writing skills—who still worked factory. It never occurred to her, or if it did, she never let on to us children, that race was any factor in reducing one's chances for success.

And in terms of rearing her three light-skinned chestnut-haired children, we in fact did not have to fear, like my cousins, racial discrimination. On the surface of things we could pass as long as we made no point of our Mexican heritage. As long as we moved my father's English surname through our lives like a badge of membership to the white open-door policy club.

In fact, I had never fully realized until this year, when I went back to California and the words tumbled out of my mouth to my sister, that color had anything to do with the reason my sister and brother and I were *the* success stories of the family. We have received the most education and work in recognized professions. I had acknowledged this inequity between myself and my mother's generation, but not within my own.

I remember my friend Tavo's words only two years ago, "You get to choose." He told me he didn't trust güeros, that we had to prove ourselves to him in some way. And I felt that challenge for proof laid flat on the table between us.

So, I said, "Well, I understand that because it's awfully hard to be in this position under suspicion from so many." This constant self-scrutiny, digging deeper, digging deeper.

Then Tavo said to me, "You see, at any time, if they [meaning me] decide to use their light skin privilege, they can. You can decide you're suddenly not Chicana."

That I can't say, but once my light skin and good English saved me and my lover from arrest. And I'd use it again. I'd use it to the hilt over and over to save our skins.

"You get to choose." Now I want to shove those words right back into his face. You call this a choice! To constantly push up against a wall of resistance from your own people or to fall away nameless into the mainstream of this country, running with our common spilled blood?

But I *have* betrayed my people.

Rita Villareal and I used to go to the roller rink together. I never noticed how dark she was until my mother pointed this out to me, warning me against her. How her jet-black straight hair and coffee bean skin marked her as a different grade of mexicana. *Una india, de clase baja.* It was the first fight about race I ever had with my mother. When I protested, she said to me, "It isn't her color and I never tell you about your friends, but this girl is going to get you in trouble. She's no good for you." Our friendship soon broke off, me keeping a distance from Rita. Later, she got into boys and booze. *Was my mother right?*

Maybe this was what my best friend Vivian had feared/expected in me, my turning my back on her, like I had on that Wizard Rocky.

Many years later, when I was already in college, I had come home for the weekend and went on a short run to the neighborhood supermarket for my mom. There, for the first time in at least three years, I ran into Rocky. She was pushing a shopping cart, and inside it was one of the most beautiful baby boys I had ever laid eyes on, jabbering and wide-eyed.

Rocky and I talked. It was clear we both still felt some affection for each other from those early grade-school days. I touched the kid's cheek, complimenting her on him. When she turned to enter the checkout line, I wanted to stop her, invite her to dinner, not let her out of my sight again. But I hesitated, wondering what more we would have to say to each other after so many years. I let her go.

Driving home, I remembered that there had been rumors that Rocky had been pregnant at graduation.

Traitor Begets Traitor

What looks like betrayal between women on the basis of race originates, I believe, in sexism/heterosexism. Chicanas begin to turn our backs on each other either to gain male approval or to avoid being sexually stigmatized by men under the name of puta, vendida, jota. This phenomenon is as old as the day is long, and first learned in the schoolyard, long before it is played out with a vengeance within political communities.

In the seventh grade, I fell in love with Manuel Poblano. A small-boned boy, hair always perfectly combed and oiled. His uniform shirt pressed neatly over shoulder blades jutting out. At twelve, Manuel was growing in his identity—sexually, racially—and Patsy Juárez, my one-time fifth-grade friend, wanted him too. Manuel was pals with Leticia and Connie. I remember how they flaunted a school picture of his in front of my face, proving how *they* could get one from him, although I had asked first. The two girls were conspiring to get him to "go" with Patsy, which in the end, he finally did. I, knowing all along I didn't have a chance. Not brown enough. And the wrong last name.

At puberty, it seemed identity alliances were already beginning to be made along rigid and immovable lines of race, as it combined with sex. And everyone—boy, girl, anglo and Chicano—fell into place. Where did *I* stand?

I did not move away from other Chicanos because I did not love my people. I gradually became anglocized because I thought it was the only option available to me toward gaining autonomy as a person without being sexually stigmatized. I can't say that I was conscious of all this at the time, only that at each juncture in my development, I instinctively made choices which I thought would allow me greater freedom of move-ment in the future. This primarily meant resisting sex roles as much as I could safely manage, and this was far easier in an anglo context than in a Chicano one. That is not to say that anglo culture does not stigmatize its women for "gender-transgressions," only that its stigmatizing did not hold the personal power over me that Chicano culture did.

Chicanas' negative perceptions of ourselves as sexual persons and our consequential betrayal of each other finds its roots in a four-hundred-year-long Mexican history and mythology. It is further entrenched by a system of anglo imperialism which long ago put mexicanos and Chicanos in a defensive posture against the dominant culture.

The sexual legacy passed down to the mexicana/Chicana is the legacy of betrayal, pivoting around the historical/mythical female figure of Malintzín Tenepal. As a Native woman and translator, strategic adviser and mistress to the Spanish conqueror of México, Hernán Cortéz, Malintzín is considered the mother of the mestizo people. But unlike La Virgen de Guadalupe, she is not revered as La Madre Sagrada, but rather slandered as La Chingada, meaning the "fucked one," or La Vendida, sell-out to the white race.[1]

Upon her shoulders rests the full blame for the "bastardization" of the indigenous people of México. To put it in its most base terms: Malintzín, also called Malinche, fucked the white man who conquered the Indian peoples of México and nearly obliterated their cultures. Ever since, brown men have been accusing her of betraying her race, and over the centuries continue to blame her entire sex for this historical/sexual "transgression."

As a Chicana and a feminist, I must, like other Chicanas before me, examine the effects this myth has on my/our racial/sexual identity and my relationship with other Chicanas. There is hardly a Chicana growing up today who does not suffer under Malinche's name, even if she never hears directly of the one-time Aztec princess.

The Aztecs had recorded that Quetzalcoatl, the feathered serpent god, would return from the east to redeem his people in the year One Reed, according to the Aztec calendar. Destiny would have it that on this very day, April 21, 1519 (as translated to the Western calendar), Cortéz and his men, fitting the description of Quetzalcoatl, light-haired and bearded, landed in Vera Cruz.[2]

At the time of Cortéz's arrival in México, the Aztecs had subjugated much of the Indian population, including the Mayans and Tabascans, who were much less powerful militarily. War was a religious requirement for the Aztecs in order to take prisoners to be used for sacrificial offerings to the sun-god, Huitzilopochtli. As slaves and potential sacrificial victims to the Aztecs, then, many other Indian nations, after their own negotiations and sometimes bloody exchanges with the Spanish, were eager to join forces with the Spanish to overthrow the Aztec empire. The Aztecs, through their systematic subjugation of much of the Mexican Indian population, decreed their own self-destruction.[3]

Chicana feminist theorist, Aleida Del Castillo, contends that as a woman of deep spiritual commitment, Malinche aided Cortéz because she understood him to be Quetzalcoatl returned in a different form to save the peoples of México from total extinction. She writes, "The destruction of the Aztec empire, the conquest of México and as such, the termination of her indigenous world" was, in Malinche's eyes, "inevitable" in order to make way for the new spiritual age that was imminent.[4]

Del Castillo and other Chicana feminists who are researching and re-interpreting Malinche's role in the conquest of México are not trying to justify the imperialism of the Spanish. Rather, they are attempting to create a more realistic context for, and therefore a more sympathetic view of, Malinche's actions.

The root of the fear of betrayal by a woman is not at all specific to the Mexican or Chicano. The resemblance between Malinche and the story of Eve is all too obvious. In chronicling the conquest of México and founding the Catholic Church there, the Spanish passed on to the mestizo people as legacy their own European-Catholic interpretation of Mexican events. Much of this early interpretation originated from Bernal Díaz del Castillo's eye-witness account of the conquest. As the primary source of much contemporary analysis as well, the picture we have of Mexican Indian civilization during that period often contains a strong Catholic and Spanish bias.

In his writings, Bernal Díaz del Castillo notes that upon the death of Malinche's father, the young Aztec princess was in line to inherit his estate. Malinche's mother wanted her son from her second marriage to inherit the wealth instead. She therefore sold her own daughter into slavery. According to Gloria Anzaldúa, there are writings in México to refute this account, but it was nevertheless recorded—or commonly believed—that Malinche was betrayed by her own mother.[5] This myth of the inherent unreliability of women, our natural propensity for treachery, has been carved into the very bone of Mexican/Chicano collective psychology.

Traitor begets traitor.

Little is made of this early betrayal, whether or not it actually occurred, probably because no man was immediately affected. In a way, Malinche's mother would only have been doing her Mexican wifely duty: *putting the male first.*

There is none so beautiful as the Mexican male. I have never met any kind of mexicano who, although he may have claimed his family was very woman-dominated ("mi mamá made all the real decisions"), did not subscribe to the basic belief that men are better. It is so ordinary a statement as to sound simplistic and I am nearly embarrassed to write it, but that's the truth in its kernel.

Ask, for example, any Chicana mother about her children and she is quick to tell you she loves them all the same, but she doesn't. *The boys are different.* Sometimes I sense that she feels this way because she wants to believe that through her mothering, she can develop the kind of man she would have liked to have married, or even have been. That through her son she can get a small taste of male privilege, since without race or class privilege that's all there is to be had. The daughter can never offer the mother such hope, straddled by the same forces that confine the mother. As a result, the daughter must constantly earn the mother's love, prove her fidelity to her. The son—he gets her love for free.

After ten years of feminist consciousness and activism, why does this seem so significant to me—to write of the Mexican mother favoring the son? I think because I had never quite gone back to the source. Never said in my own tongue, *the boys, they are men, they can do what they want . . . after all, he's a man.*

JOURNAL ENTRY: APRIL 1980

Three days ago, my mother called me long distance full of tears, loving me, wanting me back in her life after such a long period of separation. My mother's tears succeed in getting me to break down the edge in my voice, the protective distance. My mother's pleading "mi'jita, I love you, I hate to feel so far away from you" succeeds in opening my heart again to her.

I don't remember exactly why my heart had been shut, only that it had been very necessary to keep my distance, that in a way we had agreed to that. But, it only took her crying to pry my heart open again.

I feel myself unriveting. The feelings begin to flood my chest. Yes, this is why I love women. This woman is my mother. There is no love as strong as this, refusing my separation, never settling for a secret that would split us off, always at the last minute, like now, pushing me to brink of revelation, speaking the truth.

I am as big as a mountain! I want to say, "Watch out, Mamá! I love you and I am as big as a mountain!" And it is on the brink of this precipice where I feel my body descending into the places where we have not spoken, the times I did not fight back. I am descending, ready to speak the truth, finally.

And then suddenly, over the phone, I hear another ring. My mother tells me to wait. There is a call on my father's work phone. Moments later, "It is your brother," she says. My knees lock under me, bracing myself for the fall. . . . Her voice lightens up. "Okay, mi'jita. I love you. I'll talk to you later," cutting off the line in the middle of the connection.

I am relieved when I hang up that I did not have the chance to say more. The graceful reminder. This man doesn't have to earn her love. My brother has always come first.

Seduction and betrayal. Since I've grown up, no woman cares for me for free. There is always a price. My love.

What I wanted from my mother was impossible. It would have meant her going against Mexican/Chicano tradition in a very fundamental way. You are a traitor to your race if you do not put the man first. The potential accusation of "traitor" or "vendida" is what hangs above the heads and beats in the hearts of most Chicanas seeking to develop our own autonomous sense of ourselves, particularly through sexuality. Even if a Chicana knew no Mexican history, the concept of betraying one's race through sex and sexual politics is as common as corn. As cultural myths reflect the economics, mores and social structures of a society, every Chicana suffers from their effects. And we project the fear onto each other. We suspect betrayal in one another—first to other men, but ultimately and more insidiously, to the white man.

JOURNAL ENTRY: NOVIEMBRE 1980

. . . this white man coming up over and over again. There's something about him that feels like such a suck to me. And so I ask myself, is it only that my Chicana mother fed my white father all the days of her life? Is it this model I am struck with/stuck with? The white man getting the attention that should go to the Chicana daughters, that should be shared between women?

I don't sense within our culture the same fear of a man betraying our race. It is the woman who is the object of our contempt. We can't ultimately hold onto her, not in the cosmic sense. She who could provide us with the greatest sense of belonging is never truly ours; for she is always potential chattel for the white man. As with so many of our mothers, my mother's relationship with white men made survival for her and her family possible.

It was Mr. Bowman who saved the day. Saved the day in Tijuana. Big white businessman Mr. Bowman. Not very good-looking, but did he need to be? Had money. A very good dresser, mi mamá would say. The second wife, a mexicana—or was that his mistress? No recuerdo, pero this was a man to be counted on.

Cuando se murió mi abuelo, he gave mamá the bucks for the funeral. Mi abuela never asking where it came from. Mi mamá said to me, "She didn't care how I got it. How did she think I got it? I was only a girl, hija, a girl."

'Bout the time she got to the Foreign Club, they were both older. He was no spring chicken, never, even in the early years, but by now she was close to eighteen and he thought, after all, it's about time.

The chauffeur, a mexicano, put them into the back seat of the big blue sedan and they all began their way down the coast toward Rosarito Beach. Mi mamá praying the entire way, praying "santo niño madre de dios san antonio" . . . you name it, she brought out every saint and holy person she could think of, but focusing, of course, on her patron, San Antonio. Running the rosary beads through her mind, she prayed, "San Antonio, por favor, ayúdame."

She had seen the chauffeur fill the tank with gas. They had all gone to the station together. She remembered that. She had seen him fill it up. But there they were, her praying between snatches of conversation, Big Bowman sitting next to her, pleased with himself, and the car starts sputtering and jerking to a stop. They were out of gas. Smack in the desert.

It was a day's journey back to town.

No gas. No hotel. No Rosarito. No sex with Mr. Bowman.

That time the saints saved her.

"He never laid a hand on me. It wasn't that he didn't want to," she said, "but I was very lucky. If he would of wanted me, what could I do? But I was very lucky."

So little has been documented as to the actual suffering Chicanas have experienced resisting or succumbing to the sexual demands of white men. The ways we have internalized the sexual hatred and exploitation they have displayed against us are probably too numerous and too ingrained to even identify. If the Chicana, like her brother, suspects other women of betrayal, then she must, in the most profound sense, suspect herself. How deep her suspicions run will measure how ardently she defends her commitment, above all, to the Chicano male. As obedient sister/daughter/lover she is the committed heterosexual, the socially acceptable Chicana. Even if she's politically radical, sex remains the bottom line on which she proves her commitment to her raza.

WE FIGHT BACK WITH OUR FAMILIES

Because heterosexism[6]—the Chicana's sexual commitment to the Chicano male—is proof of her fidelity to her people, the Chicana feminist attempting to critique the sexism in the Chicano community is certainly between a personal rock and a political hard place.

Although not called "the sexism debate," as it has been in the literary sectors of the Black movement, the Chicano discussion of sexism within our community has, like that movement, been largely limited by heterosexual assumption: "How can we get our men right?" The feminist-oriented material which appeared in the late 70s and early 80s for the most part strains in its attempt to stay safely within the boundaries of Chicano—male-defined and often anti-feminist—values.

Over and over again, Chicanas trivialize the women's movement as being merely a white middle-class thing, having little to offer women of color. They cite only the most superficial aspects of the movement. For example, in "From Woman to Woman," Silvia S. Lizarraga writes:

> [C]lass distinction is a major determinant of attitudes toward other
> subordinated groups. In the U.S. we see this phenomenon operat-
> ing in the goals expressed in the Women's Liberation Movement. . . .
> The needs represent a large span of interests—from those of *capi-
> talist women,* women in business and professional careers, to *witches*
> and *lesbians.* However, the needs of the unemployed and working
> class women of different ethnic minorities are generally overlooked
> by this movement.[7] (*my emphasis*)

This statement typifies the kind of one-sided perspective of the women's movement many Chicanas have given in the name of Chicana liberation. My question is, *whom* are they trying to serve? Certainly not the Chicana who is deprived of some very critical information about a ten-year grassroots feminist movement where women of color, including lesbians of color (certainly in the minority and most assuredly encountering "feminist" racism), have been actively involved in reproductive rights, especially sterilization abuse, battered women's shelters, rape crisis centers, welfare advocacy, Third World women's conferences, cultural events, health clinics and more.

Interestingly, it is perfectly acceptable among Chicano males to use white theoreticians—e.g., Marx and Engels—to develop a theory of Chicano oppression. It is unacceptable, however, for the Chicana to use white feminist sources to develop a theory of Chicana oppression. Even if one subscribes to a solely economic theory of oppression, how can one ignore that over half of the world's workers are female who suffer discrimination not only in the workplace, but also at home and in all the areas of sex-related abuse? How can she afford not to recognize that the wars against imperialism occurring both domestically and internationally are always accompanied by the rape of women of color by both white men and men of color? Without a feminist analysis, what name do we put to these facts? Are these not deterrents to the Chicana developing a sense of "species being"? Are these "women's issues" not also "people's issues"? It is far easier for the Chicana to criticize white women, who on the face of things could never be familia, than to take issue with or complain, as it were, to a brother, uncle, father.

The most valuable aspect of Chicana theory thus far has been its re-evaluation of our history from a woman's perspective by unearthing the stories of Mexican/Chicana female figures that early on exhibited feminist consciousness. The weakness of these works is that many of them are undermined by what I call the "alongside-our-man-knee-jerk-phenomenon."

In speaking of María Hernández, "a feminist and leader in her own right," Alfredo Mirandé and Evangelina Enríquez, the editors of *La Chicana*, offer a typical disclaimer: "[Still] she is always quick to point to the importance of family unity in the movement and to acknowledge the help of her husband. . . . "[8] And yet we would think nothing of the Chicano activist never mentioning the many "behind-the-scenes" Chicanas who helped him!

In the same text, the authors fall into the too-common trap of coddling the Chicano male ego (which should be, in and of itself, an insult to Chicanos) in the name of cultural loyalty. Like the Black Superwoman, the Chicana is forced to take on extra-human proportions. She must keep the cultural home-fires burning while going out and making a living. She must fight racism alongside her man, but challenge sexism single-handedly, all the while retaining her "femininity" so as not to offend or threaten *her man.* This is what being a Chicana feminist has meant in Chicano-defined terms.

In recent years, however, truly feminist Chicanas are beginning to make the pages of Chicano, feminist and literary publications. This, of course, is only a reflection of a fast-growing Chicana/U.S. Third World feminist movement. I am in debt to the research and writings of Norma Alarcón, Martha Cotera, Gloria Anzaldúa and Aleida Del Castillo, to name a few.* Their work reflects a relentless commitment to putting the female first, even when it means criticizing el hombre.[9]

To be critical of one's culture is not to betray that culture. We tend to be very righteous in our criticism and indictment of the dominant culture and we so often suffer from the delusion that, since Chicanos are so maligned from the outside, there is little room to criticize those aspects within our oppressed culture that oppress us.

I am not particularly interested in whether or not people of color learned sexism from the white man. There have been great cases made to prove how happy men and women were together before the white man made tracks in indigenous soil. This reflects the same mentality of white feminists who claim that all races were in harmony when the "Great Mother" ruled us all. In both cases, history tends to prove different. In either case, the strategy for the elimination of racism and sexism cannot occur through the exclusion of one problem or the other. As the Combahee River Collective, a Black feminist organization, states, women of color experience these oppressions "simultaneously."[10] The only people who can afford not to recognize this are those who do not suffer this multiple oppression.

I remain amazed at how often so-called "Tercermundistas" in the U.S. work to annihilate the concept and existence of white supremacy, but turn their faces away from male supremacy. Perhaps this is because when you

---

*In acknowledging these few women, I think of so many other Chicanas and other Latina feminists who were the very first in their political activism to bring up the issue of our particular oppression as brown women. Speaking up in isolation, ten and fifteen years ago, without a movement to support them, these women had little opportunity to record their own history of struggle. And yet, it is they who make this writing and the writing of my compañeras possible.

start to talk about sexism, the world becomes increasingly complex. The power no longer breaks down into neat little hierarchical categories, but becomes a series of starts and detours. Since the categories are not easy to arrive at, the enemy is not easy to name. It is all so difficult to unravel. It *is* true that some men hate women even in their desire for them. And some men oppress the very women they love. But unlike the racist, they allow the object of their contempt to share the table with them. The hatred they feel for women does not translate into separatism. It is more insidiously intra-cultural, like class antagonism. But different, because it lives and breathes in the flesh and blood of our families, even in the name of love.

In Toni Cade Bambara's novel *The Salt Eaters*, the curandera asks the question, *"Can you afford to be whole?"*[11] This line represents the question that has burned within me for years and years through my growing politi-cization. *What would a movement bent on the freedom of women of color look like?* In other words, what are the implications of looking not only *outside* of our culture, but *into* our culture and ourselves and from that place beginning to develop a strategy for a movement that could challenge the bedrock of oppressive systems of belief globally?

The one aspect of our identity which has been uniformly ignored by every existing political movement in this country is sexuality, as both a source of oppression and a means of liberation. Although other move-ments have dealt with this issue, sexual oppression and desire have never been considered specifically in relation to the lives of women of color. Sexuality, race and sex have usually been presented in contradiction to each other, rather than as part and parcel of a complex web of personal and political identity and oppression.

Female sexuality must be controlled, whether it be through the Church or through the State. The institutions of marriage and family, and neces-sarily, heterosexuality, prevail and thrive under capitalism as well as social-ism. Patriarchal systems of whatever ilk must be able to determine how and when women reproduce. For even "after the revolution," babies must be made, and until they find a way of making them without us (which is not that far off into the future), we're here for the duration. In China, for example, married couples are now being mandated by the State to limit their children to one. Abortions are not only available, but women are sometimes forced by family and friends to undergo an abortion or meet with severe economic recriminations from the State. In the U.S., the New Right's response to a weakening economic system, which they attribute in part to women's changing position in the family, is to institute legislation to ensure governmental control of women's reproductive rights. Unlike China, however, the New Right is "morally" opposed to abortion. The form their misogyny takes is the dissolution of government-assisted abortions for the poor, bills to limit teenage girls' right to birth control, and the advocacy of the Human Rights Amendment, which allows the fetus greater right to life than the mother. These backward political moves hurt all women, but most especially the poor and "colored."

The white man's so-called "benevolent protection" of the family and the role of women within it has never extended to the woman of color. She is most often the victim of forced pregnancy and sterilization. She is always the last to "choose."

Unlike most white people, with the exception of the Jews, Third World people have suffered the threat of genocide to our races since the coming of the first European expansionists. The family, then, becomes all the more ardently protected by oppressed peoples, and the sanctity of this institution is infused like blood into the veins of the Chicano. At all costs, la familia must be preserved: for when they kill our boys in their own imperialist wars to gain greater profits for American corporations; when they keep us in ghettos, reservations and barrios which ensure that our own people will be the recipients of our frustrated acts of violence; when they sterilize our women without our consent because we are unable to read the document we sign; when they prevent our families from getting decent housing, adequate child care, sufficient fuel, regular medical care; then we have reason to believe—although they may no longer technically be lynching us in Texas or our sisters and brothers in Georgia, Alabama, Mississippi—they intend to see us dead.

So we fight back, we think, with our families—with our women pregnant, and our men, the indisputable heads. We believe the more severely we protect the sex roles within the family, the stronger we will be as a unit in opposition to the anglo threat. And yet, our refusal to examine *all* the roots of the lovelessness in our families is our weakest link and softest spot.

Our resistance as a people to looking at the relationships within our families—between husband and wife, lovers, sister and brother, father, son and daughter, etc.—leads me to believe that the Chicano male does not hold fast to the family unit merely to safeguard it from the death-dealings of the anglo. Living under Capitalist Patriarchy, what is true for "the man" in terms of misogyny is, to a great extent, true for the Chicano. He, too, like any other man, wants to be able to determine how, when, and with whom his women—mother, wife and daughter—are sexual. For without male-imposed social and legal control of our reproductive function, reinforced by the Catholic Church, and the social institutionalization of our roles as sexual and domestic servants to men, Chicanas might very freely "choose" to do otherwise, including being sexually independent *from* and/or *with* men. In fact, the forced "choice" of the gender of our sexual/love partner seems to precede the forced "choice" of the form (marriage and family) that partnership might take. The control of women begins through the institution of heterosexuality.

Homosexuality does not, in and of itself, pose a great threat to society. Male homosexuality has always been a "tolerated" aspect of Mexican/Chicano society, as long as it remains "fringe." A case can even be made that male homosexuality stems from our indigenous Aztec roots.[12] But lesbianism, in any form, and male homosexuality which openly avows both the sexual and emotional elements of the bond, challenges the very foundation of la familia.*

The question remains. Is the foundation as it stands now sturdy enough to meet the face of the oppressor? I think not. There is a deeper love between and amongst our people that lies buried between the lines of the roles we play with each other. It is the earth beneath the floorboards of our homes. We must split wood, dig bare-fisted into the packed dirt to find out what we really have to hold in our hands as ground.

Family is *not* by definition the man in a dominant position over women and children. Familia is cross-generational bonding, deep emotional ties between opposite sexes and within our sex. It is sexuality that involves, but is not limited to, intercourse or orgasm. It springs forth

---

*The "maricón" or "joto" is the object of the Chicano/mexicano's contempt because he is consciously choosing a role his culture tells him to despise, that of a woman.

from touch, constant and daily. The ritual del beso en la mejilla and the sign of the cross with every coming and going from the home. It is finding familia among friends where blood ties are formed through suffering and celebration shared.

The strength of our families never came from domination. It has only endured in spite of it—like our women.

LA MALINCHISTA

Chicanos' refusal to look at our weaknesses as a people and a movement is, in the most profound sense, an act of self-betrayal. The Chicana lesbian bears the brunt of this betrayal, for it is she, the most visible manifestation of a woman taking control of her own sexual identity and destiny, who so severely challenges the anti-feminist Chicano/a. What other reason is there for the virtual dead silence among Chicanos about lesbianism? When the subject is raised, the word is used pejoratively.

For example, Sonia A. López writes about the anti-feminism in El Movimiento of the late 60s:

> The Chicanas who voiced their discontent with the organizations and with male leadership were often labeled "women's libbers," and "lesbians." This served to isolate and discredit them, a method practiced both covertly and overtly.[13]

This statement appears without qualification. López makes no value judgment on the inherent homophobia in such a divisive tactic. Without comment, her statement reinforces the idea that lesbianism is not only a white thing, but an insult to be avoided at all costs.

Such attempts by Chicana feminists to bend over backward to prove that criticism of their people is love (which, in fact, it is) severely undermines the potential radicalism of the ideology they are trying to create. Not quite believing in their love, suspecting their own anger, and fearing ostracism from Chicano males (being symbolically "kicked out of bed" with the threat of "lesbian" hanging over their work), the Chicana's imagination often stops before it has a chance to consider some of the most difficult, and therefore some of the most important, questions.

It is no wonder that the Chicanas I know who *are* asking "taboo" questions are often forced into outsiderhood long before they begin to question el carnal in print. Maybe like me they now feel they have little to lose.

It is important to say that fearing recriminations from my father never functioned for me as an obstacle in my political work. Had I been born of a Chicano father, I sometimes think I may never have been able to write a line or participate in a demonstration, having to repress *all* questioning in order to prevent the ultimate question of my sexuality from emerging. Possibly, some of my compañeras whose fathers died or left in their early years may never have had the courage to speak out as lesbians of color the way they do now had their fathers been a living part of their daily lives. The Chicana lesbians I know whose fathers *are* very much a part of their daily lives are seldom "out" to their families.°

During the late 60s and early 70s, I was not an active part of la causa. I never managed to get myself to walk in the marches in East Los Angeles (I merely watched from the sidelines); I never went to one meeting of MECHA on campus. No soy tonta. I would have been murdered in El Movimiento at the time—light-skinned, unable to speak Spanish well enough to hang; miserably attracted to women and fighting it; and constantly questioning all authority, including men's. I felt I did not belong there. Maybe I had really come to believe that "Chicanos" were "different," not "like us," as my mother would say. I fully knew that there was a part of me that was a part of that movement, but it seemed that part would have to go unexpressed until the time I could be a Chicano and the woman I had to be, too.

The woman who defies her role as subservient to her husband, father, brother, or son by taking control of her own sexual destiny is purported to be a "traitor to her race" by contributing to the "genocide" of her people—whether or not she has children. In short, even if the defiant woman is not a lesbian, she is assumed to be one; for, like the lesbian in the Chicano imagination, she is *una Malinchista.* Like the Malinche of Mexican

°I certainly don't mean to suggest that Euro-American fathers are less patriarchal or homophobic than Chicanos, only that Chicanas' fear of betraying our own cultura in a white racist America may be more viscerally experienced when the "patriarch" we are confronting is not theoretical, but a flesh-and-blood mexicano padre.

history, she is corrupted by foreign influences which threaten to destroy her people. Norma Alarcón elaborates on this theme of sex as a determinant of loyalty when she states:

> The myth of Malinche contains the following sexual possibilities: woman is sexually passive, and hence at all times open to potential use by men whether it be seduction or rape. The possible use is double-edged: that is, the use of her as pawn may be intracultural—"amongst us guys"—or intercultural, which means if we are not using her then "they" must be using her. Since woman is highly pawnable, nothing she does is perceived as choice.[14]

Lesbianism can be construed by the race, then, as the Chicana being used by the white man, even if the man never lays a hand on her. *The choice is never seen as her own.* Homosexuality is *his* disease which he sinisterly spreads to Third World people, men and women alike. (Because Malinche is female, Chicano gay men rebelling against their prescribed sex roles, although still considered diseased, do not suffer the same stigma of treason.) Further, the Chicana lesbian who has relationships with white women may feel especially susceptible to such accusations, since the white lesbian is seen as the white man's agent. The fact that the white woman may be challenging the authority of her white father, and thereby could be looked upon as a potential ally, has no bearing on a case closed before it was ever opened.

The first dyke I remember in school was Sally Frankel, whom everyone called "Frank," the way she liked it. She could play the meanest game of four-square of them all—built lean and solid as an eighth-grade boy, and smart too. And very, very clearly white. *Were all lesbians white?* I remember thinking that I had never quite met a girl like Frank before—so bold, somehow freer than the rest of us. She was an "army brat" and so had lived many places, even in Europe. While all my Chicana friends were leaving me high and dry for the guys, this girl—although not particularly interested in me—represented a life beyond the tight group discussions of girls, locked arm-in-arm, where the word "chinga" was dropped like a slug in my throat. (Even at fourteen, I was still wondering if I could get pregnant slowdancing with a boy, having picked up my knowledge of sex from these cryptic, closed-circled conversations.) The desire I felt for women had nothing and everything to do with the vulgarity of intercourse; had nothing and everything to do with the naked dreams that rocked my bed at night. Somehow Frank connected with all this—as did the "funny couple" I had encountered surreptitiously one hot afternoon a few years before.

At the time we were living in the Kenwood Hotel, a kind of "drifter" hangout, down on Main Street in Huntington Beach, California, long before there was any development there. Just a few bars, a little drugstore, "The Paddock" restaurant, and a surfboard shop. My mom was managing the Kenwood.

One day I was making my way down the long hallway to go play out on the big sundeck when I suddenly stopped short of the screen door. Some "new" people were out there who were not the "regulars." Hiding behind the screen door, I decided to observe.

One woman looked like a Marilyn Monroe type—50s style. Her hair was brassy blonde and pressed into a kind of permanent wave. Her yellow sundress was very tight around her waist and low-cut. The other person next to her I knew was really a woman, although she looked mostly like a man: white dress shirt with sleeves rolled up, pack of cigs in her front breast pocket, black men's trousers. She was a big woman, about twice the size of Marilyn, except her head was small—dark haired and greased back.

Marilyn had her dress hiked up above her knees and between her thighs she had put an open jar of Skippy peanut butter. I watched as Marilyn dipped the knife into the jar, pulled out a thick glob of the brown mass, then ran her tongue along it luxuriously like she had all day to eat the stuff. She then gave it to her partner to lick in the same place. All I could think about were the germs that were being passed back and forth.

The next day, I learned that the "funny" women in room six had sneaked out in the middle of the night without paying. They had stolen the alarm clock too. My momma said she had tried to give them the benefit of the doubt, but "never again." *Were all lesbians white? And decent ladies, Mexican? Who was I in this?*

But it was la mexicana I had loved first.

Sandra García and I used to make out after school. I think we mostly put a pillow between our faces so our lips wouldn't touch, but our bodies would get all enwrapped with each other. At eleven, Sandra was already "stacked" and, very innocently, we would take the role of movie stars—she playing Deborah Walley and me, James Darren, lusting after each other. Sandra's young body seemed a miracle of womanhood to me, the bow of her pink brassiere always poking out the opening of her too-small white uniform blouse. I wanted Sandra and as long as she was interested, I'd throw myself on the couch with her and make out until my cheeks were sore.

My cousin Teresa and I made out too; and this was for real. Making up stories about shipwrecks and sailor/saviors of young French women, we would shut ourselves up in our abuelita's bedroom and press our lips long and hard against each other's. One time we touched tongues, which I remember so delighted us that we even demonstrated this to my mom, who happened into the bedroom. "Mira, tía," Teresita said, and we touched tongues tip-to-tip and giggled uproariously. My mother, of course, reprimanded us immediately, and it was only then that I realized that the strange sensation running through me had something to do with "down there." Our games soon came to an end, my feeling guilty for taking advantage of my cousin, who was three years younger than me.

Still, I can see now that these experiences with Sandra and Teresa were brief moments of sexual connection with other Chicanas that were to be systematically denied me for the next twenty years of my life.

The Mexican women in my life, a pain I don't want to get to.

It seems my life has always been a kind of catch-22. For any way you look at it, Chicanas are denied one another's fidelity. If women betray one another through heterosexism, then lesbianism is a kind of visible statement of our faithfulness to one another. But if lesbianism is white, then the women I am faithful to can never be my own. And we are forced to move away from our people. As Gloria Anzaldúa once said to me, "If I stayed in Hargill, I would never have been able to be myself. I had to leave to come out as the person I really was." And if I had stayed in the San Gabriel Valley, I would have been found for dead, at least the walking dead.

I have always known too much. It was too clear to me—too tangible—too alive in the breath of my nose, the pulse between my thighs, the deep sighs that flowed from my chest when I moved into a woman's arms.

JOURNAL ENTRY: PRIMAVERA 1980

I don't know what happened to make me this way. I do fear for my life sometimes. Not that a bullet will hit my brain, but that I will forget to be afraid of the enemy. I dreamed last night of a hostility in me so great that on the job I put a pen through the skull of a white man. I have felt like an outcast on my job lately. The new manager wants to fire me for my "politics." I am a lesbian. I love women to the point of killing for us all.

An old friend came to visit me yesterday. She is leaving her good husband for the wild love of a woman. We were both very sad together. Not for the separation from her husband but for so many years of separation from women.

Some people try to convince me that the secrets I hold about loving women do not put me in a position of threat to my life. You see, you can't see this condition—this posture of mind and heart and body—in the movement of my joints or on the surface of my skin. (And then again, sometimes you can.) But I know they are wrong.

I feel very threatened and very threatening . . .

My mother does not worry about me; she fears me. She fears the power of the life she helped to breathe into me. She fears the lessons she taught me will move into action. She fears I might be willing to die rather than settle for less than the best of loving.

The line of reasoning goes:

Malinche sold out her indio people by acting as courtesan and translator for Cortéz, whose offspring symbolically represent the birth of the bastardized mestizo/mexicano people. My mother then is the modern-day Chicana Malinche marrying a white man, my father, to produce the bastards my sister, my brother and I are. Finally, I—a half-breed Chicana —further betray my race by *choosing* my sexuality, which excludes all men, and therefore most dangerously, Chicano men.

I come from a long line of Vendidas.

I am a Chicana lesbian. My being a sexual person and a radical stands in direct contradiction to, and in violation of, the woman I was raised to be.

INOCENCIA MEANT DYING
RATHER THAN BEING FUCKED

Coming from such a complex and contradictory history of sexual exploitation by white men and from within our own race, it is nearly earth-shaking to begin to try and separate the myths told about us from the truths; and to examine to what extent we have internalized what, in fact, is not true.

Although intellectually I knew different, early on I learned that women were willing collaborators in rape. So over and over again in pictures, books, movies, I experienced rape and pseudo-rape as titillating, sexy, as what sex was all about. Women want it. Real rape was dark, greasy-looking bad men jumping out of alleys and attacking innocent blonde women. Everything short of that was just sex; the way it is: dirty and duty. We spread our legs and bear the brunt of penetration, but we do spread our legs. In my mind, inocencia meant dying rather than being fucked.

I learned these notions about sexuality not only from the society at large, but more specifically and potently from Chicano/mexicano culture, originating from the myth of La Chingada, Malinche. In the very act of intercourse with Cortéz, Malinche is seen as having been violated. She is not, however, an innocent victim, but la culpable—ultimately responsible for her own sexual victimization. Slavery and slander is the price she must pay for the pleasure our culture imagined she enjoyed. In *The Labyrinth of Solitude*, Octavio Paz gives an explanation of the term "chingar," which provides valuable insights into how Malinche, in being represented as La Chingada, is perceived culturally. He writes:

> The idea of breaking, of ripping open. When alluding to a sexual act, violation or deception gives it a particular shading. The man who commits it never does so with the consent of the chingada. . . . Chingar then is to do violence to another, i.e., rape. The verb is masculine, active, cruel: it stings, wounds, gashes, stains. And it provokes a bitter, resentful satisfaction. The person who suffers this action is passive, inert and open, in contrast to the active, aggressive and closed person who inflicts it. The chingón is the macho, the male; he rips open the chingada, the female, who is pure passivity, defenseless against the exterior world.[15]

If the simple act of sex then—the penetration itself—implies female debasement and non-humanness, it is no wonder Chicanas often divorce ourselves from the conscious recognition of our own sexuality. Even if we enjoy having sex, draw pleasure from feeling fingers, tongue, penis inside us, there is a part of us that must disappear in the act, separate ourselves from realizing what it is we are actually doing. Sit, as it were, on the corner bedpost, watching the degradation and violence some "other" woman is willing to subject herself to, not us. And if we have lesbian feelings— want not only to be penetrated, but to penetrate—what perverse kind of monstrosities we must indeed be! It is through our spirits then that we escape the painful recognition of our "base" sexual selves.

When I was about twelve years old, I had the following dream:

I am in a hospital bed. I look down upon my newly developing body. The breasts are large and ample. And below my stomach, I see my own cock, wildly shooting menstrual blood totally out of control. The image of the hermaphrodite.

In another context, I could have seen this dream as a very sexually potent vision, reflecting a desire for integration of my male and female aspects. But in my child's imagination, I am incapable of handling such information emerging from my unconscious. Up to that point I always knew that I felt the greatest emotional ties with women, but suddenly I was beginning to consciously identify those feelings as sexual. The more potent my dreams and fantasies became and the more I sensed my own exploding sexual power, the more I retreated from my body's messages and into the region of religion. Sexual fantasy and rebellion became "impure thoughts" and "sinful acts." By giving definition and meaning to my desires, religion became the discipline to control my sexuality.

I was raised within a very strict brand of Mexican, mixed with Irish, Catholicism. This was in many ways typical for Chicano children whose parents are of my mother's generation. We were taught by the Irish nuns to seek the love and forgiveness of the Father. But after confession, I went straight home to my Mexican mother, knelt before her and asked pardon for my sins against her. It seemed the real test was to kneel down on the flesh and bones of your knees, to be relieved by lágrimas, por un besito en la cocina de mi mamá.

The contradiction between what I experienced as a very female-centered living Mexican Catholicism and the lifelessness of the disembodied Euro-American Church plagued me as a young adolescent. I remember once in the sixth grade, the nun was conducting a religion class on "doubting the existence of God." In fact, I had been doubting for years that there was a god to be touched. Whoever He was, was becoming increasingly remote as the touch of men began to fall hungrily and awkwardly upon my body. The touch of women, however, moved like fire in my veins. God had never actually once forgiven me, but my mother had.

I confess that it was during this class as the nun proceeded to describe the various forms of atheism, that for some unspeakable reason I saw my life in a flash of revelation that filled me with horror. I pictured myself lying flat on my back on a kind of surgery table, and people—like white-uniformed doctors—stood around my body, putting dreams into my head. The dream that made up my life—the people, the sensations, the emotions that gripped my heart: all these things were no more than figures in my imagination, thoughts that formed pictures of bodies that could not actually be touched. Love in this case was impossible. I was crucially and critically alone and powerless.

In retrospect, I see this fantasy as a revelation on one hand, and on the other, the beginning of the way I was to learn to cope with my burgeoning sexuality. The revelation was that, yes, in fact, the Chicana *is* manipulated by a white God-Father, white president-father, under whose jurisdiction she is nearly powerless and alienated from the dominant society. In a way, the fantasy was a foreshadowing of what oppression awaited me as a young Chicana growing into womanhood. The coping mechanism is more difficult to describe, but I see now that in order not to embody the *chingada*, nor a femalized, and therefore perverse, version of the *chingón*, I became pure spirit—bodiless. For what, indeed, must my body look like if I were both the *chingada* and the *chingón*?

In my early adolescence, my fears moved me farther and farther away from the living, breathing woman-in-the-flesh, and closer and closer to the bodiless god. The confessions of box and curtain cloth. The strange comfort that the church would be standing there, just around the turn from the cemetery. That it would be expecting me—grand, square, predictable as stone. That the end of mass would find a palm placed in my hand. The sure knowledge of the spines of leaf bending into my grip. The comfort and terror of powerlessness.

La niña chooses this time not to kneel in the pew. Having started for her knees, she breaks the bend, scooting back against the hard-boned wood of the pew bench: "O-my-gaw-i'm-hartly-sorry . . . " No, the child chooses this time not to begin this way. Breaking the line, she says nothing. Waiting, she lets the visions come.

Y los diablos begin to parade before her. As common to her now as the space she'd grown to picture like a circle of flesh the size of communion host inside her ribcage—the place where she thought her soul to sleep. Thinking white, thinking empty, thinking quiet, clean and untouched. It was this spot she protected from the advancing intruders: blood-pumping, wild-eyed things. The parts of men, like animals rearing, ramming into anything that could swallow them. The parts of women, quartered, stripped and shamed.

La niña shook the pictures from her mind, intervening before they could slip below and infect the sacred place inside her chest. She, the caretaker of her soul. The warrior. The watchdog, overburdened, beaten by now.

No resistance. Not this time. Not lifting her eyes, she only looked toward her hands, repeating to herself, "just look at your hands," repeating as the only language she would allow herself until words slipped from her altogether, until she knew only the touch of her red, cold hands against the wool thighs of her uniform skirt, until she knew only her body, without fire, her face dropped between her knees, her arms wrapped 'round her thin calves rocking, rocking, rocking.

Forgive us, Father, for how badly we need tenderness.

How does one describe a world where the mind twists like a rag dry of any real feeling? Only an absent inarticulate terror. A mouth hung open with no voice breaking through?

When I was nineteen, I lost my virginity. It was during those early years of heterosexual activity that the estrangement and anguished alienation I had experienced in puberty revisited me. In awakening to the touch of a man, my sexual longings for women, which I had managed to suppress since puberty, resurfaced. The sheer prospect of being a lesbian was too great to bear, as I fully believed that giving in to such desires would find me shot-up with bullets or drugs in a gutter somewhere. Further, although I *physically* found sex with men very satisfying, I couldn't quite look at what I was doing, having turned against my Church and my mother in the act. Instead I began to develop fantasies about it. Like the white doctor visions of my childhood, I became in my imagination a dark and sinister priestess, her flowing robes of toads and sequins draped loosely over my naked shoulders. Her menacing laugh fell hungrily from my lips whenever I saddled up upon my boyfriend's lap, riding him.

But not the first time. The first time I felt the feeling, that surge of pure pleasure, coming out from behind my heart and through my open legs, gripping the bone of the boy wanting me, I fell into deep sobbing. I remembered I had felt this somewhere, some time before. I had waited nearly ten years for its return, holding my breath back between my pursed lips, praying, now remembering . . .

. . . *when as a child, at first without touching myself, the pain that tugged gently at my ovaries (not maliciously, but only with an alive sense of their existence), the pressure I felt in my bowels, and the heat in my lower back—all commingled into a delicious kind of pleasure.*

Today it has a name. At eleven, I only hoped the strange uncontrollable feeling would come back. It was an *accident* of pleasure. I wondered if other girls got this feeling too. If my sister, one year older, ever did. If it was a fact of growing up, like the thick red dirt smudge of blood that I had only months before found on my underpants. I would barely touch myself, except in the beginning when the feeling first occurred, my fingers instinctively moving down to the place where the slightest amount of pressure drew the sensation deep from out of the pit of my stomach and into my vagina in cool streams of relief. If I held my knees together tight enough to feel the lips puffed and throbbing between them, the feeling would sometimes replay itself in echoes of kindly, calling voices—momma voices—growing more and more faint as they departed.

"Mi'jita . . . Chorizito . . . Hijita . . . "

Months later, or was it years, my mother warned after I had spent some time locked in the bathroom that it was not good to push yourself too hard when you were trying to "go." She mentioned "piles," but not knowing what that was, I figured she knew about the pleasure, the pain, the pushing brought on and it was bad. It was years later before I ever reenacted my private bathroom ritual again.

Only occasionally, through high school, pretending it wasn't quite happening, I would sit with one foot under me, placing the wedge of the sole of my hard oxford school shoe up between my labia. For hours, I would allow myself at least this secret comfort through TV shows and homework late into the night, my sister on the other side of the dining room table.

At what point does the fear become greater than the flesh and the flesh of the fantasy prevail? The more vividly the sinister priestess fantasies appeared to me, the more viciously I would fuck to obliterate them from my mind. I was always wanting sex: in cars, behind the bleachers of the neighborhood ballpark, my boyfriend and I breaking into the park office where he worked to use its floor. Somehow I felt that if I fucked long and hard enough, I might being to *feel* again.

Occasionally, I would go through days, sometimes a week, of reprieve from these obsessions, but they would never last. Seemingly without my control, I would be in a conversation with someone and begin to feel as though I were being sucked down into a hole in the ground where I could always still *see* the person, but they would be shrinking farther and farther away from my hearing. Their body framed by the lip of the tunnel I had fallen into. Their mouth moving soundlessly. These feelings of outsiderhood became the lens through which I saw most of my waking life, like a thin film between me and the people I longed to touch, to reach to for help.

> *we never spoke again, really*
> *after the time I pulled up in front*
> *of our mother's house, hands still*
> *on the wheel*
> *Sister, I need*
> *to talk with you and told her*
> *there was a devil on my tail*
> *riding me.*
>
> *I know she saw it clear as me*
> *I know she'd seen it in my younger years*

always creeping too close to her, like I was
some crazy infection,

and I guess I am, crazy
that catches.

In my "craziness" I wrote poems describing myself as a centaur: half-animal/half-human, hairy-rumped and cloven-hoofed, como el diablo, the symbols emerging from a deeply Mexican and Catholic place. My recurring sense of myself outside the normal life and touch of human beings was again, in part, a kind of revelation. A foreshadowing of the marginal place, within my culture and in society at large, my sexuality was to eventually take me.

Sometimes a breakdown can be the beginning of a kind of break-through, a way of living in advance through a trauma that prepares you for a future of radical transformation. The third time I broke was many years after I had stopped seeing men. I had been out as a lesbian for a while and had examined, I thought, what this made me in the world at large, but I had never actually looked into the eyes of what this made me in the world of my cultural community. Since I was so busy making room simply to live a lesbian life safely—coming out to my family, friends, at school, in print, to my employers, etc., I had never wrestled with the reality of what being a *Chicana* lesbian meant.

All this changed, however, when I thought I saw in a lover, a woman, the chingón that I had so feared to recognize in myself: "the active, aggressive and closed person," as Paz writes, "who inflicts [the wound]." I had met my match. I was forced to confront how, in all my sexual rela-tionships, I had resisted, at all costs, feeling la chingada—which, in effect, meant that I had resisted fully feeling sex at all. *Nobody wants to be made to feel the turtle with its underside all exposed, just pink and folded flesh.* In the effort to avoid embodying la chingada, I became the chingón. In the effort not to feel fucked, I became the fucker, even with women. In the effort not to feel pain or desire, I grew a callous around my heart and imagined I felt nothing at all.

What I never quite understood until this writing is that to be without a sex—to be bodiless—as I sought to escape the burgeoning sexuality of my adolescence, my confused early days of active heterosexuality, and later my panicked lesbianism, means also to be without a race. I never attributed my removal from physicality to anything to do with race, only sex, only desire for women. And yet, as I grew up sexually, it was my race, along with my sex, that was being denied me at every turn.

I was plagued with sexual contradictions. Lesbianism as a sexual act can never be construed as reproductive sex. It is not work. It is purely about pleasure and intimacy. How this refutes, spits in the face of, the notion of sex as productive, sex as duty! In stepping outside the confines of the institution of heterosexuality, I was indeed *choosing* sex freely. *The lesbian as institutionalized outcast.*

During those years as an active feminist lesbian, I became increasingly aware of the fact that not only had my sexuality made me an outcast from my culture, but if I seriously listened to it, with all its specific cultural nuances, it would further make me an outcast from the women's movement—a movement which I had run to for dear life to avoid the gutter of utter social ostracization I had feared was waiting for me. With no visible Third World feminist movement in sight, it seemed to me to be a Chicana lesbian put me far beyond the hope of salvation.

TIRED OF THESE ACTS OF TRANSLATION

What the white women's movement tried to convince me of is that lesbian sexuality was *naturally* different than heterosexual sexuality. That in lesbianism the desire to penetrate and be penetrated, to fill and be filled, would vanish. That retaining such desires was "reactionary," not "politically correct," "male-identified." And somehow reaching sexual ecstasy with a woman lover would never involve any kind of power struggle. Women were different. We could simply magically "transcend" these "old notions," just by seeking spiritual transcendence in bed.

The fact of the matter was that all these power struggles of "having" and "being had" were being played out in my own bedroom. And in my psyche, they held a particular Mexican twist. White women's feminism did little to answer my questions. As a Chicana feminist my concerns were different. As I wrote in 1982:

> What I need to explore will not be found in the lesbian feminist bedroom, but more likely in the mostly heterosexual bedrooms of South Texas, L.A., or even Sonora, México. Further, I have come to realize that the boundaries white feminists confine themselves to in describing sexuality are based in white-rooted interpretations of dominance, submission, power-exchange, etc. Although they are certainly *part* of the psychosexual lives of women of color, these boundaries would have to be expanded and translated to fit my people, in particular, the women in my family. And I am tired, always, of these acts of translation.[16]

Mirtha Quintanales corroborates this position and exposes the necessity for a Third World feminist dialogue on sexuality when she states:

> The critical issue for me regarding the politics of sexuality is that as a Latina Lesbian living in the U.S., I do not really have much of an opportunity to examine what constitutes sexual conformity and sexual defiance in my own culture, in my own ethnic community, and how that may affect my own values, attitudes, sexual life and politics. There is virtually no dialogue on the subject anywhere and I, like other Latinas and Third World women, especially Lesbians, am quite in the dark about what we're up against besides negative feminist sexual politics.[17]

During the late 70s, the concept of "women's culture" among white lesbians and "cultural feminists" was in full swing; it is still very popular today. "Womon's history," "wommin's music," "womyn's spirituality," "wymyn's language" abounded—all with the "white" modifier implied and unstated. In truth, there was/is a huge amount of denial going on in the name of female separatism. Women do not usually grow up in women-only environments. Culture is sexually mixed. As Bernice Reagon puts it:

[W]e have been organized to have our primary cultural signals come from factors other than that we are women. We are not from our base, acculturated to be women people, capable of crossing our first people boundaries: Black, White, Indian, etc.[18]

Unlike Reagon, I believe that there are certain ways we *have* been acculturated to be "women people," and that there is therefore such a thing as "women's culture." This occurs, however, as Reagon points out, *within* a context formed by race, class, geography, religion, ethnicity and language.

I don't mean to imply that women need to have men around to feel at home in our culture, but that the way one understands culture is influenced by men. The fact that some aspects of that culture are indeed oppressive does not imply, as a solution, throwing out the entire business of racial/ethnic culture. To do so would mean risking the loss of some very essential aspects of identity, especially for Third World women.

JOURNAL ENTRY: JULIO 1981

New England. Boston to be exact. Pouring summer rain. We are all immigrants to this town—una hermana de Chicago, una de Tejas, una de Puerto Rico, y yo, de California. And the four of us move out into the rain under the beat of the downpour on the roof of the porch. Cooling off from the evening of enchiladas. I make up a little concoction of a summer drink: jugo de naranja, tequila, limón. Tossing in all kinds of ice cubes, "Try this," I say.

Y mis hermanas drink it up. Dos Chicanas y dos puertoriqueñas getting a little high from the food and the rain and the talk, hablando de nuestras madres.

Sitting out on the porch that night, what made me at home and filled me with ease where I forgot about myself in a fine and fluid way was not just that the Spanish sounds wrapped around the English like tortillas steaming in flour sacks, not just that we all had worked hard to get here from hard-working homes, not just that we understood the meaning of familia, but that we were women—somos mujeres. This is what women's culture means to me.

In failing to approach feminism from any kind of materialist base, failing to take race, ethnicity, class into account in determining where women are at sexually, many feminists have created an analysis of sexual oppression (often confused with sexuality itself) which is a political dead-end.

"Radical Feminism," the ideology which sees men's oppression of women as the root of, and paradigm for, all other oppressions, allows women to view ourselves as a class and to claim our sexual identity as the *source* of our oppression and men's sexual identity as the *source* of the world's evil. But this ideology can never then fully integrate the concept of the "simultaneity of oppression" as Third World feminism is attempting to do. For, if race and class oppress the woman of color as much as her sexual identity, then the Radical Feminist must extend her own "identity" politics to include her "identity" as oppressor as well. (To say nothing of having to acknowledge the fact that there are men who may suffer more than she.) This is something that, for the most part, Radical Feminism as a movement has refused to do.

Radical Feminist theorists have failed to acknowledge how their position in the dominant culture—white, middle-class, often Christian—has influenced every approach they have taken to implement feminist political change—to "give women back their bodies." It follows then that the anti-pornography movement is the largest organized branch of Radical Feminism. For unlike battered women's, anti-rape, and reproductive rights workers, the anti-porn "activist" never has to deal with any live woman outside of her own race and class. The tactics of the anti-pornography movement are largely symbolic and theoretical in nature. And the needs of the woman of color are a lot easier to represent on paper than in the flesh. Therefore, her single-issue approach to feminism remains intact. It is not that pornography is not a concern to many women of color; but the anti-materialist approach of this movement makes little sense in the lives of poor and Third World women. Plainly put, it is *our* sisters working in the sex industry.

Many women involved in the anti-porn movement are lesbian separatists. Because the Radical Feminist critique is there to justify it, lesbianism can be viewed as the logical personal response to a misogynist political system. Through this perspective, lesbianism has become an "idea"— a political response to male sexual aggression, rather than a sexual response—a woman's desire for another woman. In this way, many ostensibly heterosexual women who are not active sexually can call themselves lesbians. Lesbians "from the neck up." This faction of the movement has grown into a kind of cult. They have taken whiteness, class privilege and an anglo-american brand of "return-to-the-mother" (which leaps back over a millennium of patriarchal domination), attempted to throw out the man, and called what is left female, while still retaining their own racial and class-biased cultural superiority.

The lesbian separatist retreats from the specific cultural contexts that have shaped her and attempts to build a cultural-political movement based on an imagined oppression-free past. It is understandable that many feminists opt for this kind of asexual separatist/spiritualist solution rather than boldly grappling with the challenge of wresting sexual autonomy from such a sexually exploitative system. Every oppressed group needs to imagine through the help of history and mythology a world where our oppression did not seem the preordained order. Aztlán for Chicanos is another example. The mistake lies in believing in this ideal past or imagined future so thoroughly and single-mindedly that finding solutions to present-day inequities loses priority, or we attempt to create too-easy solutions for the pain we feel today.

Just as culture—our race, class, ethnicity, etc.—influences our sexuality, so too do heterosexism, marriage and men as the primary agents of those institutions. We can work to tumble those institutions so that when the rubble is finally cleared away we can see what we have left to build on sexually; but we can't ask a woman to forget everything she understands about sex in a heterosexual and culturally specific context or tell her what she is allowed to think about it. Should she forget and not use what she knows sexually to untie the knot of her own desire, she may lose any chance of ever discovering her own human (sexual and spiritual) potential.

FEEDING THE PEOPLE IN ALL THEIR HUNGERS

History has taught us that the effectiveness of a movement often depends on its ability to provide what, at least, feels at the time like a spiritual imperative. Spirituality that inspires activism and, similarly, politics that move the spirit—that draw from the deep-seated place of our greatest longings for freedom—give meaning to our lives. Such a vision can hold and heal us in the worst of times, and is in direct opposition to an apolitical spiritualist view of the world or a totally materialistic perspective.

The Civil Rights Movement is probably the best recent example in this country of a movement that was able to reach masses of people through its spiritually uplifting vision. The power of that vision, however, was based on the fact that in a very profound sense, it was deeply rooted in Black culture, and therefore, of necessity, Black spirituality. Religious fervor was not manufactured for the purposes of social or revolutionary change, but instead grew directly out of Black people's experience, influencing all those who became a part of that movement.

Major missing elements in the Civil Rights Movement, however, were consciousness and activism around specifically female and sexual concerns, as well as an understanding of the entrenchedness of white power and how to move against it. Although the race-related movements that jumped off from the Civil Rights Movement in the late 60s, such as the American Indian Movement, La Raza and Black Power, were thoroughly coming to terms with the extent and depth of white power, the role of women of color was subject for neither debate nor activism except as women functioned as female members of the race.

But times have changed. The women's movement and lesbian and gay liberation movements in the 70s brought both the subject of women's rights and sexuality, respectively, to the political light of day. Furthermore, in the 80s, with the increasing conservatism of the country manifested in the reign of Reagan and the rise of the Moral Majority, U.S. Third World organizations and organizers can no longer safely espouse the heterosexual family and, therefore, homophobia as a strategy of cultural resistance without linking themselves with the most reactionary and, by definition, the most racist political sectors of this country.

The emergence of U.S. Third World feminism, then, seemed imminent. Third World lesbians' disillusionment with the racism and classism of the women's and gay movements and the sexism and homophobia of Third World movements did much to force us to begin to organize ourselves autonomously in the name of Third World feminism.

If any movement, however, could provide a "spiritual" reference point for Third World feminism, it would be the Civil Rights Movement in its culturally based, anti-separatist and "humanist" (not to be confused with liberal) approach to political change. As Black feminist activist and writer Barbara Smith explains:

> I was trying to figure out what the connection was/is for me between the Civil Rights movement and the Black feminist movement. It is among other things, this. That the Civil Rights movement was based upon the concept of love and deep spirituality. It was a movement with a transcendent vision. *A movement whose very goal was to change the impossible, what people thought could not be changed.* . . .
>
> The women's movement has some of these same qualities, a belief in the human. Actually Black feminism is a kind of divine coalescing of the two because as Blackwomen we have an identity and therefore a politics that requires faith in the humanness of Blackness and femaleness. We are flying in the face of white male conceptions of what humanness is and proving that it is not them, but us.
>
> That's what the Civil Rights movement was getting to through its divine patience and fortitude—although tactically and strategically it was, at times, flawed—the constant demonstration that we are really the human ones.
>
> Black feminism, lesbian feminism in particular, moves in that direction. . . . We will show you what it means to be human, what it means to really care about humanity.[19]

As a Chicana who grew up in a very religious household, I learned early on to respect the terrain of the spirit as the place where some of the most essential aspects of one's life are enacted. The spirit world—my sleeping dreams, my waking fantasies, my prayers and compulsive preoccupations—was and is very rich for me. A place from which I derive strength and perseverance. A place where much internal torture has taken place.

Women of color have always known, although we have not always wanted to look at it, that our sexuality is not merely a physical response or drive, but holds a crucial relationship to our entire spiritual capacity.

Patriarchal religions—whether brought to us by the colonizer's cross and gun or emerging from our own people—have always known this. Why else would the female body be so associated in Christianity with sin and disobedience? Simply put, if the spirit and sex have been linked in our oppression, then they must also be linked in the strategy toward our liberation.

To date, no liberation movement has been willing to take on the task. To walk a freedom road that is both material and metaphysical. Sexual and spiritual. Third World feminism is about feeding people in all their hungers.

BRINGING THE STRAINS TOGETHER[20]

Contrary to popular belief among Chicanos, Chicana feminism did not borrow from white feminists to create a movement. If any direct "borrowing" was done, it was from Black feminists.

In 1977, the Combahee River Collective wrote: "The most profound and potentially most radical politics come directly out of our own identity." They go on to say that they "are committed to struggling against racial, sexual, heterosexual and class oppression and see as [their] particular task, the development of integrated analysis and practice based upon the fact that the major systems of oppression are interlocking."[21]

This "Black Feminist Statement" had considerable impact in creating an analysis of U.S. Third World women's oppression. It first appeared in *Capitalist Patriarchy: A Case for Socialist Feminism*, edited by Zillah Eisenstein, and has been reprinted numerous times in leaflet form and in other feminist publications. When I first discovered it in 1978, there were three things that struck me profoundly: one was the lesbian visibility of its authors; second was their expressed solidarity with other women of color; and third was a concern for what might be considered the *psycho-sexual* oppression of women of color. The statement asserts: "We are all damaged people merely by virtue of being Black women."[22]

The appearance of these sisters' words *in print*, as lesbians of color, suddenly made it viable for me to put my Chicana *and* lesbian self in the center of a movement. I no longer had to postpone or deny any part of my identity to make revolution easier for somebody else to swallow. I had heard too many times that my concern about specifically sexual issues was divisive to the "larger struggle" or wasn't really the "primary contradiction" and therefore, not essential for revolution. That to be concerned about the sexuality of women of color was an insult to women in the Third World literally starving to death. But the only hunger I have ever known was the hunger for sex and the hunger for freedom and somehow, in my mind and heart, they were related and certainly not mutually exclusive. If I could not use the source of my hunger as the source of my activism, how then was I to be politically effective? But finally here was a movement, first voiced by U.S. Black women, which promised to deal with the oppression that occurred *under* the skin as well, and by virtue of the fact that that skin was female and colored. For the damage that has been done to us sexually and racially has penetrated our minds as well as our bodies. The existence of rape, the veil, genital mutilation, sterilization abuse and violence against lesbians, has bludgeoned our entire perception of ourselves as female beings. As Barbara Smith writes, "It is Third World feminism that is bringing the strains together."[23]

One of the major components of Black feminism is that women of color embody the coalition essential for revolution and that each form of oppression is part and parcel of the larger political strategy of capitalist and racist patriarchy. What women of color suffer in our families and relationships is, in some way, inherently connected to the rape of women in our neighborhoods, the high suicide rate of American Indians on reservations, attacks on Black gays and disabled people in New York City bars, and the war in El Salvador. Whether one death is sexually motivated and the other the result of U.S. imperialism, women of color are always potential victims.

Each movement, then, that tries to combat an aspect of women of color's oppression offers an organized strategy for change that women of color cannot afford to ignore. The difference now is that as we begin to organize and create our own programs and institutions, we are building a political base so that we will no longer have to fall prey to the tokenism and invisibility we have encountered in other movement work. Without the political autonomy of oppressed groups, coalition politics are a bankrupt notion.

But organizing ourselves is no easy task. The homophobia of heterosexual sisters and the racism among us cross-culturally are two major obstacles toward our being a unified movement. To begin with, we are profoundly ignorant about one another's cultures, traditions, languages, particular histories of oppression and resistance, and the cultural adaptations each people has had to make in the face of total cultural obliteration. But even this would only be a matter of education, if our prejudices against one another had penetrated only our minds, and not also our hearts.

Quite simply, the oppression of women of color, especially as we have internalized it, holds the greatest threat to our organizing successfully together, intraculturally as well as cross-culturally. I think what is hardest for any oppressed people to understand is that *the sources of oppression form not only our radicalism, but also our pain.* Therefore, they are often the places we feel we must protect unexamined at all costs.

Recently, I was strutting down the street in my neighborhood in Brooklyn when, out of the side view of my eye, I caught sight of an old Irish woman with a garbage bag about the same size as her. She was trying to maneuver this huge thing down the ten steps which made up the stoop to her building. "Want some help?" I stop. And she gladly accepts, touching my cheek in thank you, telling God to bless me at least three times until I finally settle the bag there by its fellows at the bottom of the stoop. I move on down the street, feeling like the good child I was raised up to be. Then the thought came and turned the pleasantness of the encounter—the "isn't-it-good-to-be-alive-and-in-new-york" feeling— cold in my chest. I thought, *if you looked as colored as you think, she'd maybe not have let you close enough to help her. The first gesture of the open hand, seen by the woman as a move to attack/you see the fear in her face/your hand closes up/your heart. You soon learn not to volunteer your help.*

Oppression. Let's be clear about this. Oppression does not make for hearts as big as all outdoors. Oppression makes us big and small. Expressive and silent. Deep and Dead.

Even the economic restraints seem to be less of a deterrent to our successful organizing than this more insidious, invisible obstacle. The more desperate the economic times, the greater our incentive is to challenge the system simply to put bread on the table. In do-or-die situations, women of color can be relied upon to throw ourselves down in the face of fire for family. Our instincts are solidly in the right place.

But on a daily basis, have we learned to take the race hatred, the class antagonism, the fear of our fiery sexual passion and not beat ourselves down with it, not maintain our place with it, not keep one another in line with it?

JOURNAL ENTRY: JUNE 1981

And we line the women we love along the tips of our fingers, counting five to ten of the most dangerous brave women we know and we want to crawl under a rock, each. You see, to take a stand outside of face-to-face crisis, outside of dying for your children, outside of "Bolt me, landlord, outta my house? Well, cabrón, I'll show you." And she takes a sledgehammer from the neighbor's yard and blows her way back into her home.

"We'll eat beans, but we'll eat! And nobody's throwing us out!"

This stand we understand. The power is plain.

But after our bellies are full, our children well-fed and grown. After we've learned to walk with our face exposed, having beaten off the man who tried to beat it one too many times. After we've learned to stand alone. Known loneliness and borne it as a matter of course. Been nearly convinced not to expect a damn thing better from your people or yourself. Learned these lessons ten and twenty times over and still come up kicking, then what?

"Our survival is our contribution to our struggle," a South African woman freedom fighter once said.

But what of passion? I hunger to ask. There's got to be something more than hand-to-mouth survival.

MORE THAN HAND-TO-MOUTH SURVIVAL

The right to passion expressed in our own cultural tongue and movements is what this essay seems, finally, to be about. I would not be trying to develop some kind of Chicana feminist theory if I did not have strong convictions, urgent hunches and deep racial memory that the Chicana could *not* betray a sister, a daughter, a compañera in the service of the man and his institutions if somewhere in the chain of historical events and generations, she were allowed to love herself as both female and mestiza.

What might our relationships with one another look like if we did not feel we had to protect ourselves from the violent recriminations of our fathers, brothers, bosses, governors? What might our sexuality look like? Audre Lorde, Black lesbian poet, writes:

> In order to perpetuate itself, every oppression must corrupt or distort those various sources of power within the culture of the oppressed that can provide energy for change.[24]

The extent to which our sexuality and identity as Chicanas have been distorted both within our culture and by the dominant culture is the measure of how great a source of our potential power it holds. We have not been allowed to express ourselves in specifically female and Latina ways or even to explore what those ways are. As long as that is held in check, so is much of the rest of our potential power.

I cannot stomach the twists sexual repression takes in the Latina. It makes us too-hot-to-handle. Like walking fire hazards, burning bodies in our paths with the singe of our tongues, or the cut of our eyes. Sex turned manipulation, control—which ravages the psyche, rather than satisfies the yearning body and heart.

In the wee hours of the morning my lover and I fight. We fight and cry and move against each other and a torrent of pain. The pain doesn't stop. We do not shout at midnight. We have learned to keep our voices down. In public. In the public ear of the building where we try to build a home. We fight quietly, urgently. The latina who lives below us—who catches sight of us in the hall and turns her pale cheek away from us, whose eyes are the eyes of my enemy—is pounding on the ceiling. Again. A frantic hateful beating below us, under our bed. She knows we are up, up to something. She hates us. And my lover's eyes staring back at me are red like apples from tears. The pounding—more vicious—continues. Our neighbor wants to remind us. She is there with her husband, her children in the next room. Decent people sleep at this hour. My lover says, "We are two women. We have no right to care so much about each other that the pain could keep us up."

"Those women or whatever they are," she describes us to the lady next door the next morning.

If they hurt me, they will hurt me in that place. The place where I open my mouth to kiss and something primordial draws the lips back, causes a woman to defend herself against the love of a woman. I am everybody's pesadilla. Jota. Pata. Dyke. Walking through the rooms of my puertorriqueña friend's house, her grown son says to her, "Don't you let her (meaning me) put her hands on you." He fears his mami's eye will turn on him. To me. To me. For once, mujer, turn to me. Choose. Choose me. Cara a cara con el hombre.

The distortion and repression of our sexuality is so commonplace a fact in our lives that as young Chicanas we learn to accept it as "culturally natural" as we grow into womanhood. In a letter on my thirtieth birthday, my sister wrote to me:

> I remember the shock when you slowly began to need a bra. I can see you wearing that T-shirt I brought you from Arizona—two little round mounds sticking out from under the shirt. And mom mentioned that after she had rubbed you down, she had been surprised to find two tiny hairs sprouting. I hated to hear her speak of it. As a painfully growing adolescent, I hoped that you, who always looked like such a child, would be spared the curses I was having to face.

Is it possible to build a movement that grapples with *this* kind of silent suffering, the "damage" the Third World woman suffers, as the Combahee River Collective describes it? The visibility of lesbians of color choosing our sexual partners against the prescribed cultural norms and our examining the political implications of such a choice can provide, I believe, the kind of political space necessary for other women of color to begin to ask themselves some profound and overdue questions about their own psycho-sexual identity. The Third World lesbian brings colored female sexuality with all its raggedy edges and oozing wounds—for better or for worse—into the light of day.

I once had a very painful conversation with my mother—a conversation about moving away from her. I am the only person—male or female—among my relatives who ever left home for good without getting married first. My mother told me that she felt in some way that I was choosing my "friends" (she meant lesbian lovers) over her. She said, "No one is ever going to love you as much as I do. No one." We were both crying by then and I responded, "I know that. I know. I know how strong your love is. Why do you think I am a lesbian?"

Dead silence. But I knew, I felt in the air, that it was the silence of an unspeakable recognition. Of understanding, finally, what my being a lesbian meant to me. I had been "out" to my mother for years, but not like this.

I knew at that moment that this kind of thing has happened for generations among Chicanas. It is our tradition to conceive of the bond between mother and daughter as paramount and essential in our lives. It is the daughters that can be relied upon. Las hijas who remain faithful a la madre, a la madre de la madre.

When we name this bond among Raza women, from this Chicana feminism emerges. For too many years, we have acted as if we held a secret pact with one another never to acknowledge directly our commitment to one another. Never to admit the fact that we count on one another *first*. We were never to recognize this in the face of el hombre. But this is what being a Chicana feminist means—making bold and political the love of our women. Possibly the words of one Latina to another will come closer to the cultural/female connection I am trying to describe:

> There is something I feel for you or with you or from you that I experience with no one else, that I need and crave, that I never get enough of, that I do not understand, that I am missing at this very moment . . . perhaps it's spiritual openness, two souls touching, love that transcends the boundaries of materiality, ordinary reality and living.[25]

No one else can or will speak for us. We must be the ones to define the parameters of what it means to be, and love, la mestiza.

A political commitment to women does not equate with lesbianism. As a Chicana lesbian, I write of the connection my own feminism has had with my sexual desire for women. *This is my story.* I can tell no other one than the one I understand. I eagerly await the writings by heterosexual Chicana feminists that can speak of their sexual desire for men and the ways in which their feminism informs that desire. What is true, however, is that a political commitment to women must involve, by definition, a political commitment to lesbians as well. To refuse to allow the Chicana lesbian the right to the free expression of her own sexuality, and her politicization of it, is in the deepest sense to deny one's self the right to the same. I guarantee you, there will be no change among heterosexual men, there will be no change in heterosexual relations, as long as the Chicano community keeps us lesbians and gay men political prisoners among our own people. Any movement built on the fear and loathing of anyone is a failed movement. The Chicano movement is no different.

The secret agenda of denial which has so often turned the relationships between mother and daughter, sister and sister and compañeras into battlegrounds has got to come to an end.

For you, mamá, I have unclothed myself before a woman
have laid wide the space between my thighs
straining open the strings held there
taut and ready to fight

Stretching my legs and imagination so open
to feel my whole body cradled
by the movement of her mouth, the mouth
of her thighs rising and falling, her arms
her kiss, all the parts of her open
like lips moving, talking me into loving.

I remember this common skin, mamá
oiled by work and worry.
Hers is a used body like yours
one that carries the same scent
of silence   I call it home.

The first women I loved were the women of my race. Fui muy lejos de mi pueblo en busca del amor por la mujer, pero ahora . . . ahora.

Regreso a mi pueblo . . . a la mujer mestiza.

EPILOGUE: LA MUJER SALIENDO DE LA BOCA

There resides in her, as in me, a woman far greater
than our bodies
can inhabit.
So I stay
and take what I can
in thick drops
like oil that leaks
from the cave of anger
wrestling between her legs.

Women agitate my consciousness. What I am willing to work out on paper/in life has always been prompted by women: la mujer en mi alma, mis sueños—dark, latina, lover, mother. Tengo miedo.

In conclusion, quiero decir que these changes scare me. Returning to la mujer scares me, re-learning Spanish scares me. I have not spoken much of la lengua here, possibly because my muteness in Spanish still shames me. In returning to the love of my raza, I must confront the fact that not only has the mother been taken from me, but her tongue, my mother-tongue. I yearn for the language, feel my own tongue rise to the occasion of feeling at home, in common with other latinas . . . and then suddenly it escapes me. The traitor-voice within me chastises, "¡Quítate de aquí! You don't belong!"

JOURNAL ENTRY: 1 DE SEPTIEMBRE 1981
I called up Berlitz today. The Latino who answered refused to quote me prices over the phone. "Come down and talk to Mr. Bictner," he says. I want to know how much it's going to cost before I do any train riding into Manhattan. "Send me a brochure," I say, regretting the call.

Paying for culture. When I was born between the legs of the best teacher I could have had.

Quiero decir que I know on the surface of things, this may not make any sense. I spoke English at home. On the surface of things I am not supposed to feel that my language has been stripped from me. I am "born American," college English educated, but there is something else, deep and behind my heart that I want to hold hot and bold in the hands of my writing, in the circle of my mouth, and it will not come out sounding like English. Te prometo. No es inglés. And I have to wonder, is it so that I have felt "too much," "too emotional," "too sensitive" because I was trying to translate my feelings into English cadences?

Mi amiga says to me, she could never go back to not fucking in Spanish. And I think about this. Yo recuerdo a Carmela—su mano trazando los círculos de mis senos around and around bringing her square small hands down, moving my legs apart, opening my lips hovering, holding me there, her light breath on my thighs. No me lame, pero espera, mirándome, diciendo, "¡Qué rica! ¡Ay mujer, qué rica tú eres!" And I can't quite believe my ears, she is talking about the taste of me *before* su boca lo sabe. She knows *before* hand and mouth make it possible. She tells me my name, my taste, in Spanish. She fucks me in Spanish. And I am changed. It is a different kind of passion . . . something remembered. I think, *soy mujer en español.* No macha, pero mujer. Soy Chicana—open to all kinds of assaults.

In recent months, I have had a recurring dream that my mouth is too big to close; that is, the *outside of* my mouth, my lips, cannot contain the inside—teeth, tongue, gums, throat. I am coming out of my mouth, so to speak. The mouth is red like blood; and the teeth, white like bones, the skeleton of my feelings clattering for attention.

Returning from the Latin American Women Writer's Conference, I say to my friends as I drive down 91 South, "The mouth is like a chocha." La boca spreads its lips open to talk, open to attack. I remember Malinche, that ancestor-woman of words and sex. "I am a lesbian. And I am a Chicana," I say to the men and women at the conference. I watch their faces twist up on me. "These are two inseparable facts of my life. I can't talk or write about one without the other."

My mouth cannot be controlled. It will flap in the wind like legs in sex, not driven by the mind. It's as if la boca had lodged itself en el centro del corazón, not in the head at all. The same place where the vagina beats.

And there is a woman coming out of her mouth.

Hay una mujer saliendo de la boca.

Brooklyn, New York,
March 1983

RIVERPOEM

En el sueño mi amor me pregunta
   "¿Dónde está tu río?"
and I point to the center of my chest.
I am a river cracking open.

Before, all the parts of me, just thin tributaries.
lines of water like veins running barely beneath the soil
skimming the bone surface of the earth
 —sometimes desert creek
 —sometimes city-wash
 —sometimes like sweat sliding
    down a woman's
    breast
    bone.

Now I can see the point of juncture.
Comunión.
And I gather my forces
to make the river
run.

FEED THE MEXICAN BACK INTO HER

para mi prima

what I meant to say to her as she reached
around the cocktail glass to my hand, squeezing it
> saying, *it makes no difference to me.* what I meant to say
> is that it must make a difference,
> but then I did say that and it made
> no difference, this difference
> between us.

what I meant to say to her is I dreamed we were children. I meant to tell
her how I took her thin brown hand in mine and led her to the grocery
store—the corner one, like in l.a. on adams street, where I remember her
poor and more mexican than ever. we both were. I meant to remind her of
how she looked in her brother's hand-me-downs—the thin striped tee
shirt, the suspenders holding up the corduroy pants, literally "in suspen-
sion" off her small frame.

I meant to sit her down and describe to her the love, the care with which
I drew the money from my pocket—my plump pink hand, protective,
counting out the change. I bought tortillas, chiles verdes. I meant to say,
"Teresita, mi'jita, when we get home, I'll make you a meal you'll never
forget."

Feed the Mexican back into her.

I meant to tell her how I thought of her as not brown at all, but black—
an english-speaking dark-girl, wanting to spit the white words out of her,
be black angry. I meant to encourage.

Teresita

there is a photograph of us
at seven, you are skinny
at the knees where the brown wrinkles
together black,
my hand like a bright ring around yours

we are smiling.

In the negative, I am dark
and profane/you light & bleached-boned
my guts are grey & black coals glowing.

I meant to say, *it is* this *fire you see*
coming out from inside me.

Call it the darkness you still wear
on the edge of your skin
the light you reach for
across the table
and into my heart.

AND THEN THERE'S US

for LaRue and Elvira

Nobody would believe it
to look at us

how our families'
histories
converge.

> Two women on opposite south
> ends of the continent
> working cotton
> for some man.

                                    Nobody would believe it.

> Their backs
>   and this country
> collapsing

> to make room for us together.

QUERIDA COMPAÑERA

Para Papusa Molina en respuesta

> *. . . fue como rencontrar una parte de mi misma que estaba perdida, fue el reafir-*
> *mar mi amor por las mujeres, por la mujer, por mi raza, mi lengua, el amor que*
> *me debo, a mi misma . . .*
>
> —una carta de mi compañera, mayo 1982

¿qué puedo decirte in return
stripped of the tongue
that could claim lives
de otras perdidas?

la lengua que necesito
para hablar
es la misma que uso
para acariciar

tú sabes.
you know the feel of woman
lost en su boca
        amordazada

it has always been like this.

profundo y sencillo
lo que nunca
pasó
por sus labios

but was
        utterly
        utterly
        heard.

A Flor de Labios
1995-1999

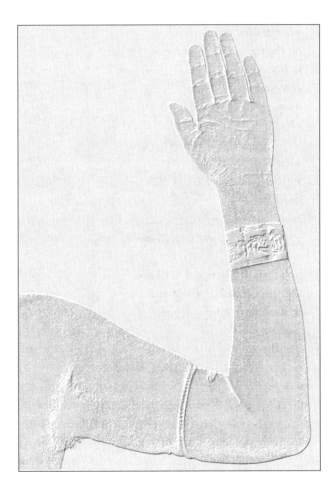

CANTO FLORIDO

1

a flor de labios
vivo yo
poeta de palabras
silenciosas
            I do not sing
what resides always
on the tip   of the tongue,
la ausencia
contenida en la cuna
de cuerpo

            it is always
what is not   said
what we remember
fleetingly
as the flower.
            a petal drops between my teeth.

(the Spanish Poets did not know
this, the Spanish Poets tasted
dust on their stingy tongues.)

2

la flor fugaz.

en la boca del río
that is our bed
we return a la tierra salada,

a los huesos molidos.
we turn ancient mitos'
fertilizer pa' flora born of the sea.

you are not so much sea
as desierto, the hot
animal-glove que me cubre
por la noche   Cihuacoatl.

membrane molten onto fist,
the sieve of my pored-skin left
wanting
nothing.

cells reorganize.
we prepare to die.

tú tú
mi flor
en la flor de su edad
ya   *a petal drops between my teeth*

mi querida

muerte.

LOOKING FOR THE INSATIABLE WOMAN[1]

One day a story will arrive in your town. There will always be disagreement over direction—whether the story came from the southwest or the southeast. The story may arrive with a stranger, a traveler thrown out of his home country months ago. Or the story may be brought by an old friend, perhaps the parrot trader. But after you hear the story, you and the others prepare by the new moon to rise up against the slave masters.

—Leslie Marmon Silko, *Almanac of the Dead*[2]

Most of us can name the story that came into the town of our hearts which changed our lives forever. For me, they were the earliest stories I can remember of my mother's childhood as a farmworker, so little the family used to drag her along between the rows of crops like the sack of potatoes they were picking. Thirty years later, those stories would become the farmworker families of my plays. The place the same: the central valley of Califas; the people—composites of stories told, remembered, witnessed and invented.

Ironically, the story of La Llorona, the Mexican Weeping Woman, was never told to me by my mother or any member of my family; and yet, it has had a more profound impact upon my writer's psyche than any story she recounted. One traditional Mexican version of La Llorona tells the tale of a woman who is sexually betrayed by her man, and, in what was either a fit of jealous rage or pure retaliation, she kills their children by drowning them in a river. Upon her own death, she is unable to enter heaven because of her crime. Instead, she is destined to spend all eternity searching for her dead children. Her lament, "Mis Hijos!" becomes the blood-chilling cry heard along irrigation ditches and country creeks, warning children that any misbehavior (straying too far from camp, for example) might lead to abduction by this female phantom.

The story of La Llorona first arrived in the "town" of my heart quite by accident, through the mouth of an almost-stranger. She was a "traveler," as Leslie Marmon Silko writes, "thrown out of (her) home country" of bible-belt California years before. At the time, the mid-70s, I was working as a waitress in a vegetarian restaurant on the borderline between San Francisco's gay Castro district and el barrio de la misión. The "traveler" was a white woman who'd come in every other weeknight for a bowl of brown rice and stir-fry vegetables and a cup of tea. I liked the look of the woman from the start: thirty-somethingish, bleached-blond and permanented hair, broken-toothed and full-chested. She had a big ol' smiling face. I spied the button she wore on her too-tight tee shirt, which read "Commie Dyke," and I instantly knew the girl was family. Amber (I'll call her by her real name because she'd like being the protagonist of her own story) came in most nights after she closed up shop at the collectively owned commie bookstore in town. She'd walk in, throw a load of new titles onto the decoupage tabletop and crack open one of those revolutionary texts. The books drew me to her. I remember one title in particular, the blue and red letters against the silver background, *The Romance of American Communism*.[3] There in the post-rush-hour lull, over a cup of darjeeling and within ear shot of a few scraggly-looking hippies, I got my first real introduction to Mr. Karl Marx as told to me by Ms. Amber Hollibaugh,[4] an honest-to-god member of the working class. She informed me that I, too, had been holding membership without ever fully knowing until it poured from this girl's lips like salve for the wounded and ignorant. *But that's another story.*

The story I want to tell is how this white-girl from the "asshole of nowhere," as another working-class friend's momma used to call anywhere not Los Angeles or New York, opened my heart to the story of La Llorona. Not that this girl from some truck stop in the Central Valley *consciously* knew anything about the Mexican myth, but what she told me shook loose that memorybone in me that had stored the cuento for at least one generation.

At the time, Amber was doing prison support work for a 39-year-old lesbian, who had been locked up in an Oregon prison for half her life. Jay was a child-killer. A contemporary La Llorona. And the required betrayal involved not a man, but what looked more like a kind of self-betrayal—as feminist philosopher María Lugones calls internalized homophobia—between two female lovers. Twenty years earlier, the dyke and her lover got into some mess of a fight. It seems. The kids were involved. It seems the couple drove the kids to a cliff and, each taking that innocence into their hands, threw each a child off the cliff. They were drunk no doubt. Crazed. No doubt. And they both no doubt were guilty of the crime. But it's redneck Oregon. And the biological mother takes the stand and testifies that "the dyke made me do it." Under the spell of the "pervert," she was forced to commit the gravest female crime against nature—infanticide. The biological mother walks. The lesbian lover, twenty years later, is still in jail. Twenty years a model prisoner and each time she is up for parole the word gets out, "lesbian child-killer to go free," and public pressure keeps her behind bars.

Today, another twenty years later and I don't know if Jay's still in prison. Amber's in New York now and still working with prisoners and dykes, I hear.[4] And I am left here, still unraveling this story. In 1976, I wrote a poem about it, called the "Voices of the Fallers."[*] Couldn't get the kid or the killer out of my head, that child falling. "I'm falling," he cries, "can't you see? I'm falling?" The child's plea echoes the voice of my high school classmate, another manly woman, crying as she tossed herself off a cliff in Baja California. (But that's another story.) I couldn't get those voices out of my head because I know what it's like to be a lesbian mom, biological and not. I know when the kid and the homophobia and the fear and shame of ourselves can lead to blows against the walls, against each other, against the child. It's not so far away from me. But the poem didn't satisfy my hunger to know the story, the real story, the story of why a woman kills her child. The story of La Llorona.

Why did I need to know the story? I am a sub-urban Chicana. Kids drowned in the local plunge, not the nearby river. I never heard anyone say "La Llorona's gonna get you." It was the "Boogie Man" in our neighborhood, or that simple inarticulate terror inspired by some *Twilight Zone* episode (the original ones), where the short trip down the hall to the bathroom became a long, labyrinth-like journey into the unknown.

"C'mon, walk down the hall with me. I gotta go."

"Okay, but you go first."

"No, you first."

* Included in this volume.

"No, you."

"You."

"Then hold my hand."

But as the daughter of a thoroughly Mexican mother, I did know about women being punished for the rest of their lives for some sin that happened somewhere in our collective history. "Eres mujer." That's all we need to know. That's the crime we feministas are still solving. I echo here Helena María Viramontes' story, "Growing," where she writes of a father reprimanding his daughter:

> *Tú eres mujer,* he thundered, and that was the end of any argument, any question, and the matter was closed because he said those three words as if they were a condemnation from the heavens and so she couldn't be trusted.[5]

When I first learned the Mexican story of La Llorona, I immediately recognized that the weeping woman, that aberration, that criminal against nature, was a sister. Maybe by being a lesbian, my identification was more easily won, fully knowing my crime was tantamount to hers. Any way you slice it, we were both a far and mournful cry from obedient daughters. But I am convinced that La Llorona is every Mexican woman's story, regardless of sexuality. She is sister to us all.

I began to investigate the myth. From the first paragraph I ever read on the subject in *Literatura chicana texto y contexto,* to José Limón's analysis and Rudolfo Anaya's fictionalization,[6] to interviews with farmworkers in Oregon, to finally sitting for days in the San Francisco public library scanning roll upon roll of that neon blue microfilm for every account of infanticide ever printed in the daily news—no version ever told me enough.

The official version was a lie. I knew that from the same bone that first held the memory of the cuento. *Who would kill their kid over some man dumping them?* It wasn't a strong enough reason. And yet everyone from Anaya to Euripides was telling us so. Well, if *traición* was the reason, could infanticide then be retaliation against misogyny, an act of vengeance not against one man, but man in general for a betrayal much graver than sexual infidelity: the enslavement and deformation of our sex?

A partera friend posed another possibility to me. As a woman who had worked as a nurse-midwife for many years among mechicanas, she was intimately connected with the full range of maternal instincts, both sanctioned and taboo. "Infanticide is not a homicide," she told me, "but a suicide. A mother never completely separates from her child. She always remains a part of her children." But what is it then we are killing off in ourselves and why?

The answer to these questions resides, of course, in allowing La Llorona to speak for herself, to say something other than "mis hijos" for all eternity. When this dawned on me, so did the beginnings of a play I began four years ago and still has me working and wondering. I called it a "Mexican Medea"[7] in reference to both the Greek Euripedean drama, where the "protagonist" kills her children and the Llorona story. As Euripides' dramatization of the story of Medea turned to the Greek gods as judge and consul, I turned to the pre-Columbian Aztec deities. In my research, I discovered another story, the Aztec creation myth of "the Hungry Woman;" and this story became pivotal for me, an aperture in my search to unlock la fuerza de La Llorona in our mechicana lives.

In the place where the spirits live, there was once a woman who cried constantly for food. She had mouths in her wrists, mouths in her elbows, and mouths in her ankles and knees. . . .

Then to comfort the poor woman [the spirits] flew down and began to make grass and flowers out of her skin. From her hair they made forests, from her eyes, pools and springs, from her shoulders, mountains and from her nose, valleys. At last she will be satisfied, they thought. But just as before, her mouths were everywhere, biting and moaning . . . opening and snapping shut, but they [were] never filled. Sometimes at night, when the wind blows, you can hear her crying for food.[8]

Who else other than La Llorona could this be? It is always La Llorona's cries we mistake for the wind, but maybe she's not crying for her children. Maybe she's crying for food, sustenance. Maybe que tiene hambre la mujer. And at last, upon encountering this myth—this pre-capitalist, pre-colonial, pre-catholic mito—my jornada began to make sense. This is the original Llorona y tiene mucha hambre. I realized that she has been the subject of my work all along, from my earliest writings, my earliest feminism. She is the story that has never been told truly, the story of that hungry Mexican woman who is called puta/bruja/jota/loca because she refuses to forget that her half-life is not a natural-born fact.

I am looking for the insatiable woman. I am reminded of Mexican artist Guadalupe García's cry in her performance piece, *Coatlicue's Call*.[9] She laments, "I am looking for a woman called Guadalupe." Maybe we're all looking for the same woman. When La Llorona kills her children, she is killing a male-defined Mexican motherhood that robs us of our womanhood. I first discussed this desire to kill patriarchal motherhood in relation to another Mexican myth, the "Birth of Huitzilopotchli."[10] The Mexican myth recounts the story of Coyolxauhqui, the Aztec moon goddess who attempts to kill her mother, Coatlicue, when she learns of her aging mother's pregnancy. As we feministas have interpreted the myth, Coyolxauhqui hopes to halt, through the murder of her mother, the birth of the War God, Huitzilopotchli. She is convinced that Huitzilopotchli's birth will also mean the birth of slavery, human sacrifice and imperialism (in short, patriarchy). She fails in her attempt and instead is murdered and dismembered by her brother Huitzilopotchli and banished into the darkness to become the moon.

This ancient myth reminds Mexican women that, culturally speaking, there is no mother-woman to manifest who is defined by us outside of patriarchy. We have never had the power to do the defining. We wander not in search of our dead children, but our lost selves, our lost sexuality, our lost spirituality, our lost sabiduría. No wonder La Llorona is so irrefutably punished, destined to walk the earth en busca de sus niños. To find and manifest our true selves (that "woman before the fall," I wrote elsewhere),[11] what might we have to change in the world as we know it? "¡Mis Hijos!" Llorona cries. But, I hear her saying something else. "¡Mis hijas perdidas!" And I answer. "Te busco a tí también, madre/hermana/hija." I am looking for the hungry woman.

"La Llorona," "The Hungry Woman," "The Dismemberment of Coyolxauhqui"—these are the stories that have shaped us. We, Chicanas, remember them in spite of ourselves, in spite of our families' and society's efforts to have us forget. We remember these stories where mothers worked in factories, not fields, and children played in city plunges, not country creeks. The body remembers.

Each of my plays, each poem, each piece of fiction has been shaped by a story. Most writers will tell you the same. My play *Shadow of a Man*[12] grew out of an extended image, a story my mother told me of her dead father appearing to her at the foot of her bed. He was silhouetted against the darkness, hat dipped over one eye, a shadow across his face. "I knew it was a sign of death," she said. "But I didn't know whose." Another of my plays, *Heroes and Saints,*[13] whose protagonist is a seventeen-year-old Chicana without a body, began in response to a play Luis Valdez wrote, entitled *The Shrunken Head of Pancho Villa.*[14] In it, he is looking for the missing head. In *Heroes,* I am looking for the missing body, the female one. In both plays, Valdez and I are looking for a revolution.

What does it take to uncover those stories with the power to inspire insurrection?
How do we breed a revolutionary generation of Chicana art?

Stories inspire stories, and the best and most revolutionary of stories are recuperated from the deepest places of our unconscious, which is the reservoir for our collective memory. The best writers speak with a "we" that rises up from all of us. So that when we truly succeed at our storytelling, we cannot wholly take the credit. I grow impatient with Chicano and Chicana literature that is purposely colloquial, the tourist literature, written for audiences who are strangers to the cultural and political geography of our symbols, images and history. When we write in translation, we never move beyond our colonized status. When we write for ourselves, our deepest selves, the work travels into the core of our experience with a cultural groundedness that illuminates a total humanity, one which requires a revolution to make manifest. Our truest words and images are suppressed by the cultural mainstream. They do not *entertain* and only entertainment yields profit. As a result, we learn to write less well, less deeply, less truly ourselves.[15]

Still, I know our promise. I have glimpsed it. Sometimes in the first few "forbidden" chapters of an unfinished novel by the published poet.

Sometimes in the roughly scripted monologue of a sixteen-year-old Xicana-Navajo dyke thinking she's a vato loco. Sometimes in the bleeding trails of watercolor taking the shape of a severed vulva-heart on a piece of mata paper. Sometimes. I still believe in the power of story to change our lives, whether it's a story you stumble across spilling out of the mouth of a commie dyke at a vegetarian restaurant or one your bisabuela told your abuelita and your abuelita told your mami, but your mami "forgot" to mention to you. There is revolutionary potential in the story. True stories empower, the way lies disempower. Thus, when we come across a true storyteller, she must be protected and nurtured.

Today, we Chicanas may romanticize our grandmothers as cuentistas, but our granddaughters still have few teachers in the art of storytelling. A generation after El Movimiento and a generation of affirmative action have created a body of literature to read, but who will guide these young readers in the art of *writing*? The programs and political movements that once fostered the cultivation of artists twenty-five years ago are virtually nonexistent today. The NEA has been butchered[16] and anti-affirmative action in California links arms with Proposition 187 in waging a class war against Raza to ensure that only the most privileged and "American" will be allowed access to the arts and education.[17] There are few cultural centers left, little creative writing, teatro, or visual arts being offered through Chicano/Latino studies programs. Universities across the country may be preparing a cadre of literary critics, political and social scientists, historians and lawyers (lots of lawyers) to negotiate a settlement, but where are our artists to predict the next uprising?

University ethnic studies departments need to renew their commitment to harbor a few working artists in their program to ensure that cultural critics continue to work in tandem with the cultural producers. Artists need to be given space to speak for ourselves on our own terms directly to a new generation of story-makers. You may say, isn't that what Fine Arts programs are for? I assure you, el llanto de La Llorona will not be heard in the most traditional M.F.A. programs. Our students need teachers who can recognize the signs of the "hungry woman" in all her disguises and disfigurations. Our students need Maestras who are familiar with the history of our mythology and mythology of our history and have made home, as artists, in the meeting place between the two.

At the time of this writing, I am still working on my Llorona story. Of course, I want to believe it is revolutionary, but at some point, I may have to accept that "Mexican Medea" may only succeed in capturing a splinter of what I know in my bones about Llorona.[18] I confess, it's a harder story to write now, being a mamá in the flesh with all the beauty and burden of those lessons of Mexican motherhood. Pero sigo adelante. And if this play doesn't satisfy my hunger for La Llorona's story, maybe another later work will. Maybe it's a story I'll work on for the rest of my life in many shapes and voices and styles. Maybe, as James Baldwin once said, we each have just one story to tell and every writing effort is just an attempt to say it better *this time.* Maybe somewhere in me I believe that if I could get to the heart of Llorona, I could get to the heart of the mexicanaprison and in the naming I could free us . . . if only just a little. Maybe the effort is a life well spent.

ENTRE NOS

I am not

the indian she is
but am witness to the story
of the dirt
and the trees
and the land
before the road
they built
through the mountain.

SOUR GRAPES:
THE ART OF ANGER IN AMÉRICA

Here is a fruit for the crows to pluck
for the rain to gather
for the wind to suck
for the sun to rot
for the tree to drop.
Here is a strange and bitter crop.

—"Strange Fruit" as sung by Billie Holiday[1]

But for the shared history of miscegenation, Pulitzer Prize-winning play-wright August Wilson and I have little in common, at least at face value. He is a man, a man of large stature. (He must be over 6-2; 200 lbs.) He is an African American, a heterosexual, born in the East. I am a short, half-breed Mexican woman (I won't note my weight), born and raised in the Southwest. I am a lesbian. And yet, sitting in the last row of the packed 500-seat McCarter Theater at Princeton University, I cried and called him "brother" out loud. I cried as he said to an audience of theater professionals, overwhelmingly white, "I am a race man" and "The Black Power Movement . . . was the kiln in which I was fired."[2] I cried out of hunger, out of solidarity, out of a longing for that once uncompromising cultural nationalism of the 60s and 70s that birthed a new nation of American Indian, Chicano, Asian American and Black artists.

I describe here my experience of August Wilson's keynote address at the Theatre Communications Group's conference in June 1996. My unexpected tears forced me to acknowledge my longing for a kind of collective mutual recognition as a "colored" playwright writing in White America. It is a longing so wide and deep that every time Wilson mentioned "Black," I inserted Chicana. With every generic "he," I added "she." Wilson spoke of Black artists who insisted on their own self-worth in what he referred to as the "culturally imperialist" world of American theater, as "warriors on the cultural battlefield." Although I knew he wasn't thinking of me, guerrera and embattled, I knew I carried the same weapons (more crudely made than his) and the same armor (mine surely more penetrable in my colored womanhood, in my sexuality). I knew, whether he recognized me or not among the ranks, that I was a "sister" in that struggle against a prescription for American theater that erases the lives of everyone I call my "pueblo."

In his address, Wilson went on to cite the history of slavery, distinguishing between those slaves who entertained in the big house for the master and those who remained in the slave quarters, creating song, dance, story for one another. He proclaimed, "I stand . . . squarely on the self-defining ground of the slave quarters." The day before, I had gone to see his latest play, *Seven Guitars*, on Broadway, surely the "Big House" by mainstream theater standards; still, the language of word and body in the play, as is the case in all Wilson's plays, reflected an "un-translated" conversation among African Americans. It is a conversation white audiences may be privileged to witness, but are prohibited from shaping, even as they "consume" it through their ticket purchase.[3]

As a Black *American* writer, Wilson sees himself in the trajectory of Western theater, which finds its foundation in the Greek dramatists and Aristotle's *Poetics*. Possibly this shared theatrical foundation is what makes Wilson's work, although challenging in thematic content, accessible in form to Euro-American audiences. Still he "reserve[s] the right," as he puts it, "to add [his] African consciousness and . . . aesthetic to the art [he] produces." A right he freely and powerfully employs.

The American theater establishment enjoys using August Wilson as the example of the ultimate democracy of American theater: that even a one-time member of the slave-class of this country can make the "big time." Meanwhile the aesthetics of Euro-American theater—what is considered "good art"—remain institutionally unaltered and secured by the standard theatergoer who pays "good money" to see it; that is, a theater which reflects the world as middleamerica understands it, a world which at its core equates free enterprise with freedom. As Chicano theater historian Jorge Huerta puts it: "If theater is a temple, it is now dedicated to corporate greed."[4] A few "darkies," a few "commies" and "perverts" may slip through the cracks, but the gestures are token attempts to keep the marginalized in this country—that growing discontented "minority"—pacified. Exceptions to the rule never become the rule.

Sometimes I marvel at my own naiveté. Throughout my twelve years of writing for the American theater, over and over again I am referred to the Aristotelian model of the "well-made play." So, good student that I am, I track down Aristotle's *Poetics*. I read it, re-read it, take copious notes. But not until I read the Marxism of Brecht, then Augosto Boal's *Theater of the Oppressed*, does my discomfort with the Aristotelian system begin to make any sense. Aristotle created his poetics within the context of a slave-based economy, an imperialist democracy, not unlike the corporate-controlled democracy we are living under in the United States today. Women and slaves were not free citizens in Aristotle's Greece.[5] I am reminded of my own character's words in a recent play, as she struggles to remember the dance of her O'odham ancestors, "I just keep moving my feet like this . . . ignorant feet . . . in order to do something other than theirs on this stage."[6] What does the theater of the oppressed really *look* like? Can the forms of our theatrical storytelling take on a shape distinct from the slave master's stage? Today, the very people (Mexican *and* American at once) who take center stage in my plays daily have their citizenship denied, questioned and/or inauthenticated. These are me, my mother, my cousins, my ancestors and my children. These are my characters—like Wilson's, the children of slaves. And when the children of slaves become playwrights, even our literary ancestors are proffered freedom.

I'm watching this freedom-struggle take space on stage. I'm watching history in the making, watching child-of-slave-little-brother-son take pen in hand and write. For us.

In *Fed Up: A Cannibal's Own Story*, Chicano playwright Ricardo A. Bracho gives voice to a character whom he refers to as "the first woman of color of the outer colonies of Western Theater," Sycorax of *The Tempest*:[7]

You know [silence] goes way back. . . . I used to think that was my name, but it ain't. . . . The name's Sycorax. Silence. Silence. Sycorax.

Close, huh? Particularly when you're not allowed the chance of sounding it out. See on account of one whiteboy who went by the name of William Shakespeare I been . . . shut-mouthed for centuries. He wrote a play about me n mine [indicates the "Cannibals"]. My island. My sex. And this fantasy he and his call my race.[8]

When the children of slave women begin to speak, they point fingers as deadly as knives. The knives pierce to core depth of silence. It hurts all around. And they will care more passionately about their love for one another than their hatred for their onetime "master." Bracho's play attests to this colored-centric passion. In *Fed Up* his "cannibals" (i.e., modern-day Calibans and the children of Sycorax whom the playwright characterizes as gay men of color) make a meal out of the body of the Dead White Writer, a gay man. Historically the white man's prey, the "Cannibals" revolt through their ritualistic consumption of the writer's remains. A rage generated by the colonization of the colored body motivates the writing of the play and the action of the characters.

CorporateAmerika is not ready for a people of color theater that holds members of its audiences complicitous in the oppression of its characters. *Who would buy a ticket to see that?* Audiences grow angry (although critics as their spokespeople may call it "criticism") when a work is not written *for* them, when they are not enlisted as a partner in the protagonists' struggle, when they may be asked to engage through self-examination rather than identification, when they must question their own centrality.

. . . . .

The next day, at the same TCG conference, I was on a playwrights' panel where we were to discuss the motivation or inspiration for our playwriting. Without hesitation, I responded "absence." Like in those children's games where you are shown a picture, study it, then turn the page, and you are shown the same picture again, but this time you have to figure out what is missing. You are asked, *"What's missing in this picture?"* That question sums up my entire experience as a Chicana feminist playwright. With every play produced, whether on Broadway or in the barrio, I ask the question, what's missing in this picture? And the answer is invariably, "we." Suzan-Lori Parks echoes this sentiment in a 1995 interview in *The Drama Review*:

> It's a fabricated absence. That's where I start from. . . . It's the hole idea. . . . It's the story that you're told that goes, "once upon a time you weren't here . . . and you didn't do shit." [9]

I don't go to theater looking for other Chicana lesbians. (Or at least I don't look for them *on stage*.) But I do look for glimpses of colored-woman-centered realities without white male translations. Stories of colored womanhood that are complex, contradictory and compellingly told by equally complex, contradictory and compelling colored woman writers. Certainly in the late 1990s, we can witness some of this on the pages of a book, but theater remains what seems to be the last bastion of cultural imperialism in the American art world, with the visual arts a close second. Is it because it is a three-dimensional live form which, like film, requires real live women of color as actors, writers, directors? The novel requires only one tenacious colored woman and some significant support along the way. The collaborative art forms require a small army.

I most viscerally experienced this "what's missing in this picture?" phenomenon as an audience member of Tony Kushner's *Angels in America* on Broadway. Of course, I loved the play, as did most of the audience that Sunday matinee, as has most of the theatergoing public of the United States in the last few years. The play is undeniably and unabashedly queer and dangerously "commie" in perspective, which I relish and respect about Kushner's work. But what I anticipated would make the audience uncomfortable was precisely what made the audience hysterical. Every dick joke, even every *Jewish* dick joke, even every *homosexual* Jewish dick joke, tore the audience up. They weren't offended. They were entertained.

So, I thought to myself, well, Jewish humor is synonymous with New York and so even non-Jews "get the joke" on Broadway. The same is true, to a certain degree, across the United States, where prime-time TV abounds with Jewish and "kind of" Jewish guys cracking jokes, written by Jewish writers. To the degree that a Jewish sensibility—the exquisite timing in the telling of a joke, the witticism, the occasional Yiddish term, the sharp-tongue, the self-denigrating comment, etc.—has penetrated the family evening TV hour, Kushner's *Angels* has to do little cultural translation to be understood by mainstream audiences. (Except for the fact that the playwright is better read than 99 percent of most Americans.) I would also interject here that Jewish-American *drama* is another story all together; Jewish culture for the most part remains "ghettoized" within the genre of comedy. Further, I must also add before any inferences of "Jewish conspiracy theories" be extrapolated from this writing, that I am engaging with a leftist queer Jewish writer in this comparison precisely because he is *not* a WASP. Because he is specific about his cultural "otherness" from WASP-Amerika and the history of genocide that prohibits his complete assimilation. Because Kushner's work is the closest I, as a Chicana lesbian playwright, can get to a mainstream counterpart, like August Wilson—which still is, of course, very far away.

Okay, so culturally, *Angels* is translatable. Everyone's laughing at the Jewish jokes, but the dick jokes? The homo jokes? I look around at this Broadway audience, mostly straight, overwhelmingly white, upper middle-class (your typical theater crowd); and again, I can't believe it, they're all laughing. Are they laughing because the play is a Tony Award winner and they think to be cool and hip, they'd better laugh? Maybe. Still, to my amazement two guys start to "fuck" on stage (as Kushner describes it in the stage directions: "They fuck.") and everyone is fine with it. Of course, we know theater is not real life and those same laughing lawyers and stockbrokers in the audience may very well cry at the real news of having a real gay son. But theater is what I am looking at here. So, I did a little private experiment. Every time I heard the word or a reference to "Jewish dick," I replaced it with "Mexican pussy." Jewish dick . . . Mexican pussy. Jewish dick . . . Mexican pussy. Jewish dick . . . Mexican pussy. And nobody was laughing. That's me on Broadway. That's my people on Broadway. That chilling silence. Nobody is laughing. Pussy ain't funny unless a man tells the joke. Mexican ain't funny unless a gringo's talking. Put a Mexican woman downstage center wanting some pussy and nobody's gonna laugh, unless she is laughed at, i.e., ridiculed, objectified, scorned. *And who the hell's gonna translate that Spanglish those Chicanos speak anyway?*

Of course, prick, like pussy, is always racialized and, therefore, politicized; and not for a minute do I imagine Kushner is not critically aware of the racialized history of Jewish genitalia and the sexual exploitation and distortions suffered by Jews (male and female alike) through anti-Semitism. Nevertheless, in contemporary mainstream U.S. society, there is also a profound identification with dick, from both men and women, and a comfort in the "normalcy" of its whiteness. After all, we aren't talking black dick here, which is, eurocentrically speaking, altogether more dangerous.

"Sour Grapes," this is what the little diablito (internalized-racist) voice keeps whispering in my ear, throughout this writing. "Ah, Moraga, this is all just sour grapes." And I think, "Yes, exactly." Sour grapes: the bitter fruit artists of color are forced to eat in this country.

Zoot Suit, by Luis Valdez, the only Chicano work that ever made it to Broadway, was a sell-out long-running success in the late 70s in Los Angeles; however, it only lasted a few weeks on Broadway. Why? It was not culturally translatable. Even with the play's concessions to the mainstream —including a few redeeming and redemptive white characters with whom the typical theatergoer might relate—weren't sufficient to "de-Chicano" the play. Who would pay for it? Not New York. New York won't even pay to see Puerto Ricans, whom ostensibly they should know better by sheer geographic proximity and demographic representation. (Of course, there is always the occasional revival of *West Side Story*.) The reviews killed *Zoot Suit* because the reviewers were being asked to step outside their cultural myopia in order to not only evaluate a work, but actually "see" it.

If the agreed-upon assumption is that good theater is a good time, a good cry, a good laugh, then the writer must create characters with whom his* audience can identify to create that emotional connection. And the reviewer, representing the concerns of the typical audience, is being entrusted with that responsibility to ensure a "good time" to his readers and ward off the "bad." Although the majority of theatergoers are white, middle-class females, the producers are overwhelmingly white and male and expect all of us cultural consumers to digest the works we witness on

*Throughout this essay, the masculine is used intentionally not to reflect the generic, but the majority, i.e., male writers and critics.

stage as they do, i.e., as white men. This doesn't require great cross-cultural leaps for most viewers, regardless of gender or race. We know how white men think because white men have had the privileged opportunity to tell us so through our educational system, every manner of media, all forms of literature and the arts. Similarly, the white-male-minded writer has to do little cultural translation to elicit his audience's identification and sympathies. We slide effortlessly into the well-worn shoes of his protagonist. The story moves us. Leaving the theater, we feel better. Again, Aristotle's Theater of Catharsis.

When the subject of a work is a woman of color, however, a poor or working-class woman, maybe even a lesbian, and the character is not constructed within the white male imagination (neither exoticized, eroticized nor stigmatized), how much harder must the playwright work to convey the character's humanity, for she is from the onset perceived as "other"— i.e., not a suitable subject for identification. In this case, playing before a mainstream theater audience, how much more difficult it is to establish that emotional connection with the audience. The spectator and the reviewer don't care about her life. She is foreign. The play is judged as inferior. "I wasn't moved," writes the critic. Chicanas' multigenerational conversation around a kitchen table is referred to as "banter" because the critic isn't interested in it. The only significant male figure in an otherwise all-Chicana play (in this case, my own *Shadow of a Man*) is mistakenly viewed as the protagonist because he's the closest the male reviewer can get to caring. "He's a weak character," the reviewer states. "He doesn't hold the play together." He wasn't supposed to. In *Shadow,* the father's (intentional) weakness as a character is fundamental to the plot; it is the women who must hold the family *and the story* together. But the reviewer wasn't following the plot lines of those whom he was accustomed to viewing as auxiliary to the "real" (the man's) story.[10]

I have never felt so strongly about the cultural tyranny of theater reviews as with the premiere production of my play *Watsonville: Some Place Not Here.*[11] Probably more than any other of my work, *Watsonville,* to the credit of Brava Theater Center, the producer, generated in its six-week run in San Francisco the most diverse audience I have ever witnessed. It included the mainstream theatergoer, all the major press, the arts community, the politically active Chicano community, student groups, youth groups from the barrios of San Francisco and Watsonville, queers of all kinds, feminist activists, women's groups and a steady base of Mexican immigrant workers from the greater Bay Area. Each audience created a different gestalt. Each new configuration of all the sectors mentioned above made for a different experience of the play. This is, I'm reminded, the marvelous beauty and danger of theater: the audience as collaborator in the experience. Teenagers snickered nervously at the lesbian kiss. Cannery workers from the real town of Watsonville whispered in Spanish to their comadres, "Así se sucedió." "It happened like that," referring to the 18-month strike upon which the play was based. Chicana lesbians laughed out loud when the heterosexual cannery worker, a single mother, wants to know how you can tell who's who in a lesbian relationship. "If some women are your friends and some are your lovers, how do you know when to be celosa [jealous]?" Her innocence is familiar and familial; we see her in our cousins, our aunts, the young women of our barrios. In post-show discussions, lefties commented on their identification with the middle-aged drunken nostalgia of two Chicano organizers who mourn the increasing poverty and isolation of Cuba due to the U.S. embargo. "Ay pobre de Cuba. The only island left in the world."

JOURNAL ENTRY. MAY 27. THE MORNING AFTER.

I don't remember the opening night party, I only remember the performance. What was on a different night too long, last night captured all our attention, our minds & hearts—those of us so hungry to see our lives, our people reflected. I felt vindicated. Yes, I believe that is the word: "vindicated." "You see. Ya ves," I want to say to all those who doubt us, our complexity, render us invisible. "We exist . . . y más." The reviews tomorrow, no doubt, will say they saw something else. But, I must remember the work. I am getting closer, I hope, to some more profound portrait of who we are as a people. That's all that really matters: the writing.

My journal entry predicted correctly. When the reviews for *Watsonville* came out, the only official judges on the play's significance were middle-class Euro-Americans who regarded the play as outsiders, without once questioning the cultural bias and ignorance that influenced their opinions. The play's structure didn't adhere to the requirements of a "well-made play," they complained. (Otra vez, Aristotle.) "Who is the main character?" "Too many stories." "Epic in dimension," but "the playwright just doesn't pull it off."

Okay, who needs them—these reviewer guys and (sometimes) gals? Progressive theater needs them because they bring in the middle-class ticket buyers, those who can afford to pay full-price on a Saturday night and cover the cost of all the group rates and freebies that bring in the audiences who do see their lives reflected in the work. Without governmental support for the arts, community-based theaters striving to create an art of integrity and beauty are forced into dependent relationships with whiteuppermiddleclassamerica. Still, this is not just a question of exploiting the monied classes for the advancement of the disenfranchised; there is also a moral and aesthetic obligation here. If critics refuse to learn the traditions, the languages, the sensibilities of the artists they critique, how are they then to educate their own readers?

As August Wilson states, "The true critic does not sit in judgment. Rather he seeks to inform his reader, instead of adopting a posture of self-conscious importance in which he sees himself a judge and final arbiter of a work's importance or value."[12] Simply put, how can a critic judge a work he knows nothing about? And how can s/he call something representative of American theater when his definition of "American" remains a colonial one—i.e., White America perceiving Blackness through the distorted mirror of its own historical slaveowner segregationist racist paranoia and guilt, while all other people of color remain invisible.

Sour Grapes? Oh, most definitely.

I attended that TCG conference in Princeton one week before the closing of *Watsonville* in San Francisco. In the best of scenarios, we'd hoped the play might run all summer. Due to the lukewarm critical reception of the play, ticket sales dwindled and the play closed after the sixth week. In retrospect, I understand that the proximity of the conference to my disappointment in the reviews is one reason August Wilson's words brought tears to my eyes and the shape of an "old-fashioned" raised fist to my hand. Few theater professionals really comprehend the obstacles to creating a colored (and I would add female) theater in white America, except those who have suffered at its hands. I do not turn to this writing to discuss the merits or weaknesses of my dramatic works, for I know the body of my writings contains both. I turn to these words to discuss the politics of trying to write and produce theater in a country where the people you speak of, with, and for are a theatrical non-event—or worse, in "real life" are the object of derision and scapegoating.

This is real life.

I am a half-breed Chicana. The difference between my gringo immigrant side and my native Mexican is that when gringos came to the United States, they were supposed to forget their origins. My whitedaddy isn't quite sure what he is. Orphan son of a British Canadian, he thinks. His mother . . . French, yes French for sure, cuz there was some French grandmother somewhere, but Missouri is where they all end up. She meeting my grandfather, whom I only met once . . . they say . . . I was too young to remember . . . my Dad's history too vague to remember because they came to this country to forget.

Mexicans, however, don't forget. Anything. We remember our land daily in the same smells, same seasons, same skies, same sierras, same street signs . . . San Francisco . . . Alameda . . . El Presidio . . . the Spanish sounds slip and slide away. It is a colonial language, but of an Indian people. And the measure of our "Americanism" (in U.S. terms), the testimony to our acculturation to U.S. culture, is our eventual forgetting.

But I remember . . .

one smog-laden sticky-thighed childhood afternoon, sitting inside the cool stone walls of the Old San Gabriel Mission, our parish church. The nun tells us, "There are dead Indians buried down there, too." She said this "too" like an after-thought, after roll-calling the rolling r's of each of the Spanish friars' names carved into the man-sized plaque filling the center aisle floor. "Down there," she said. Down there under my white oxford missionschoolgirl soles, shuffling against the creaking wooden pews and a buried history.

I am neither Spanish friar nor mission Indian, but it's Indian history I'm diggin' up, diggin' for, thirty-five years later. Or maybe I'm just hunting for some woman somewhere some breed some mixed-blood mixed-up mess of a woman-loving-woman like me.

I am once twice three times removed. But I know, I ain't all immigrant.

To me, one of the greatest and most bitter ironies is that the Mexican immigrant daily reminds us U.S.-born Mexicans that we are not really immigrants at all. What most immigrants from México share is poverty and what most poor people share in the nation-state of México is their Indianism. They may be calling themselves "Mexican," but their blood is speaking Indigenous American. And the shape of the head, the nose, the cheekbones, the shade of skin is talking back.

So, I'm angry and I write about it. I write when little in the national picture reflects back anything I understand as common sense. What was initiated by California's Proposition 187[13] in the mid-90s and nationalized in Congress is the lie in the line, the borderline. When I first began this essay in the fall of 1996, Congress had already made recommendations that would require a national ID, repeal the 14th Amendment's guarantee of citizenship to U.S.-born children of undocumented parents, limit due process for asylum seekers, deny undocumented children a public education, and increase, yet once again, border patrol enforcement. Ironically, this turn-of-the-century "witch hunt" against "illegal immigrants" is being mounted primarily against Mexicans and Central Americans, people with roots in this continent that surpass the Anglo-American by millennia. The real truth is, Americans are being kept out of América. As the century comes to a close, California emerges as the mastermind of a legislation of fear and scapegoatism. Prop 187 laid fertile ground for the unrestrained xenophobia and racism of Propositions 209 and 227,[14] which followed a few years later. The abolition of both affirmative action and bilingual education in our public schools ensures that the Latino/a student, in particular (the largest minority in California), will remain firmly situated in the underclass of this country. We will remain "illegal" and "illiterate," which is exactly where CorporateAmerika prefers its working poor, if not in prison. In the meantime, U.S. corporations, thanks to NAFTA, can cross the border, without restraint, in order to exploit Mexican labor and land. The maquiladoras are a case in point, but Mexicans cannot return the favor by freely seeking a livable wage in the U.S.

Generated by the same cultural arrogance and greed exhibited by U.S. corporations and their legislators, the so-called progressive American Art World, perpetrates admittedly more benign but equally insidious acts of exclusion on Chicano/a and other "colored-identified" Latino artists.* It is precisely the indigenism of Chicano art and its opposition to Euro-American cultural dominance that renders it "foreign" and of little interest to the dominant U.S. culture, a culture of European immigrants.[15] Ironically it is the same indigenism that makes much of Chicano culture fundamentally "American" in the original native sense of the term, not the Constitutionally constructed one. While regional theaters complain as federal legislators hack away at their government funding, those very institutions subscribe to the same narrow definition of American culture that their so-called enemies on Capitol Hill do.[16] They want us to forget our origins and, in the act of forgetting, make our work palatable to an American consumer culture. But I/we are not so easily eaten.

. . . . .

I am a third-generation Mexican born in the U.S. My mother was born in Santa Paula, California, in 1914; my maternal grandmother was born in the Sonoran desert in 1888. Was it Arizona then? Was it México? In the 19th century, borders were drawn like fingered lines in the sand, and erased with every wagon wheel. In the 1840s, U.S. land had been Mexican land; a generation before that, it was Spanish territory; and before that and always Apache, Yaqui, Seri, O'odham. Same land. Same folk. But shifting geopolitical borders, slavery, rape, intermarriage and Catholicism name the land and its dwellers differently and our identities change along with the changes. But never, never thoroughly.

This is the American landscape: this califaspomo land upon which the United States imposes itself; this "nation" born in 1776; this "frontier" appropriated in 1848; this "New Spain" stolen in 1519. The history of conquest in América constitutes so little time compared to the indigenous

---

* I make a distinction here between Chicano, U.S. Latino and Carribbean artists and writers who posit their work in resistance to Western aesthetic dominance, and "Hispanics" who identify with whiteness and situate themselves culturally as any other European immigrant to the U.S.

history that preceded it. And yet, this is all America (even liberal America) seems to remember. To counter the racism laid bare by recent national anti-immigrant measures, progressives assert, "But it was immigrants who built this country." In order to justify the integration of new immigrants into U.S. society, liberals portray the United States as a nation constructed exclusively by immigrant-labor, while slavery, the contributions of Native peoples and the theft of Native lands are conveniently ignored. Further, there is little public discussion about which immigrant groups are made welcome in the United States and when. What do economics and politics have to do with it? What does U.S. intervention in the Third World have to do with it?[17]

Five days and five hundred years ago in América, immigrant whites and their ancestors considered themselves welcome in this continent. Call it manifest destiny, call it the gold rush, call it the godly thing to do, call it convert los indios, call it sugarcane, banana plantations, call it Phoenix-Arizona and Club Med, the dot-com gentrification of La Misión de San Panchito, call it New Age Spiritualism, call it whatever you want, Indigenous Americans continue to suffer as a consequence of European-immigrant cultural and political domination. Witness the neocolonization and cultural appropriation of the U.S. Southwest by East Coast immigrant artists: the "New New Mexico."

How quickly we Native-born and immigrants of color are required to forget our place of origin to guarantee our Americanism. But what does a culture of forgetfulness produce except suburban shopping malls and more and more violent video games? True, every nation of people living within U.S.-imposed borders must reckon with the monolith of the nation-state, but we do not have to believe that a "nationality," a mono-culture of people, was invented with the signing of the Declaration of Independence. If the Bill of Rights could be altered to give human rights to a U.S.-conceived fetus, while denying those same rights to a U.S.-born child of an undocumented immigrant, how much confidence should we put into the Constitution as a reflection of the cultural/ethical values of the peoples of the United States of America?

On my more lucid days, when my ideas are less controlled by pre-scribed modes of conventional thinking, I ask myself, how it could happen that a new nation was invented to hold complete dominion in a land where verifiable nations already existed? How is it that the spiritual practices, ethical beliefs, systems of government, gender roles and ecology of the original peoples of this land, as well as the peoples themselves, were not elemental to the construction of this invented nation? The Iroquois influence in the writing of the Constitution seems thoroughly remote from the actual implementation of that document. These are purposely naive questions because the answers are equally simple. Such coexistence requires a humility of spirit and a sense of communal responsibility with other living beings which totally counter what we've come to understand as American Culture.

Sour Grapes. The fruit of the labor del pueblo mechicano.

Highway 5, heading north from L.A. to San Francisco. I am on cruise-control, speeding through the California landscape. Grapes growing, thinking . . . Mexicans dying.

Cruising . . . and vineyards turn to endless miles of yellow dirt and graying tumbleweed. The backdrop: sentinels of electrical towers. There is a faint, very faint, mirage-like outline of what could be the Sierras, somewhere east of this cloudless central valley white-blue stillness. It's not desert here exactly, too much food growing, but the same trucks barrel through I-5 as I-80 with their oversized loads of trailer houses split into two for transport.

Five miles later, I can't name what crop borders the stone river of this highway, yellow-flowers blooming from irrigation, then fruit trees . . . almonds? Back to yellow dirt. Broken barbed wire and stick fences hold in fields of burnt brush.

Cruising . . . I pass a sign reading, "Pleasant Valley State Prison," an institutional oxymoron, then pull into an Arco station. A man hops out of the late-model van next to me and slides open the passenger door. And I find the woman I have been looking for.

The van is packed hip-to-hip with Mexican farm workers coming back from the fields. It is the end of the day. She is squeezed among them, the only woman. She is the face of the best looking of us Mexican women. Her body draped in a loose flannel shirt and oversized khaki trousers. She is covered from shoulder to delicate wrist to ankle. I can't see her ankles, but want to. She could've been my mother sixty years ago. Same black eyes, black rope of hair. "You don't belong here," I hear my mother's words rise to the surface of my own lips. I want to tell her, "You don't belong here." Meaning out there, in the fields. Like they told my mother, her delicate-boned back bent over the potato, the cotton plant, the brussel sprout. Her artist's hands hooked into the shape of hoes.

The native beauty of this land reduced to labor undersold and stolen. The native beauty of this land reduced to labor: parceled plots of pesticide poison.

Land has memory. And the original peoples of that land, and those who daily live its lessons, are the memory carriers. The failure to remember, the failure to respect and defend the memory carriers, destroys cultures, ecological environments, destroys lives. The United States' record of genocide against the original peoples of this land and the ecological devastation it has wreaked upon it are testament to this fact.

Today, our memory carriers, often removed from their place of origin, are more and more difficult to encounter. If we are fortunate, we may find elders in our own families who still carry stories with them. Our storytellers are the chief purveyors of memory and, as a consequence, vision. But the memory carriers are also our youth, if they can find forms in which to express themselves. And this is where art comes in; for through art cultural memory is transmitted and our stories are told. I do not want the Vietnamese, the displaced Palestinian, the Jew or Gypsy, the Quiché Maya to forget their cultures when they take residence on this North American continent. And with even greater passion I do not want their artists to forget. I want this country to remember its origins and its peoples to remember theirs.

. . . . .

Recently, I saw a rerun of an interview with Toni Morrison on public TV; it had originally taken place a number of years ago, upon the publication of her book, *Beloved*. As always, Morrison's eloquence awed me. But what most astounded were her words: "What is really infinite is the past." And

I thought of how un-American that way of thinking is; for this "nation" was built upon the belief that one could and should forget the past and invent a future.[18] By contrast, she spoke of the future as something finite; and indeed it is, from an artist's perspective. Because history in all its limitlessness determines the future. And unraveling history, the multitude of versions of the story, the story from multifarious perspectives, this is limitless. And how great is our task to remember if we are people of color artists, if we are artists without a written history, if we are artists who have been forced into exile (three or three thousand miles) from our ancestral lands.[19] Because our version of the story has never been told. Still.

Finding the path to memory is my task as an artist. Writing for the "Ancestors," as playwright August Wilson has said, that's my job. To remember ancestral messages, to counter the U.S. culture of forgetfulness. Sometimes memory is no more than a very faint scent. You sniff it, take a step, stop and sniff again, and gradually make your way along a path to a people. You are blind and hand-and-tongue-tied. You just keep sniffing toward the warmth of the light on your face, the scent of heat on the stone-packed dirt beneath your feet, the cooling of a summer central valley evening drawing a sudden chill to your skin. You go backwards in time. You write. You're right. Even if you never read it in a book, saw it on stage or at the movies, you're on the right road.

"Bitter Fruit."
We are "a strange and bitter crop," Billie
we, the children of slaves, the survivors of genocide.

And we don't forget how we got here.

THISTLE

thistle
she tells me
with thistle they awaken
the mind back
into the living body

I see it bloom purple
like flowering bruises

here

and here.

OUT OF OUR REVOLUTIONARY MINDS
TOWARD A PEDAGOGY OF REVOLT[1]

HISTORY

In the beginning was the letter. A conversation between Nat Turner and a slave from the play, *Insurrection: Holding History:*

> NAT: [Hammet,] you been studin' 'em letters?
> HAMMET: I been studin' em.
> NAT: let me see one 'em A's then.
> (*HAMMET moves to NAT's Back.*
> *With his Finger he begins Drawing the letter "A.")*
> HAMMET (*Slowly*): . . . arrow.
>   . . . stick.
> NAT: nah do me one 'em B's.
> HAMMET (*Concentrates*): . . . stick.
>   . . . rock. rock.
> NAT: do that one again and don't speak it this time. . . .
>   okay nah befo' we split i'm gon' teach you a new one.
>   (*NAT begins drawing the letter "C" on HAMMET's Back.*)
>   moon
>   this letter "C."
>   (*He points to sky.*)
>   think "see" "moon."
>   "C."[2]

And the letter was made flesh. And became the word. And the word was "insurrection" because literacy was forbidden. "If you teach [a slave] how to read," Fedrerick Douglass's "master" admonished, "[i]t would forever unfit him to be a slave."[3] The slaveholder fears: to use the master's words is to take up the master's tools to destroy the master's house. However, a century and half later, poet Audre Lorde warns: "[But] the master's tools will never dismantle the master's house."[4]

Maybe it is more complicated than we ever imagined: this practice of the pen.

For playwright Robert O'Hara, author of *Insurrection,* the bent back of Nat Turner is the metaphor for revolution, where the lash is repulsed and replaced by the letter. More than a hundred years later, literacy was still viewed as the best escape from our enslavement as people of color; that is, until the slaveholder of racist profiteering began to re-channel (and re-chain) youth of color energies into dreams of sudden wealth through professional sports contracts, hip hop and ghetto/barrio drug dealing.

Education was the mantra I heard growing up in the voice of my mother's counsel: "If I'd only had the education, hija . . . nothing could've stopped me." This is the rare gift the undereducated (my mother got no further than the third grade) can offer to the next generation: "ganas."* The desire for that which was not their god-given (read: class-secured) right, and so all the more coveted. I, too, learned to covet education, not for the job out of the factory, but for a world wider than the confines of my neighborhood working-class rituals of work and worry. "No one had to make *me* do my homework," I remind my ten-year-old, slumped begrudgingly over her Oakland City Schools xeroxed handout homework (again).

In my innocence, as a first-generation college student, I imagined books as that stolen inner-world sanctum where one was allowed to *contemplar:* one's existence, the meaning of one's life, the source of one's suffering, el propósito de estar aquí, here inside what was then a blossoming female body. In the 1970s I read imaginative literature because it was more complex than pyschology, truer than history, and as hungry as any art; and as such, literature and its makers became my teachers. So I fell in love with literature, looked to literature for personal insights into political contradictions, as I also sought to extract from poems, novels and essays the political meaning of my most intimate personal preguntas.

Twenty-five years ago, however, there was little personal "me" to read. That "me," Chicana and lesbian, had not been invented. But race and

---

* The truest thing said by Mr. Escalante, through the mouth of Edward James Olmos, in the film *Stand and Deliver.*

racism had. Passion and perversion had. And hunger, always hunger. So, I rifled the pages of a 1928 edition of *The Well of Loneliness* for some remote acknowledgment of what could be defined as lesbian desire in the body of a ruling-class Englishwoman-wannabe-man. Or better, found my own "otherness" reflected in the hunch-backed and queer figures of Carson McCullers novels. I did not know at that time, that she, too, was a lesbian. And for colored womanhood . . . , I read Black women.

In 1975, with so little "me" to read, I wrote. To fill in the blanks. Hélène Cixous reminds us: "Writing and reading are not separate, reading is a part of writing. A real reader is a writer. A real reader is already on the way to writing."[5] For many of us, that ability to read and write was not passed down as our family herencia. As Chicana poet Lorna Dee Cervantes puts it, "[We] come from a long line of eloquent illiterates / whose history reveals what words don't say."[6] My generation, coming of age in the 60s and early 70s, the age of affirmative action and bilingual education, may be the first to have suffered en masse the promise of union and threat of separation from our origins proffered by our collective literacy. But the proximity of our literacy to that eloquently illiterate generation that preceded us served as a continual reminder of our questionable and questioning relationship to the gringo world of arts and letters. It kept us humble before the work-worn faces and fingers of our parents and grandparents, but more importantly, critical of the unilateral authority of academic knowledge. Our crianza had proven there were other ways of knowing. "Survival is not an academic skill."[7]

Significantly, in those early years of Chicano cultural production, that one-generation-working-class proximity served as a kind of barometer to gauge the significance of our work in relation to the people we supposedly represented. If our "letters," i.e., our art and thought, continued to emerge from the flesh, as described in *This Bridge Called My Back* nearly twenty years ago, then our work would remain grounded in the mechicano/a body (our history, memory, instincts and intuitions) and would hold the promise of servicing the freedom of that body. Ideas *could* inspire insurrection, as O'Hara suggests.

The academy, then, as a house of ideas, should (theoretically) be able to house the study of insurrection, as thought by the body of the

Chicana/o, the African and Asian American, the American Indian. Or so the plan was, thirty years ago. When the Third World Strike took place on the UC Berkeley campus in 1969, students demanded a "Third World College," a relatively autonomous organization within the larger university system. "Ethnic Studies" was the compromise. And compromise it was and continues to be as Ethnic Studies programs are required to adhere to the same set of cultural assumptions and values about knowledge—i.e., what's worth knowing and how one comes to know—as any other academic program on campus.

One does not pass through the university system unchanged. It is the intellectual factory of Corporate America, whose intention is to educate us to be law-abiding consumer-citizens. More insidiously, the university functions to separate us from the people of our origins, which in effect neutralizes whatever potential impact our education might have on them. The university allows a benign liberalism, even a healthy degree of radical transgressive thought, as long as it remains just that: *thought* translated into the conceptual language of the dominant class to be consumed by academics of the dominant class, and as such rendered useless to the rest of us.

If the study of insurrection must occur within the conceptual framework and economic constraints of the patrón-university—e.g., tenure tracking, corporate-funded grants and fellowships, publishing requirements, etc.—insurrection can never be fully conceived and certainly never realized.[8] Lessons and strategies for sedition can be partially garnered from the texts made available at the university, but our most defiant thoughts—those profoundly intuitive insights, those flights of the unrestrained imagination—generated through life's lessons and remembered history can never be fully explored or expressed in their original tongue at the university. By the time we have succeeded in translating "revolution" to adhere to appropriate academic standards, it ceases to be revolutionary. Then where *do* we find the teachers and students of revolution? Today, Ethnic and Feminist Studies programs across the country are, for the most part, full members of the academy (while still experiencing discrimination), but as such have been required to abandon their radical agendas. Again, Lorde's words resonate here: "The master's tools will never dismantle the master's house."

I know that most of the students of color I teach at the university turned to books for the same reasons I did. Most of them have a love for language and ideas and an innate sense of social responsibility that was, in part, inspired by books that responded in radical ways to the contradictions and inequities in their lives. Kafka writes:

> I think we ought to only read the kind of books that wound and stab us. If the book we are reading doesn't wake us up with a blow on the head, what are we reading it for? . . . We need books that affect us like a disaster, that grieve us deeply, like the death of someone we loved more than ourselves, like being banished into the forest far from everyone, like a suicide. A book must be the axe for the frozen sea inside us.⁹

A book must be the axe for the frozen sea inside of us. My question is, how many of such books are our students still reading? How many of such books are still left unwritten by us, Chicana/Lesbian/Native, when we aren't supposed to be whole bodies, with our cultural histories intact, doing the reading and writing?

When the Chicana writer sits down to table with tinta or text in hand, she brings the history of "eloquent illiteracy" with her. The body of her literature is not only decoded from those imported black glyphs pressed upon the dead leaves of american trees, it is also experienced spontaneously from the home-grown language of cuento and canto and a philosophy that resides within the physical body of history. Why should 21ˢᵗ century radical thought require such separation from its most regenerative source, the body of our history and our arts? And yet, this is precisely the lament of most poets and politícos who *have* "darkened the doorways" of the academy. Imaginative literature and the arts as expressions of the body, i.e., the whole organism of the Chicana/o, have become, as my friend Alberto Sandoval suspects, merely "a pretext for do[ing] theoretical work." Further, most artists are habitually banished from the campuses and conferences where the theoretical discussions of our art occurs. We don't have the teaching credentials.¹⁰

BODY

At the "Crossing Borders" conference at The City University of New York,[11] that same Alberto Sandoval—poet, político and scholar—referenced his ten-year battle with AIDS, stating, "Alberto had become a body." He spoke of the dis-ease ironically, as a kind of ally in his relentless reckoning between his physical self and the life of the mind. AIDS was the rude awakener that put his entire academic life into question. He openly admitted a kind of contempt toward the academy, which is, by definition to him and Webster, "theoretical . . . without practical purpose or intention," and as such, remains incompatible to the body and its needs.

So, AIDS gave Alberto a body and as such, practical purpose. He states: "I am dying to write. I am not dying to be published. It is a popular misconception that to be published is to achieve immortality. For me, immortality is in the moment of writing, an act that confirms I am alive." In Alberto's daily confrontation with death and in his survival of the assaults the academy has visited upon his erased body, Alberto has uncovered an enormous amount to teach us. But does the academy want to hear the dying's lessons, especially if those lessons are coming from an HIV-infected gay man of color?

If the academy, in its very mission, denies the body, except as the object of theoretical disembodied discourse, The Body with a capital "B," then what is the radically thinking "othered" body (the queer, the colored, the female) doing there?[12] What skills does the academy offer for our survival? Is not the academy the locus of cultural genocide for non-dominant cultures? Ethnic Studies has not ensured the cultural survival of U.S. peoples of color; it has mostly served to produce a cadre of professors of color unwittingly wielding the whiteman's tools to, as Alfred Arteaga puts it, "define [our] world for the benefit of the colonizer."[13] *"See how we suffer, patrón. . . ."* The body has been lost in the language of the academy because Art (as well as the Art of Writing) and the social-political movements it incites—that meeting place of mind and matter—cannot find expression there.

LANGUAGE

I am a writer. Language matters to me. I am acutely aware of those moments when language illuminates, gives body to something which was before vaguely known to me, like a dream that stays, but stays distant, indecipherable. I am grateful when words teach me something I forgot I knew. I am equally aware of the times when language kills, diminishes, truncates the creative impulse and the dream of change. I know when someone uses language to do violence against me. In response, language becomes my form of self-defense, a mechanism of survival.

I am reminded of N. Scott Momaday's story about the "man made of words," the Arrowmaker whose survival is utterly dependent upon language.[14] It is late at night. He is alone in his tepee with his wife. A human shadow appears on the other side of the tepee wall. If the shadow understands the arrowmaker's language, there is nothing to fear. If the shadow doesn't respond when the Arrowmaker addresses him in his Native tongue, the shadow will receive an arrow into his heart.

Language and survival. Is this not still the metaphor for our own survival, seeking out those whose language we can trust? I put my faith in the stories, that language of the body, where the word is made flesh by the storyteller. "Words are intrinsically powerful," Momaday writes. "They are magical. By means of words one can bring about physical change in the universe. . . . To be careless in the presence of words . . . is to violate a fundamental morality."[15]

I think often of the immoral waste of words in academic life: the so-called "postcolonial" (postmodern) methods of inquiry one must employ to critique the neocolony;[16] the foreign eurocentric sources that must be cited to substantiate one's own so-called unauthorized (what may be intuitively known) ideas; the ways once powerful words can be appropriated to the point of impotence.

In *Borderlands/La Frontera*, Gloria Anzaludúa aptly describes the "border" as a "1,950-mile-long open wound." She writes: "The U.S.-Mexican border *es una herida abierta* where the Third World grates against the first and bleeds. And before a scab forms it hemorrhages again, the lifeblood of two worlds merging to form a third country—a border culture."[17] That was fifteen years ago. Her meditations on the border emerged from her *direct* experience living en la frontera. Her metaphoric imaginings of the border genuinely grew out of a kind of poetic prophecy of the world's citizens in the state of mass migration, where geopolitical boundaries between nation-states define less and less who their inhabitants are ethnically and culturally. This text, visionary in many respects, gave all of us something to think about. And write about. And teach about. And use as titles for conferences. And think and write some more about. Until the academic appropriation of Anzaldúa's "border" metamorphosed the concept of "border" and "borderlands" into a kind of 1990s postmodern homeland for all displaced peoples of mixed blood and mixed affinities; a mythologized location, much easier to inhabit, ideologically and much more comfortable politically than that oh-so-70s Nation of Aztlán, the realization of which would mandate armed conflict.

In contrast to an appropriated, amorphic borderland, Tejana writer Norma Cantú describes her border home-town of Laredo as a police state, where five kinds of law enforcement agencies patrol the streets: the INS, the border patrol, the Texas rangers, the city police and the state police.[18] This is a real geopolitical "choque" between two worlds, becoming the site of increasing surveillance, human rights abuse and concomitant terror. The border is not the idealized metaphorical site of a new hybridity. Laredo, Nogales, Juarez, Mexicali, Calexico, Tijuana, National City are not figures of speech. They are first and last physical locations of great economic, social and cultural strife.[19] Still, it is all for a purpose: this facile use of language. The "border" as a metaphor poses no threat to the cultural and economic dominance by Euro-America.

Moral words, as Momaday tells us, "can bring about physical change in the universe." In an unjust society, moral words would bring about justice. In a slave society, moral words would bring about freedom or at least a 21st century abolitionist movement. And this is what the academy must avert, the cultivation of moral, i.e., ethically responsible, words. Words that require a radical revisioning of how, why and what we learn and who gets to decide.

In academic life, theoretical language is, as a rule, profane. It is used to obfuscate rather than illuminate. It does not bring about physical change in the universe, except an increased deadening . . . deadening . . . deadening. My own "unauthorized" opinion, one garnered not through degrees, but through twenty years of non-tenured university work, is that some of the finest "colored" minds in this country are being held captive within the university system. Moral words would free them from their enslavement to Western Thought. Free words would bring about revolutionary change. Free words are sacred. That's why we aren't allowed to say them in a place donde nuestro sagrado is not respected.

"Go home to your Maya grandmother," I tell my Guatemalan-born-U.S.-raised Stanford undergrad. "She'll teach you what you want to know. You don't have to suffer their words any longer."

Still, we tell ourselves (queers, feminists, colored folk) that we are here at Stanford, at Yale, at Dartmouth, at Duke, at Cal, to engage in radical re-visions of history in the effort to construct a radical agenda for the future, *once we get* their *theory down.*

From *Insurrection: Holding History,* a dialogue between a graduate student and his 189-year-old ex-slave great-great grandfather (the character of Mutha Wit speaks as the voice of Ron's grandfather):

RON: I just gotta finish my thesis.
MUTHA WIT: What's a thesis?
RON: It's a long paper I gotta write.
MUTHA WIT: Then what you do after you don' wrote it?
RON: Then I gotta show it to a bunch of white folks.
MUTHA WIT: Then what?
RON: Hopefully I can get paid like one of them white folks.
MUTHA WIT: Then what?
RON: . . . Gramps . . .
MUTHA WIT: Then what?
RON: Then nuthin. What you mean then what? Then I'm done. I git a job. I live, become fabulously rich and mildly famous.
MUTHA WIT: Then what?
RON: Then I drop dead I guess I don't know.[20]

THIRD WAVE?

Some Chicana and Chicano scholars, in their effort to politically justify their philosophical engagement with the postmodern paradigm, refer to their turn-of-the-century academic inquiries as the "Third Wave" Movement, a movement of scholars.[21] For me, it is impossible to think of the theoretical work being done on campuses today by Chicano/as as the "third wave" of any movement, when it seems so clear that the gains of our "first" movement, if we consider the "movimiento" of the 60s and early 70s as such, were systematically dismantled by the Reaganism of the 80s and brought to a complete halt in California through the anti-Latino legislation of Governor Pete Wilson in the 90s. Further, reforms made during those years of movement activism were just that: reformist gains subject to conservative-era losses, liberal concessions within the context of an unaltered system. So, as far as I can see, the Chicano Movement barely got started. The one public television documentary series on the subject of Chicanos depicts the Movement as beginning in 1965 and ending in 1972.[22] It briefly examines UFW organizing, the school walkouts, Tijerina's Land-Grant movement, Corky Gonzales, César Chávez and Dolores Huerta, and provides a few passing shots of Brown Berets. All this reflects the sum total of movement activity. Seven years. That ain't a movement. It's the beginning of a movement that went into a kind a deadening recession, with periodic ruptures of rage rising to the surface, like the Los Angeles Rebellion of 1992.°

In the meantime, feminism and gay and lesbian liberation took to the streets. (Was this the *second* wave?) Although they marched down different neighborhood blocks, there were places of convergence for Chicano/a and queer folk, male and female. This history of raised consciousness and activism will fundamentally impact any viable resurgence of a Chicano Movement.

In the meantime, a few colored folk have made strides within capitalism. So what? There are continued assaults against our Spanish surnamed selves and the future of our youth: anti-affirmative action; anti-bilingual

---

° These outpourings of collective anger, catalyzed by gross executions of injustice, like the Rodney King verdict, are not the product of a strategic process, i.e., a veritable political movement; but they do bring public visibility to our collective condition and force a response from the powers that be.

education; virulent campaigns against immigrant rights, and most recently against our youth and queer folk in the passage of California Propositions 21 and 22.[23] There is continued systematic collective amnesia about our Indian selves and relatives, the theft of what was once our México and before that and still Tierra Tarahumara, Yaqui, Seri, Pima, O'odham. . . .

No, I don't believe the movement of young scholars on our university campuses is setting the stage for radical action. (On our more cynical days, my artist friends and I describe that "movement" as no more than shuttling from office to office and conference to conference.) I believe the best of our young academics are struggling to get their Ph.D.'s with their original tongue, cultural beliefs and basic humanity intact. At times I wonder how equipped they are for a world of real political confrontation when, at places like Stanford and Cal, they have been separated from the streetlife of their communities. They know the inside of libraries and school classrooms, the honors tracking system has seen to that, where they study the whiteman's culture at the cost of separation from their own.* The question is: are they prepared to return home? Is the university system not a kind of "post-modern Indian boarding school for Raza?"[24] This is certainly not the case for all Raza students, students who have squeezed out an intellectual life in spite of a childhood that centered around economic survival and the threat of violence: incest, wife battering, gang-related death, police brutality, la migra and basic poverty. I've seen these students, whose retention in the university is the hardest to secure, because they cannot integrate into their academic discourse the greatest source of their knowledge: life experience.

This alienation from the university is not the exclusive terrain of twenty-year-old undergrads, but affects faculty and middle-aged students as well. I can't help but consider here the two suicides that occurred among the Latina Stanford community in the last two years: Lora Romera, a Chicana, who died in 1997, followed by Cuban-born Raquel Mendieta, in 1999. Lora was a "junior" faculty member of the English Department and Raquel, a returning Ph.D. student. Both Latinas. Both queer. Both

---

*Richard Rodriguez and his autobiography about his educational process, *The Hunger of Memory*, provides testimony to this.

dead. I know I am *supposed* to think of these self-inflicted deaths as "unre-lated." There is no way to *prove* how much or little the alienation from "real life" a place like Stanford *might have* contributed to what was surely a complex and intimate web of despair experienced by these two highly visionary and impassioned women. Still I wonder. I wonder about an unnamed hostility they experienced toward their queer and colored lives (bodies) in places like Stanford. I know that is why I do not make my home there.

RAZA: LA CULTURA DE POVERTY

The majority of Raza isn't teaching at or attending elite universities. The majority of Raza wrought its education from the same extended community where it eats and sleeps. Today, within a capital-based cul-ture, state and community colleges remain a kind of factory in the accu-mulation of units toward a degree that should ostensibly provide the graduate, should s/he survive the college system, with some economic buffer in the world. Few students have the privilege (time, space and economic support) to really "study," that is, pursue the life of the mind, however briefly.

Community and state college faculty are overworked and underpaid, with impossible class loads and overloaded classes without teaching assis-tants. The embattled condition of teaching at such institutions discour-ages many of us from teaching the very communities to which we are ded-icated. *If you teach full time at City College,* my writer's self reminds me, *that's all you do.* Basic skills—what should have been acquired in elementary and secondary schools (another point of critical concern)—are severely lack-ing. This was even the case at UC Berkeley when I taught there in the late 80s; so that every course becomes an English composition class, whether or not the teacher is prepared or willing to teach it.

20 MARZO 1999
It is 5:21 am. In the darkness, I am awakened by the ridiculous and the profound.
Conversations replaying from my five-year-old son. He is pure survival instinct and
struggling ego. All hurt feelings and uncomplicated joy. All still speak-what-is-on-your-

mind. Do not repress. And for that I should be grateful. But the words he says . . . they
have me awake at 5 o'clock in the morning.

The night before, he stands upon a small stool to brush his teeth, drier-warm flannel paja-
mas draping him, shoulder to ankle. He hops from one ball of foot to the other, barely
balancing . . . a constant fidget. We discuss "race" before going to bed: "I look down at my
hands," he says, "and I was afraid in the beginning that they were going to kick me out."
"Who?" I ask. "Where?" He means his private after-school program, mostly white mid-
dle-class kids. Three months later and he still remembers the feeling. I remember, too, him
refusing to speak Spanish for fear that that, too, would distinguish him from the others,
"kick him out."

Three times in the same conversation, my son explains his difference
from other kids by referring to himself as Black. Because at his public
school where he attends kindergarten, not-white means Black. In the
meantime, I'm on the phone to the school board, politicking to get my
son transferred out of our neighborhood school, not to separate him
from Blackness, but to situate him in Latinidad. Still, better identifying
Black than white, I think, for a Chicano kid: it is a stronger position of
survival, that self-acknowledgement as a "colored" child in this Amerika.
I make another mental note: *it's the after-school program that's gotta go.*

Months later, I do manage to get Rafael transferred to a Latino elementary school within the same Oakland school district. A month after
being there, he is still without books, in a classroom with no windows,
speaking English with second-graders who do not have first-grade skills.
This was the first/second grade combination class I elected to transfer
him into after discovering that the nicaragüense Spanish-speaking first-
grade teacher conducted her classroom according to a 200-year-old
Mission model of acquiescent obedience. Passing her classroom, I always
assumed it empty. How could any one manage to keep 30 six-year-olds
that quiet? Needless to say, I removed my son from the school and, without other options, returned him to the public school where he was
before. I was humbled by the process, realizing the Chicano school I
sought for my son no longer existed, not locally anyway. I was looking
for the Revolutionary Escuelita of the 70s, where my age-peers had sent

their children, kids who managed to get into Cal, Stanford, Harvard, UCLA with their culture and sanity intact. But the 70s was a long time ago, or so it seems.

When my son was to enter preschool two years earlier, I had encountered the same problem in San Francisco. The only Latino preschool available required parents to be in a lower economic bracket than mine. Although I, of course, support culturally specific educational programs for low-income Latino families, why is it middle-class Latinos can't even *pay* to get their kids a Latino-identified education? Since such programs do not exist, we are usually forced to send our kids *and our money* to white programs, like the one from which my son felt so alienated. In my search for bilingual/bicultural education for my son, I was reluctantly forced to conclude: the only way you can "stay Latino" in the state of California (at least in the Bay area) is to "stay poor." It appears that class ascendency for the Latino/Chicano requires our hispanization at best and our agringación at worst.

The construction of identity. My baby boy trying to make his way as a Mexican child in a society where Black is divided from white and the rest of us are required to fall inside that great divide. *So who's gonna break our fall?* What are Chicanos doing to counter the cultural poverty of this system of education? With the continued reduction of bilingual/bicultural education, where are our cultural schools? Schools of philosophical thought?

I fantasize a calmecac,[25] a 21st-century Xicano cultural school based on indigenist *and* xicanafeminista filosofía. A kind of "Saturday school" for Chicanitos/as but all week long. Asian and African Americans do it. I flip through the pages of those freebie parent newspapers: Japanese schools, Chinese schools, Jewish cultural programs, even some Afro-centric alternative education programs. These communities seem to understand that cultural pride is the key to strong self-esteem and ultimately to success in the United States. I'm not looking for capitalist-defined success for Razita; but I am looking to eradicate inferiority complexes disguised in macho bravado. I'm looking for an alternative to prison and teenage pregnancy as statements of cultural resistance.

REVOLUTIONARY BODIES

I came of age with images of brave. Brave in the face of scared. Student sit-down strikes, Civil Rights activists bludgeoned by police, Chicanos picketing lettuce fields, Vietnam protests, Black Panthers. So many billy clubs, young faces streaked with blood, burning flags, riot gear and sharp shooters peering off of inner-city and campus rooftops. Images of violent protest; that is, protest which produced a violent response from a violent culture. Martin Luther King was moving from an integrationist nonviolence to a critique of imperialism when they violently murdered him. Because Martin Luther King was not going to be happy with "Negroes" eating from a poisoned pie. A piece of the American Dream was not. The Dream.

Real political struggle always poses the threat of violence, danger real and imagined. The Chicano Moratorium of 1970 (which I witnessed ten miles away on television news reports) was real and highly imagined. Real heads were beaten in, real girls my age were dragged away by helmeted, baton-swinging police. I imagined myself so near and far from them.

There are less dramatic dangers, visible and invisible and many fronts of struggle. But always hard sacrifices are made . . . for change:

• Undocumented workers challenge the eviction of a fellow worker. Block the entrance to the factory. Stand face-to-face with police. Danger.

• A woman hangs off a redwood in a protest of protection. Chainsaws buzz in the background. Danger.

• It's 1968 and he burns a draft card. It's 1998, she won't scab in the strawberry fields. She needs a job. Bad.

I think the only real dangerous moves I've ever made in my life were out of necessity, so they felt not very dangerous at all. When you have time to think about it, you think better of it, you think yourself out of danger. You don't move. So sometimes it's better not to think at all. At times, I ask myself, have I ever really been brave? Words have hurt me. The worst. Words by lovers, brothers, intimates. Words that were hurled at me because I spoke up. First. At all.

Getting arrested in protest against an unconscionable war was not brave. It was performance. A rehearsed act of resistance, as Valdez has written.[26] What wasn't rehearsed was my claustrophobia. I didn't know how jammed we'd be in the police van. I hadn't thought about being restrained, how the plastic of the make-shift handcuffs behind my back would turn my hands swollen and blue and make me want to crawl out of my skin, being confined so. But all that was an *accident* of courage. And basically not dangerous.

It was brave of me the first time to sit down in a circle of women of color and say "we" without apology. Brave each time. Brave to do so without titles of books in my hand. Like proof. Of what? Authenticity? Belonging?

• Brave giving the enemy ammunition to hurt me, my child. I am a lesbian mother and practice both out loud. Brave to leave my lover of eight years.

• Brave to tell my mom I was a lesbian. Brave at 22.

• Brave to refuse to give up my wages to my boss who decided, when his business was failing, he wanted to collectivize all our earnings. Brave at 27 to be the only one.

• Brave to eat medicine when I was afraid and didn't know nothing.

• Brave to speak Spanish like a fool in front of people who knew plenty.

These are pitiful examples.

These are me.

I'm scared all the time and when I am not scared, there is no chance for change. In me. That's how I teach writing. "Go toward the fear," I tell my students. "Feel its pulse. Let it speak to you." Bravest in my writing. But that's not the same as action, only that writing can sometimes force action in yourself and others. Sometimes. Sometimes you read or write words you got to live up to. Never know what it's going to dig up. Dig up the dirt of memory, the dirt of land. Make you want some for us. Make you fight to have it.

THE PEDAGOGY OF REVOLT

Revolt: verb. To refuse to acknowledge someone or something as having authority over you.

I have taught professionally for twenty years. I have taught high school, poets-in-the-schools, the Marxist school, myriad youth programs, so-called "gang-prevention" and "high-risk" programs, theater for queer youth and immigrant women, writing groups for Indígenas and other women of color, and playwrights' groups. I've served as an adjunct instructor (mostly) in Women's Studies, Ethnic Studies, Creative Writing, Drama, and in Spanish and English Departments from the "country club" of Stanford University to the innercity campuses of community colleges and state universities on both coasts.

I love teaching and remain in conflict with it. Fundamentally, it takes me away from my primary vocation, which is to write. To make art. I teach well, I believe, and chose teaching over political activism in the fourth decade of my life, because I couldn't do both *and* write . . . *and* be a mama . . . *and* support an extended family. One could effect political change, I believed, through teaching, while making some semblance of a living. Now, I wonder. Over the successive years of teaching, I have found that the profession, in its increasing corporatization, has moved further and further away from a radical agenda. Since I have been situated primarily in Ethnic Studies or Women's Studies, I have witnessed academic programs that emerged out of political struggle separate themselves from that struggle, even at a time when assaults against people of color and our right to education have escalated to point of verifiable government-instituted racist paranoia.

A movement doesn't happen in a book, but it doesn't happen without books either.[27]

Through the writing of this essay, I have been conscious of the possibility of my ideas being mis-interpreted as a kind of anti-intellectualism. Bueno, should my words be misconstrued as such I have no one to blame but my poet's passion to the speak the unspeakable, expose the Academic Emperor in all his nakedness, even at the risk of the generalization which belies the exception and the exceptional. There *are* exceptional students and exceptional faculty. There are remarkable moments where "critical consciousness," as described in Paulo Freire's *Pedagogy of the Oppressed*,[28] is awakened, where the most visionary and dangerous of faculty inspire thoughts that directly affect the bodies sitting in front of them. The bodies think. They stand up. They are not afraid of freedom. They act.

In recent years, students of color can't help but be aware of the increase in the state-sanctioned violation of their right to an education and a future. Last winter, with the introduction of yet another assault on the rights of youth (Proposition 21), students took to the streets and filled campus plazas in protest. Most impressive was students' willingness to connect Props. 21 and 22—and the struggle against racist and homophobic legislation —to basic shared human rights concerns. I attribute this to the coalition-activism initiated by queer students of color. It was their bodies, after all, that provided the living connection between the issues.

The revolutionary body. The revolutionary body that reads and writes.

I saw it happen. In April 1999, in recognition of the 30th anniversary of the Third World Strike at UC Berkeley, students occupied Barrows Hall to protest the "state of regression" of Ethnic Studies at the Berkeley campus. Stating that "the systematic decline of [Ethnic Studies] pro-grams [was] causing a slow and steady death" of the Department,* pro-testers demanded a substantial increase in funding and faculty for Ethnic Studies to be implemented immediately and continued over a five-year period. To press their demands, students held daily protests and nightly vigils, suffered mass arrests for civil disobedience, and maintained a 10-day hunger strike until the administration was forced to concede.

The rescue of Ethnic Studies is not, in and of itself, revolutionary. It does not alter the racist *system* of higher education in this country. It is, however, an impressive act of revolt, requiring a radical consciousness. It challenges the unilateral authority of the university to determine *what* and *how* we learn and by *whom*.[29]

In the 60s, from the Third World Strike to the school walkouts in East Los Angeles in 1968, education remained the fundamental concern of young Raza. Because education was about the future of a people. And we saw ourselves as such, as a people distinct from mainstream America, requiring culturally specific methods of intellectual inquiry. Questions were raised then that remain unanswered because we have not, as the Marxists mandate, continued to question the question. However, these acts of revolt in the last few years by students of color and their allies have

* This was especially true for the Native American Studies, which had been reduced to hav-ing no full-time faculty.

given me renewed hope that possibly the "questions" have not been buried forever beneath the depoliticized rhetoric of postmodernism.

What is worth knowing? Who are our teachers? Where do they reside within our communities? How do we find and support them? How does one acquire knowledge? How does knowing increase within our communities? How do we best learn? And of course, for what purpose, what result, do we educate ourselves and our children? The system of education in this country from the public elementary school to the private university will not, by definition, permit a culturally autonomous approach to these inquiries. As Freire points out, "It would be a contradiction in terms if the oppressors not only defended but actually implemented a liberating education."[30]

When I think of my own Chicano/a people and the state of California's betrayal of its soon-to-be-majority Latino population, I lose patience with liberal attempts at remedy. I've come to believe that the less we see ourselves as a nation of people, the less we will be able to define the intellecutual, cultural and educational needs of our community.

EDUCATING A NATION

Today I am writing Nation. It is not a dirty word.

You choose the right word.
Mestizo.
Raza.
Border.
Hybrid.
Nation.
Sovereignty.

You choose the word most difficult to swallow and that's the one you gotta learn to eat. Eat to learn anything new; that's the one that holds the most potential for a real education. That's the one that takes guts, the one that threatens our middle-class-secured positions, the one that puts our lives in danger.

A North American Indian woman is kidnapped and murdered crossing the borders of nation-states. And the nations of people within those borders—Menominee and U'wa, Chicana and Hawai'ian—cry out in outrage. "The body of [Ingrid] Washinawatok, 41, and two others* were found bound and blindfolded Thursday in a field just across the Arauca River in Venezuela. . . . All the victims were shot multiple times with 9mm weapons."[31]

My friend Ingrid had "ignored the State Department's warnings to stay away from rural Colombia."[32] She went anyway because the U'wa people asked her, in the traditonal way, to come. She could not refuse. She had gone to Colombia, according to a family spokesperson, to develop an indigenous-based school curriculum for the tribe. Ingrid, in her many roles as an activist, had instituted models of pedagogy where the cultural integrity of indigenous people is preserved and honored. *You have a belief. You dedicate your life to the realization of that belief.* That's brave.

Ingrid believed in sovereignty, complete sovereignty of mind, body, spirit, nation. Sovereignty was *her* most dangerous word. Months before her death, she wrote: "Europeans relegate sovereignty to only one realm of life and existence: authority, supremacy and dominion. In the Indigenous realm, sovereignty encompasses responsibility, reciprocity, the land, life and much more."[33] Ingrid left her family, a son and a husband, to make good on her beliefs, to assist other Indigenous peoples in creating models of education in accord with their own traditions. It was a dangerous time to make the trip. For several years, the indigenous U'wa have been in protest against oil exploration by Occidental Petroleum Corporation on their ancestral lands in northeast Colombia and have met with U.S.-sanctioned violence from the Colombian government.[34] Ingrid could've stayed home, like the "officials" had advised, she could've minded her own business. She didn't. That's brave.

Nationhood. I stay up nights and wonder. If sovereignty could be realized, just the way Ingrid wrote about it, well, just maybe there'd be an

* Lahe'ena'e Gay (Native Hawai'ian) and Terence Freitas (California).

actual Chicano/a body to name and some land to claim to share. Ingrid returned home to her Menominee Nation in a black body bag. No American flag draped over it. At least that much was true. The United States of America was not her nation.

"Perhaps the greatest stories," Scott Momaday writes, "are those which disturb us, which shake us from our complacency, which threaten our well-being."[35] This is Ingrid's story. The greatest stories ever told. The story about a woman who got herself killed by practicing what she preached. Somebody who put into practice the art of teaching people how to teach themselves through their own cultural symbols, languages, values. The U'wa are not a people unconscious of their oppression. The invitation to Ingrid and her acceptance was a reciprocal gesture between peoples who viewed their survival as integrally interdependent and who viewed education from an indigenist perspective as critical to that survival. To teach is to empower. And to teach the oppressed in their own language with their own tools is to create (or in the case of the U'wa, sustain) an insurrectionist. Still the most valorous job I can envision.

Do we have to die to be teachers of revolt? I want to think not. I want to believe that our pedagogical and artists' acts of resistance can do some damage to the cultural hegemony of Euro-America and, in the process, do some good for the growing consciousness of our nation. So I teach Chicano/a Nation in my own language.

I am trying to find the words. I am learning to spell *revolution*.

LA DANZANTE

1

I dream red
since our return
from cactus-stone and full white
      moon
light   I awaken to red
wet between your dusted thighs.

Was it a birthing
or a death
you danced
days
ago:
the measured step, toe
to pebbled earth
knee rising to heaven
down again   this time
back to ground
again

we walk.

2

we talk about roads,
the whitebardyke of native seed
has planted the memory
in Indian ink
across the broken-edged blades
of her back
down to butt bone

there is all manner of medicine
prescribed there
eagle/águila
lobo/oso
my son's childeyes
pore over loose pale skin
a living cartoon,
his struck gaze tells me.

we wash our hands after
the naked revelation:
chain-smoking-mid-fifties-sober-dyke-once-indian
is too much regret
for either of us to carry.

how does she bear the weight
of all that medicine?

She broke her bone, I remember
she dragged a broken bone
at the end of her thigh
into the high road of the desert.
That's where I met her
on the road
she called red.

Not us Mexicans.
our road less rose, mas amarillo
in its southern descent
para sol
your sculpted slope of nalgas
more "forever" than any tatoo.

3
Behind eyes sheltered
from the sky's relentless azure

I too step toe to earth
mouth words whose meaning
becomes evident in the repetition
I wait to know
you in the light
of the darkness of sleep
death, I mean to say

and it is the simplest of knowing.

When I open my eyes
you are already walking
away from me
fifty years from now
now
it makes no difference
your face, the face of every ancestor in every stone
we stumble over with clumsy worldly feet.

At some point you'll have no need to cry over it,
the mistakes.

Of course
it is not a matter
of words
it is not of matter
when the molecules of your body
mix with the earth and the sky in a prayer I do not enter.

But
I won't forget your *red*
woven-crowned head
amid arizona
blue
the bleached *white*
sheet of cloud
rumpling snail to viejita

red
white
blue
the colors of a nation
only dreamed.

4
Nationless
I take you into my arms
in the ordinary bed of a california
valley roadside motel
unwind the crimsoncotton
wrapped 'round your hips

and I enter you as deep and as hard as we want
because you were there too dying
in the midday sun
singing to the same god

and we want to touch it somehow
because our bodies are remembering

we want to gather all the touch we can

before we go

back.

THE DYING ROAD TO A NATION
A PRAYER PARA UN PUEBLO[1]

for CHR

We, you and I, must remember everything. We must especially remember those things we never knew.

—Jimmie Durham, *A Certain Lack of Coherence*

CATHOLIC MEMORY

I remember
when I was a little esquincle in the new
mech(x)ico los angeles califas san gabriel lomas gangland
pero en el otro lado de los tracks
the missionary sisters taught me about chuy christ
and impure thoughts and que thoughts were igual
que'l real act and that was the catch-22 que te chinga every time
cuz someone tell you not to pensar en el pezón
y pues ya ves
you already got the pinche picture en tu mente
millones de pechos all sofialoren and bustin'
outta pleasant peasant campesina cotton
al estilo italiano
y bueno . . .
all this thinking on what NOT to think
caused me to consider the question of thought
unadulterated, learned later
'bout buddhism and emptying the mind de toda la mierda
which I never been good at
only good at dying
cuz
that's where my nine-ten-eleven-&-twelve-year-old-thoughts
took me to knowing that dying was all there was inside

outside was puro sueño, tú sabes:
just whitedoctors putting sadistic dreams
of paganbabies&christianconquest
inside your cabeza-head
and this was pre-race-consciousness
pre-the-body-politik
pre-puberty casi
children's faces be a dream
their vacant laughter, their causa
to humiliate the fat nun with the fat open mouth
standing stupid and oblivious
in front of our sixty-plus catholic school-girl desks,
mosca buzzing
in 'n' out
in 'n' out
it all be a dream before Martin Luther King's
I knew and kept waiting
for some jesus to save me from the word
the only word: death

SUSTO

I was raised by a fierce fighter of a woman who, already in her mid-30s having had the necessary round of babies and betrayals, knew what she believed in: a God, surely, but a God far outside the "mystical body" of the Catholic Church as I had learned it. My mother is a Mexican Catholic of humble origins which, in short, means an Indian Catholic which she would never admit but demonstrates in her basic indifference toward Church dogma and basic faith in the saints in candles in a relentless rosary more like canto than christian prayer.[2]

My mother has faith. Faith that looked, in 1961, like an 85-pound Mexican woman, just out of the hospital, walking the streets of Montebello, Southern California, dressed in the robe and rope of San Antonio de Padua. The seamstress had come to my Tía Eva's house. I remember her pulling out the yards of brown Franciscan-heavy cotton from a Woolworth's shopping bag, followed by a tape measure which she wrapped around my mother's frail frame of bone and scar tissue. And with that, she custom-designed my mother's "ofrenda."

My mother had lived. And the garment was her 30-day prayer of gratitude to the saint that had interceded in her behalf. After two surgeries and five weeks in the hospital, my mother survived what had been erroneously diagnosed as cancer which turned out to be an ulcer requiring the removal of three-quarters of her stomach. My mother had survived when we thought she wouldn't, when I had prayed hopelessly, neurotically because there was no God I already knew, only fear, only a relentless scratching scratching scratching nervously tearing into the flesh of my inner arm in the effort to dig down to some ground, some land, some "where," whole and embraced by a mother's love.

She did return. But mothers, I had already learned, *could* die. And the world of the heart could end while the world continued indifferent around you. I am every woman who was once a little girl who has lost a mother, almost lost a mother, been betrayed by a father/a brother/an uncle—who learned in a brutal unforgiving way that there is no childhood really, no innocence. There is no protection. Death teaches children this. So does incest and all those hushed abandonments. Your protector can die on you or disappear or not notice or not respond when you are in danger. You have to grow up too fast and be alone.

My only child learned this aloneness, spilling into the world three months too soon, weighing two and a half pounds. He knew. That no matter how surely his mother squeezed his toothpick-sized finger, I could not keep him on this planet.* That was between him and his God, which returns me to the subject of this reflection: death. Still the one word I understand for God.

I call God by the name of death because nothing other than death wields such unyielding power in my life. I am afraid of death, the loss of the body-life. I recognize this fear as I sit in meditation, rigidly holding onto the body of what I imagine to be myself. I am so afraid, my mind

* In 1993 my son was born three months premature. After three and a half months in the hospital and two surgeries, Rafael Angel recovered a healthy infancy, and now a growing boyhood. This journey is described in a memoir released in 1997, *Waiting in the Wings: Portrait of a Queer Motherhood* (Ithaca, NY: Firebrand Press).

conjures many images in the vain attempt to secure the parameters of "self"—delusions of my importance and conversely my own pitifulness. And language language language, which codifies raw being. But all this is oh so preferable to the promise-threat of the experience of any real "godness," and the radical re-vision of meaning it requires in our lives. My preciously guarded "me" is a world I have known intimately since my earliest remembrance of an internal reflective life. It was that place in which I held my first private anguished conversations with Catholicism, and what I came to understand as prayer. It is infinitely lonely.

Sometimes I just feel like my eyes are too open.
It's like the more you see, the more you gotta be afraid of.

—Lupe, *Shadow of a Man*[3]

SIGUEN LOS SUSTOS

At nineteen, I was sedated and had my wisdom teeth pulled out. Although a child of the 60s, the psychedelic drug culture arrived belatedly at my doorstep, so my oral-surgeon-sanctioned high came as the most unexpected pleasure . . . and the most beauteous dream. It was all shape and color and design. All movement, infinitely fascinating. While sedated I had, for the first time in my life, forgotten my "self" completely. I had disappeared. I missed no one, had no attachments to people, my name, my memory. I was a dream without a dreamer. When I came to, too soon, I found the dentist (a brutal butcher of a man) hacking away at the remains of the last impacted tooth. As consciousness returned to me, so did the pain. And an unspeakable fear. The fear that a drug could have that kind of power over me, that it could allow me to leave this planet, and not care. That one *could* leave this planet and not care. I knew it was like that in death. That indifference. That ultimate aloneness. I panicked as the dentist put me under a second time and I suffered a tortuous dream of entrapment. Still, I did extract some "wisdom" with the extraction of those impacted molars, or so I thought: the revelation of the impermanence of our earthly passions and attachments, which I speedily repressed.

In recent months, I have carried in my briefcase, like those mid-90s San Diegan comet-crazed-suicide-missionaries in Nikes,[4] everything that could identify me to an alien who reads Earth English: Passport, Certified Birth Certificate, Hospital Birth Certificate with the "Angelina" crossed out and "Cher'rie" written over it with an apostrophe instead of an accent in the wrong place with the wrong last name of an adopted grandfather ("Lawrence") whom I never met. My son's life is in the briefcase, too: five-year-old with passport, social security number, birth certificate, baptismal record. Then there are pages and pages of "documents": "Power of Attorney," "Last Will & Testament," "Custody" and "Guardianship" clauses in the event of death (mine), etc.

I have been on the way to the bank's safe deposit box for weeks now, never getting there, lugging the stuff around cuz home ain't safe enough, they say, in case of fire, they say, burglary, in the event of some unforeseen disaster . . . tragedy. But here in this briefcase, it all feels too heavy, too final, like I'm already planning my death and securing the key to the lock for my survivors to find. As my parents have done, putting *their* key in an overnight bag buried in the bottom of the back bedroom closet. Months ago, my sister and I each received in the mail a list of what the box contains, typed out on my father's Olympia manual. Am I waiting for my parents to die? To open up their safe deposit box, not for some imagined inheritance of wealth, but for the inevitable, coming to pass? The inevitable is just that.

I cry over every new arruga on the face of my mother, the ever-slowing steps of my father, straining up the stairs to my new home. I mourn the passage of time in their frail and failing bodies. I am afraid of doctor's exams in the women I love. I am afraid to miss any month of my son's growing up for sleepwalking, my days spent in useless worry. I sleepwalk anyway, fearfully.

My mother laments her imminent passing, cancels vacations and anniversary celebrations as her body continues to betray her. "My bones are showing," she says. "I can't take the trip. I look too ugly," meaning too old, and I wonder how she imagined she would look at 84. She is not ugly. She is a woman shrinking into her old age, growing in frailty and a rising anger against all that she cannot control: my sister's middle-aged and newly liberated single motherhood; the heaviness of the cast-iron pots she once used to toss effortless onto the open flame of the stove; grandchildren foreign-blonde and too-often remote. I know she thinks about dying daily. She won't admit it when I (sort of) ask. She speaks only of the overnight bag on the closet floor in the back bedroom. She's got everything under control. My mom fighting for the life of her that dying that no scratching can ward off. *She's gonna leave me after all.*

DYING LESSONS

When a revered uncle died of lung cancer, a few years after my son's almost-death, I remembered the obvious: *we live to die.* Suddenly all decisions began to matter with an urgency I hadn't experienced before. All decisions were a matter of life and death. I know (and not unconsciously) that the death of that aging uncle became the stimulus for me to act on a lesbian divorce years in coming. I know that the same mantra—*if not now, when?*—catapulted me into the arms and the family of a Mexican woman I had ignored intentionally for years, that inevitable return to my own.

I do believe in the dead and dying, their lessons. The lesson my premature son taught me upon his threatened birth: that we are not born new, but come from some place of return. That we re-live in death a memoryplace we have forgotten. I prayed for my son's life and got him long enough to learn the word "quiero" not just for leche, but love. Got him long enough to forget the promise of death I had birthed. Still, three years after his birth, I was forced again, to remember in the passing of my father-close uncle. And then again, and again . . . and again. Until I am standing face-to-face with a death that looks very much like myself.

My comadre, Marsha, comes to me in dreams. I stand in a circle of women on Indígena land in Tejas. Marsha is impatient with the group, their shocked inaction upon the news of her violent death. She tells me, "build me a dome," a round-house she means. To continue her work. There is no time to waste.

In September 1998, Marsha Gómez, artista-activista-lesbiana-madre-hermana, was murdered by the hand of her only son. Marsha

Gómez was like me, mixed-blood. Off-seasons, she could be mistaken for Jewish or something else not quite white, but not necessarily always Choctaw, not siempre the darker side of Mexican. "Cajun and Hispanic" is what her blood sisters called themselves. But unlike her sisters and mine, Marsha was 100 percent "colored girl," "red-skin," and kickin' butt. Thoroughly. And her thorough-courage frightened and compelled me because I knew Marsha was afraid, always a little, some place in her not quite convinced she belonged in either world— Mexican or Indian, No Native enrollment card. Few Spanish-language skills. Queer in both worlds. But my god, that other world, a dead world. The woman-hating white world from which she could not protect her white-skinned son. And we are left with her *and his* legacy. With desperate fingers I try to unknot the noose of this tragedy, how to change that fate, steer our sons and daughters—our nation's children— away from hopelessness.

I am learning in hard ways. Daily. That we live in a violent and unforgiving world and all our acts of heartlessness return to us. I have also learned there is a time for heartlessness, for an unmoving warrior-stance. I have learned this most palpably in relation to my son. For him I have committed unforgivable acts, denied motherhood to a white woman—for eight years, my partner—who saw herself his "mother" because she could not accompany us on the brown road I was to walk. I turned *away* from her and *toward* that disappearing Chicano tribe in which, without country or contract, I seek place, for myself and my son.

The rupture of that long-term relationship was nothing less than a death consciously chosen, a brutal sacrifice for change. Sacrifice: not the interminable suffering proffered by christianity, but sacrifice as understood within the pre-Columbian world. The severing of that relationship became my ofrenda. My spirit-gods, incensed by my ignorance, my looking away from that soul-self for so long, required nothing less.

Still
when I turn on the cold water faucet
put the toothbrush
under the winter-cold ribbon of water

when I do what I do everyday of my life
I remember the ordinary
life with her
lost.

A Change of Heart

I do not re-write history. I tell the story for the first time.
The story of holding one's self apart, to hold oneself together.

A few years ago, that same white woman partner asked me as we ended our relationship for the last time, "Just answer me one thing, do you think you are an Indian?" She was very angry with me, angrier that my new partner was someone undeniably "Indian." Mexican Indian, yes. Indian via las montañas de México, and Chicana-bred in a country where mestizos are required to lose our Indian identity.

I was humiliated by the question. To not answer would have been to suggest (by my silence) that her question and her role as interrogator were somehow legitimate. To answer the question dignified its cultural arrogance. Standing speechless and ready to bolt out her front door, the worst accusations regarding my own "authenticity," ironically, were hurled by the hand of my own self-doubt. In my mind's heart, I heard her saying: "I know your hungriest places even if I couldn't feel them/fill them. Being hungry for a thing doesn't give you it. You aint no Indian. You're a half-breed Mexican at best who, when you choose, can move effortlessly, we arm-in-arm as white women in the world."

I hold a great rage within me. A rage and shame against myself. How the whiteness of my skin and my habitual identification with it continues to seduce and betray me with its shifting disguises. Some place in me remained convinced I didn't have the right to *feel* so different from this whitewoman I loved because I didn't *look* so different. This was what she always told me. Most times without words. The question I am plagued with is why I believed her. Never totally. I was always the "lover-in-cultural-resistance" and she complained of it often, my basic sexual nationalism. Still, when the accusation of my own "racial" inauthenticity comes whirling out at me—"Do you think you are an Indian?"—I know that the question itself, and her self-authorized entitlement to ask it, *is* the critical point of departure between us. I have to choose. There is no place for ambivalence, no place for immigrant-ethnic meanderings, no place for bi-racialized maybes. We part ways, choose different paths. For life. "Conscientização," I remember Paulo Freire's term.[5] Conscientización, in Spanish, a consciousness born of a body that has a shade, a language, a sex, a sexuality, a geography and a history. And that sometimes changes everything, including with whom you love and lay.

COMING OUT

Twenty years ago, I wrote what I consider to be my first real work of "conscientización," the kind of writing that in the act itself strives to know something unknown and where the act of knowing will force a change in action. Writing "La Güera,"* I was physically sick through the entire first draft, holding back the urge to vomit a personal history that tore at my guts. Driven by an exhausted self-censorship, the writing was for me a kind of "coming out" as a half-baked brown woman and a silent collaborator in whiteness. It was also a confession and a declaration of conscientización as a Chicana in a light-skinned body, drawn relentlessly toward women by bona fide lesbian desire. I would pay (was already pay-ing) for that desire, but what most viscerally entangled my stomach in that web of knots was the unstated knowledge that I would also pay, more dangerously, for how Mexican that desire was.

Coming out is about choice(s) and running out of them. As a young woman barely out of my teens, I came out twenty-five years ago because I was just plain tired of lonely. Having sex without a body in the arms of a man, I was not going to spend the rest of my life wanting, waiting. I made the move to return to women, knowing the world was wholly bent on my separation from them. What frightened me so in the writing of that essay (now nearly a generation ago) was that I discovered that that

* Included in this volume.

return to women required a return to my people (Chicano/mexicano/indio) as well, *when the world was wholly bent on my separation from them.* The world had opened its door for me, light-skinned, college-educated and born Anglo-surnamed, and I was shutting that door in its face, as I would shut that door on that ex-lover's face twenty years later.

The latch clicks behind me. I walk down the hallway of her building for the last time. I think: *I am a traitor to my race (if color is its measure); that is what she despises in me.* There is nothing magnanimous in my betrayal of whiteness. It is about (again) plain tired of lonely. And a rage. A rage against a culture that I can only call enemy. One whose collective ego (ethnocentrism) kills spirits, lives, art. I cannot justify my actions beyond this. There is no compromise. It is finally a matter of life and death.

I don't know how much Indian I got in me. I don't know if it's called Yaqui, Seri, Apache, O'odham . . . or if the Indian people on my mother's side just gave it all up upon the conquest and were subsumed by Spanish culture which, combined with Indian people and Indian ways, became Mexican. So I do dignify the accusation with an answer, when I respond with what my "ex" already knows, but refuses to believe matters, "I am Chicana. And yes, I imagine I have Indian in me." What else is there to say when it is impossible to say all the rest, to speak of Return to one's people without our tongues tied by amerikanisms? I say, "return," and Amerika hears "nostalgia," "romantic idealism," "escapism."

So I keep myself secret, preparing the ground
in the private dream of a more generous heart.

I think of this lost love daily. She whom I used—her accusations are correct—to postpone this look at the self. No mirror reflection there. Or maybe her mirror always made me feel dark in comparison and I liked the look and feel of that. I don't know. I loved her, hard and true as I could, and stayed in the closet of my strongest desires 'cause I didn't want to be left holding them alone.

"It was not a murder but a sacrifice." I remember Linda's words when I had told her that I felt like a murderer, leaving that eight-year-loving so completely. "It was a sacrifice," she counseled. "For great change." (I think of Marsha.) And so it is. An offering up of the life I've known for something else, not there. I have become a criminal in a world whose values are the real crimes. I have chosen "nation" over prescribed Euro-American lesbian ethics about motherhood;[6] and I have lost friends and funds because of it. It was one of the hardest things to do in my life.

> But this is harder yet . . .
> *this naked step I take into a clouded mirror*
> *that is my woman, my self.*

THE RETURN

"Que vale la vida* if we can't take each other back." That's all my new love, so long in the knowing, had to say to finally bring me to her. But, how far back is Return? What radical action does Return require? What junctures of separation and connection, separation and connection do we encounter again and again on the neglected road of our mistakes and forgetfulness?

JOURNAL ENTRY.

I feel very young, unremarkable, an ordinary student nada más. I have to ask my Beloved daily many things. I have to ask her what the pain in this desert means, why do the women cry so awkwardly. I have to ask her how to enter the arbor, how to tie a prayer tie, wrap a sage stick, roll a cigarette of prayer tobacco. And I wonder how can she want me, baby that I am.

"Teach me how to pray," I say. She takes me by the hand, presses the copal between my fingertips, then releases the pebbles into the burning embers. And in the act, I am sent home to what I already learned at my mother's breast: faith. I turned to her for God. I break some taboo to write that. That God is found in bed, in the open-face of consummated desire. That death is found there, too, limpio y sencillo. That fear of death has a way of subsiding. In love. That's all. For a moment. All I prayed for was to find a woman with whom I could make familia, with whom I could wake up each morning with a shared purpose, a shared prayer, a shared

* (Translation) What's life worth . . .

practice. Sin mentiras, no illusions that death did not await us at every turn. How do we love on the dying road? What does that kind of spiritual practice look like?

I read buddhism because it calms me down, but I don't feel the land under my feet on those pages. I am an earthworshipper and the earth is Indian in América, that's all. And the ancestral tribalism of mexicanismo (as I experienced it) has saved me from the obscenity of american individualism. That's all.

"Do you think you are an Indian?" What I should have answered was that what is female and brown in me (is that Indian?) has been my Salvadora in the worst of times. This she-knowing in me, that darkness, has been my deepest prayer. A prayer against cruelties small and great. I do not speak of identity politics here. I speak of a living knowledge of *otherness* that inspires compassionate action. A knowledge that is the prayer assuming flesh.

Maybe my spiritual practice is nothing more than this writing. Maybe one wakes up every morning and really wakes up. Maybe that is the daily prayer. The "Give Us This Day Our Daily Breath." And the bread . . . something as simple as bread . . . the matter of a revolution. But the revolution begins at home.[7] A cliché born of truth.

HOME TRUTHS

You want to change your life, I tell myself. You light a candle. You pray on it. Daily. All day long. Then you do the hard work of living the prayer.

Years ago, I made a prayer. Same prayer. Every day. Bring me family. And I knew in the praying, I was inviting the sons of lovers and brothers of nation and the children of every shade to return to me. It took them a long time to arrive, but now that the time has come, I know that the hardest work is in front of me. I do not have the same trouble loving women, but the men in my family—from the darkest to the palest—keep arriving at my doorstep and pleading entrance, most profoundly in the brown body of my son. Loving him is easy. Raising him is not. The others—his father, my partner's sons, my nephews, the students I have adopted as sons—require a heart-wrenching kind of work. They are missing their fathers, angry at their mothers. They want to return home, to make a different kind of man, brother, father, son. At times they mirror in their youth and self-important arrogance what I could never assume as a woman, and for which I still resent their fathers. I miss the mexicano brothers I never had, a whole generation of men who let my generation of women down in their refusal of feminism, in their looking away from the source of their "home sickness."

I could write harder words, I could write confession, how much we envy men and their freedom, how much we, lesbians, have built our lives apart from their murderous impulses. Has it all been written before? The history of Mexican women: the colonization that tried to make Guadalupes of us all, all-forgiving madres, and those of us who rebel, Chingadas; how our men have colluded in this 500-year-old mentira.

But I remember Coatlicue, Aztec Goddess of Creation *and* Destruction, that buried knowledge of our female rage, our venganza, our inherent power as Creators of Life to take life away. I remember that pre-memory when men openly admitted that they were awed by us and our diosas. And so they were less angry then, less brutal, less frightened and frightening. I remember. . . .

And then we give birth to sons,
who become men.
And we are unable to defend ourselves
against this most intimate,
most beloved
of oppressors.

. . . . .

He used the tools of her art
to murder her.
This is not a metaphor.
He blugeoned his mother to death
with the tools of her trade.

She was a sculptor.

Marsha Gómez was murdered by her only son, that once-soft boy who saw in himself a woman's vulnerability and learned to despise it. This matricide is not a metaphor; it is an eruption of violence that speaks to the real incarcerated state of the mechicano familia: the wounded heart of our nation. There are those who will look away from this death as an aberration; but it is not an aberration. It is a gift, even it its violence—

because we cannot imagine it

because our minds can't conjure it

because she was so unworthy of it

because we see ourselves in it . . . we are forced to rethink everything about our lives, why we are standing on this road, at this hour, broken-hearted as we are.

I still want to believe that at some point Marsha made a decision toward life, that she offered up her body to save her son from himself, to save other women from the violence of his corazón inquieto. She was *not* the first woman he had assaulted. Maybe as mothers, there's a place in us where we all fear the retribution of our children: the anger from our sons never mothered enough in a motherless world of missing fathers. Maybe it's too easy to say that. Too easy to speak of genocide, matricide. But I know those responsible for Marsha Gómez's death have faces and do not have faces, that in my speechless shocked heart only one truth resounds: *that her death was not an accident, but the result of a murderous political history still in the making.*

None of us is immune to that history. I recognize myself in this sister-artist, in her aging body, in her son's rage she used as a weapon against herself. I've seen my own son's anger at only five years old. "Mom, the tears won't stop." He tells me con ojos lagrimosos. He slaps each of his own cheeks. "They just keep coming down. Make them stop. Por favor." I bring a tissue, the end of my shirttail, or maybe a sleeve to his moist puppy-nose, soaked lashes. He stops crying. For now.

Did Marsha's son ask for anything more complicated than that? "Relieve me of myself, Mom, make the tears stop coming down." But what a mother may cure at five, twenty years later is not enough. It is never enough. We women can never cure our sons of the "manhood" imposed on them.

A few days following Marsha's death, I learned from friends that hours after the murder her son was seen on a nearby country road looking for the man who killed his mother. The bitter irony is that maybe this is la búsqueda that all sons and brothers and fathers should undertake along with us, that search for their/our murdered mestiza/india mothers, sisters, daughters, lovers. . . . This is and this is not a metaphor.

Feminism and Indigenism.[8] The only tools at my disposal to construct a son, a family, a people. I take hold of them, wield them as murderous weapons. There is no room for liberalism now. All I know is that I awaken every morning remembering that there was a life before greed. Before family as private property. Before competition, linear plotlines and Romance and Western Reason. Before and After Reason. I know there was a time where "two-spirit" people like Marsha, like me, like my mujer, held a place in some tribal circles without compromise to our being.* I am fighting for my son's life and how that life is shaped. I want to walk with him through my own opening heart to a different country, one we may still only inhabit within the walls of our home or inside the circle of those with whom we pray, or on a small square of dirt not yet stolen off from us. Pero es algo. It is something to try and build a nation by heart.

The rest is just questions. I could die tomorrow and the small world who reads my work will say, "Mira, see how she suffered the same questions her whole life." I wonder about the relationship between our lives and the manner of our deaths. About a relentless exhaustion that invites death. I wonder about small and mass deaths. About genocide and every individual life lost there.

HOME PRAYER

On the Day of the Dead, we put out food for our ancestors. Tequilita for my Tía Tencha, white roses for Marsha (her favorite), tamales, chocolate,

---

* The term "two-spirit" is used to refer to contemporary Native American/First Nation gay men, lesbians, transvestites and transgendered individuals, as well as to traditions of multiple gender categories and sexualities in tribal cultures. Some Xicanas who recognize themselves as Native have also begun to employ the term. For a diverse discussion on the subject, see: *Two-Spirit People: Native American Gender Identity, Sexuality and Spirituality*, eds. Sue-Ellen Jacobs, Wesley Thomas, and Sabine Lang (Urbana and Chicago: University of Illinois Press, 1997).

water, black coffee with a tablespoon of sugar for Doña Domitila. Cigarettes for my Tío Bobby who died of lung cancer. Frijoles and pan. We pray.

I wonder if they come to visit, my relatives. Or if, upon death, they are relieved of us. Finally. I wonder if this offering is really for them or for us. I pray for the dead, that, when they come to visit us in our sleeping and waking dreams, they are large enough to hold a piece that remembers us, but where their hearts no longer ache, want, as we do now. I pray that our spirits are something much grander than this pitiful longing and all the beauteous attachment we have to it. I am a llorona, my tears, at times, my most faithful companions. I cry Marsha away from this earth. I pray that with the release (the relief) of the body, her spirit is not encumbered by the ego through which she thrived and suffered.

These prayers are my preguntas, I write this as if I were without faith, but when la curandera María Cristina carries Marsha's spirit back into our home through the few small worldly tokens of Marsha's life (a piece of hair, an earring), I am altered by the spirit's presence.

I believe in the dead and the dying. Their lessons.

LA LECCIÓN

On the way across the Bay Bridge my son asks me, "Can God count to infinity." I answer yes, since Rafael, newly acquainted with letters and numbers and long fascinated with superheroes, wants to understand the limits of power and numerical comprehension.

He goes on. "Is God more powerful than Batman?"

I answer "yes," again adding an explanation about the nature of the power to which I refer. Power of the heart, of the spirit, etcetera, etcetera, knowing on some level he just wants to know if God can kick Batman's butt. Now that would be a comfort, someone infinitely strong in charge of it all.

Since I know my son is thinking hero equals male, my feminism kicks in to remind him that God is both male and female—well, really neither male nor female but all energies simultaneously. And my indigenismo and buddhism prompt me to remind my son of the presence of God in all things living, even things that can't punch back. *Yes, even rocks breathe. I've seen them.*

My answers are pitiful as I try to separate in my mind truth from lie from myth and cuento. I teach myth's truth. I teach my son about a God personified in his mind as a superhero because that's what he understands about power. It's the best I can get for now but only because I want him to know humility. I am a mother in search of a language that finds awe in the face of beauty, art, the ongoing creativity of nature and its insistent survival, its flourishing in the face of death. Because whatever my religion is, it counters the solipsism of American greed and the egotism of the "rugged individual." Because I want him to know he is not the center of the universe, but that the universe resides within him as in the flower. I want to relieve him of the burden, but reinforce the responsibility, of knowing his interdependent place upon this planet and its consummate heavens.

He is one among many, as am I.

Superheroes and his male-identification firmly intact, my son is attracted for some of the same reasons to the image of Christ on the cross. But it is not Christ the Hero that draws my son in. But the Naked Christ. Christ the Unjustly Scorned. Christ the Martyr. At five years old, Rafael is also fascinated with child-imagined bondage and can often be found tied up with all manner of shoestring, curtain cord or discarded packing twine. My compadre and I joke that he may have inherited this need for self-imposed restraint from his mother's residual Catholicism, or, I suggest, he may be responding to a vague memory of his earliest months of premature life spent within confines of a doll-sized hospital isolette, his body tied to IV lines. Who knows? But undeniably this image of the bound Christ moves my son.

I don't have crucifixes in my house as a rule. As a rule Christ never answered a prayer I can remember. But my son discovers the one crucifix I've packed away, given to him by his grandmother when he was about two years old. I am sure my mother fully expected that I would nail the dying figure above my son's sleeping head the night that I received it. Well, I could neither display the Crucified Christ (a dream catcher hangs in its stead) nor toss it away, for the faith my mother had imbued it with in passing it onto my son. Upon spying the half-naked and bleeding figure, Rafael immediately begins hammering me with questions about him. "Who hurt him like that?" "Why doesn't he have more clothes on?" "Did his mama know?" And in spite of my rejection of Catholicism at the age of 18, the Life, Death and Resurrection of Christ is probably the best religious story I know. So, I tell him what I remember and can live with. I refer to Jesus as a holy man and explain that people were jealous of him, that they wanted to stay cruel and greedy and he wanted change and peace in the world. I'm fumbling badly, I think, when he asks why they hung him on the cross to die. I don't remember my answer; but later, when he retells the story to a friend, I overhear him say . . .

"They killed Jesus because he knew God."

And I think, maybe my answers aren't so pitiful after all.

La Ve P'atras
She Who Looks Back

Months later, I attend a Latino academic conference in New York City. I am speaking with the Critic about Nation. We are on-stage and I am trying to make a point. I turn my whole body away from the audience, a full 180 degrees. I look behind me. I am trying to illustrate the point with my body. I am trying to teach the teachers something about ourselves, about looking backward toward our Indian and Black mothers to find a future. An image stays in my mind: a Casta Painting by Miguel Cabrera of 18th-century New Spain. It is a portrait of miscegenation. In the painting, the mixed-blood child sits on the lap of his Spanish father. The child's facial features and coloring are a delicate blend of Gachupín and Indio. His mestiza-india mother stands next to the pair. This child is looking back, back at her, to his Indian antecedents. To his past and to the future he will choose. This is my own face looking back. Not all of us are compelled to return, but I am. And I want to take the others with me. I tell them so.

"Que vale la vida if we can't take each other back."

A young man in the audience is outraged. He stands in the second row from the rear and accuses me of feigning shamanhood, playing "some kind of curandera" role. He is angry that he too is white enough to move forward, effortlessly, into americanmanhood and I am his mama reeling him back in and backwards. Into darkness. *We were not always like this, stupid and forgetful.*

But there *is* nothing new. No theory, no computer program, no virtual nada that has anything more profound to teach us than what is found in the dark quietude of this ancestral prayer. This is "infinity," I want to tell my son. And as close to god as we can get.

We, you and I, must remember everything.
We must especially remember those things we never knew.

—Jimmie Durham

My family is dying. My blood and heart relations are vanishing with each passing of seasons. I am next. I know. Always next. I pray only for the courage to remember what I may never have the chance to live. And in the remembering may I know and in the knowing may I teach.

It's the little bit I have to offer the exiled and forgotten I call my nation.

NOTES

PASSAGE

1. Stephen Berg, *Nothing in the Word: Versions of Aztec Poetry*, (New York: Grossman Publishers, 1972), n.p.

2. The mythical/historical place, in the area of present-day northern New Mexico, from where the Aztecs were to have migrated before settling in what is now Mexico City. It is the mythical homeland of the present-day Chicano people.

LA GÜERA

1. Emma Goldman. *Red Emma Speaks*, ed. Alix Kates Shulman (New York: Random House, 1972), p. 388.

2. "La Güera" was originally written for inclusion in *This Bridge Called My Back: Writings by Radical Women of Color*, which was published in 1981, two years before this publication.

3. From "The Brown Menace or Poem to the Survival of Roaches," *The New York Head Shop and Museum* (Detroit: Broadside, 1974), p. 48.

A LONG LINE OF VENDIDAS

1. Norma Alarcón examines this theme in her essay, "Chicana's Feminist Literature: A Re-Vision through Malintzín/or Malintzín: Putting Flesh Back on the Object," in *This Bridge Called My Back: Writings by Radical Women of Color*, eds. Cherríe Moraga and Gloria Anzaldúa (3rd Edition. Berkeley: Third Woman Press, forthcoming, 2001; originally published in 1981).

2. See Aleida R. Del Castillo, "Malintzin Tenepal: A Preliminary Look into a New Perspective," in *Essays on La Mujer*, eds. Rosaura Sánchez and Rosa Martínez Cruz (University of California at Los Angeles: Chicano Studies Center Publications, 1977), p. 133.

3. Del Castillo, p. 131.

4. Del Castillo, p. 141.

5. Gloria Anzaldúa, unpublished writings.

6. The term "heterosexism" deserves a definition here as it, like "homophobia," has seldom, if ever, appeared in Chicano publications. Heterosexism is the view that heterosexuality is the "norm" for all social/sexual relationships and as such the heterosexist imposes this model on all individuals through homophobia (fear of homosexuality). S/he supports and/or advocates the continued institutionalization of heterosexuality in all aspects of society—including legal and social discrimination against homosexuals and the denial of homosexual rights as a political concern.

7. Silvia S. Lizarraga, "From a Woman to a Woman," in *Essays on La Mujer*, p. 91.

8. Alfredo Mirandé and Evangelina Enriquez, *La Chicana: The Mexican-American Woman* (University of Chicago Press, 1979), p. 225.

9. Since the first edition of *Loving*, a number of books by Latina feminists have been published, including: Gloria Anzaldúa's *Borderlands/La Frontera: The New Mestiza* (San Francisco: Spinsters/Aunt Lute, 1987); *Cuentos. Stories by Latinas*, eds. Alma Gomez, Cherríe Moraga and Mariana Roma-Carmona (Latham, NY: Kitchen Table Press, 1983); *Compañeras: Latina Lesbians*, ed. Juanita Ramos, (New York: Routledge, 1994); and *Chicana Lesbians: The Girls Our Mothers Warned Us About*, ed. Carla Trujillo, (Berkeley: Third Woman Press, 1991). Also see recent critical writings by Ana Castillo, Emma Pérez, Alicia Gaspar del Alba, Yvonne Yarbro-Bejarano, among others.

10. The Combahee River Collective, "A Black Feminist Statement," in *But Some of Us Are Brave: Black Women's Studies*, eds. Gloria T. Hull, Patricia Bell Scott, and Barbara Smith (Old Westbury, NY: The Feminist Press, 1982), p. 16.

11. Toni Cade Bambara, *The Salt Eaters* (New York: Random House, 1980), pp. 3, 10.

12. Bernal Díaz del Castillo, *The Bernal Diaz Chronicles*, trans. and ed. Albert Idell (New York: Doubleday, 1956), pp. 86–87.

13. Sonia A. López, in *Essays on La Mujer*, p. 26.

14. Norma Alarcón, in *This Bridge Called My Back*, p. 184.

15. Octavio Paz, *The Labyrinth of Solitude: Life and Thought in Mexico* (New York: Grove Press, 1961) p. 77.

16. Cherríe Moraga, "Played Between White Hands," in *Off Our Backs*, July 1982.

17. Mirtha Quintanales with Barbara Kerr, "The Complexity of Desire: Conversations on Sexuality and Difference," in *Conditions: Eight*, Box 56 Van Brunt Station, Brooklyn, NY, p. 60.

18. Bernice Reagon, "Turning the Century Around," in *Home Girls: A Black Feminist Anthology*, ed. Barbara Smith (Latham, NY: Kitchen Table: Women of Color Press, 1983), 361.

19. Barbara Smith, unpublished paper. For recent writings by Barbara Smith, see *The Truth that Never Hurts* (New Brunswick, NJ: Rutgers University Press, 1998).

20. Parts of this section originally appeared in a speech I gave at the Second National Third World Lesbian and Gay Conference in Chicago in November 1981. It was entitled "A Unified Rainbow of Strength."

21. Combahee River Collective, in *But Some of Us*, p. 13.

22. Combahee River Collective, in *But Some of Us*, p. 18.

23. Barbara Smith, unpublished paper.

24. Audre Lorde, *Sister/Outsider* (Santa Cruz, CA: Crossing Press, 1978).

25. Mirtha Quintanales, unpublished letter.

Looking for the Insatiable Woman

1. This essay was originally presented as an address at El Frente Latina Writers' Conference at Cornell University on October 14, 1995, organized by Helena María Viramontes, among others. Feminist philosopher María Lugones, whom I reference later in this essay, was also present at the conference. On February 22, 1996, the lecture was again delivered at the University of California, Los Angeles, sponsored by The César Chávez Center and the English Department.

2. Leslie Marmon Silko, *Almanac of the Dead* (New York: Simon & Shuster, 1991).

3. Vivian Gornick, *The Romance of American Communism* (New York: Basic Books, 1977).

4. Amber Hollibaugh, from commie dyke organizer to published writer, is the author of *My Dangerous Desires: A Queer Girl Dreaming Her Way Home* (Durham, NC: Duke University Press) to be published in Fall 2000.

5. *Cuentos: Stories by Latinas,* eds. Moraga, Alma Gómez, and Mariana Romo-Carmona (New York: Kitchen Table/Women of Color Press, 1983), p. 66.

6. *Literatura chicana, texto y contexto,* eds. Antonia Castañeda Shular, Tomas Ybarra-Frausto, and Joseph Sommers (Englewood Cliffs, NJ: Prentice-Hall, 1972). José E. Limón, "La Llorona, the Third Legend of Greater Mexico: Cultural Symbols, Women, and the Political Unconscious," in *Between Borders: Essays on Mexicana/Chicana History,* ed. Adelaida R. Del Castillo (Encino, CA: Floricanto Press, 1990), pp. 399-432. Rudolfo A. Anaya, *The Legend of La Llorona* (Berkeley, CA: Tonatiuh-Quinto Sol International, 1984).

7. The play is now entitled, *The Hungry Woman: A Mexican Medea.*

8. From *The Hungry Woman: Myths and Legends of the Aztecs,* ed. John Bierhorst (New York: William Morrow & Co., 1984).

9. *Coatlicue's Call/ El llamado de Coatlicue* (conceived and performed by Guadalupe García; written and directed by Cherríe Moraga) premiered at Theater Artaud in San Francisco, October 25, 1990. It was produced by Brava! For Women in the Arts.

10. See my essay "En busca de la fuerza femenina," in *The Last Generation* (Boston: South End Press, 1993), p. 73.

11. *The Last Generation,* p. 72.

12. *Shadow of a Man* is published in *Heroes and Saints and Other Plays* (Albuquerque, NM: West End Press, 1994).

13. Moraga, *Heroes and Saints.*

14. *West Coast Plays 11/12* (Berkeley, CA: California Theatre Council, 1982).

15. These concerns over the state of our art as Chicano/as—for whom and for what purpose we write—have plagued me for over a decade. See "Art in América con Acento" in *The Last Generation,* pp. 58-60.

16. From 1989 to 1998, a conservative-led U.S. Congress succeeded in drastically slashing federal funds to the National Endowment for the Arts (established in 1965 by the Johnson administration) in an effort to eventually dismantle the agency. As of 1998, the agency's budget stood at $98 million, as compared to $172 million in 1992. Begun in part to divert attention from a growing U.S. national budget deficit (the result of the Reagan administration's excessive military spending), the NEA was depicted as a "drain" on the U.S. domestic budget. In actuality, by 1998, taxpayers contributed roughly only thirty cents per year to the funding of the NEA. The move to defund the NEA drew its ideological foundation from the inflammatory rhetoric and "family values" of bible-banging conservatives such as Jesse Helms and Newt Gingrich (among others). At the heart of right-wing outrage was the federal funding of artists such as Andres Serrano, Robert Mapplethorpe, Holly Hughes, Karen Finley, John Fleck, and Tim Miller, whose works challenged conservatives' positions regarding "obscenity vs. art," as well as their vision of the agency's purpose. Helms later went on to attack lesbian literary artists including white southern poet Minnie Bruce Pratt, elder African American poet and essayist Audre Lorde, and Native American author Chrystos. The rampage of public charges of indecency and immorality continued, especially against art and artists of color: the Black lesbian film "Watermelon Woman" by Cheryl Dunye; Marlon Riggs's "Tongues Untied" about Black gay men's desire; and, the series "Ecce Lesbo/Homos" at Highways performance space in Los Angeles, for an image of a black gay man wearing a cross on his naked back. A resulting battle between public funding of the arts and First Amendment rights raged throughout most of the 1990s, eventually reaching the Supreme Court. Only with the resignation of NEA chairwoman Jane Alexander in the late 1990s and installation of William Ivey, who managed to placate Helms and other conservatives, has the move to eliminate the NEA been abandoned. Still, the agency's efficacy in genuinely supporting individual (non-affiliated) artists to create experimental and avant-garde work has been essentially neutralized.

17. Proposition 187 intended to deny undocumented immigrants and their families access to basic social and health care services and public education. Proposition 209 eliminated affirmative action in California's public education system and in employment. Proposition 227 outlawed bilingual education programs in California's public schools. For a more detailed discussion of these anti-immigrant and anti-Latino measures, see endnotes 13 and 14 in "Sour Grapes: The Art of Anger in América," below.

18. As this expanded edition of *Loving in the War Years* goes to press in July 2000, *The Hungry Woman: A Mexican Medea* has been completed and published, but remains unproduced. It appears in a collection of plays entitled *Out of the Fringe: Contemporary Latina/Latino Theatre and Performance*, eds. Caridad Svich and María Teresa Marrero (New York: Theater Communications Group, 2000). It will also be collected in a volume of plays entitled *Some Place Not Here: Five Plays by Cherríe Moraga*, to be published by West End Press of Albuquerque, New Mexico, in 2001.

Sour Grapes

1. "Strange Fruit," original words and music by Allan Lewis.

2. August Wilson's address was delivered on June 26, 1996. It is entitled "The Ground on Which I Stand" and was first published in the September 1996 issue of *American Theater*, pp. 14-16, 71-74.

3. A major factor in Wilson's ability to maintain an African American aesthetic in his plays is his insistence on working with Black directors which he is has consistently been able to actualize. Wilson's gift as a playwright was first nurtured under the guidance of African American director Lloyd Richards, when in 1984 Wilson submitted *Ma Rainey's Black Bottom* to the National Playwrights Conference at the Eugene O'Neill Memorial Theater Center. The play caught the attention of Richards, who served as the conference's Artistic Director. As the Dean of the Yale School of Drama and the Artistic Director of Yale Repertory Theater, Richards directed the premiere production of *Ma Rainey* at Yale. He would go on to direct the play's premiere on Broadway and would serve as director for the next six of Wilson's play premieres both at Yale Rep and in New York.

4. Jorge Huerta, "Looking for the Magic: Chicanos in the Mainstream," in *Negotiating Performance: Gender, Sexuality, And Theatricality In Latino America*, eds. Diana Taylor and Juan Villegas (Durham, NC: Duke University Press, 1994), pp. 37-48.

5. Ancient Athenian (aristocratic) women were never considered citizens of Athens. They were excluded *from all public activities* and restricted to the private sphere of the home, where their primary purpose was to bear children and maintain the household (of goods and slaves). Slaves were both laborers and a central part of the Greek household. An aristocratic household could own fifteen to twenty slaves, who functioned as servants, tutors, and guardians. They were not considered citizens of Greece, only living possessions—property. Greeks strongly believed that nature intended certain humans to be subjugated from the very moment of their birth. The presence of Athenian women and slaves at the performances of tragedies during dramatic festivals of the fifth century is a hotly contested historical debate.

6. From a play-in-progress, presented in a staged reading at The Lesbian Playwrights' Festival at the Magic Theater of San Francisco on January 13, 2000. It was directed by Irma Mayorga.

7. Euripides' Medea, however, may qualify as the first "woman of color" of all of Western theater. In Hellenic society (500-300 B.C), any person not of direct Greek origin was considered a foreigner and therefore a "barbarian," an uncivilized "Other" in relation to the cultural norms ("superiority") of the Greeks. In many versions of her story, Medea was originally from the city of Aea in a region known as Colchis on the eastern end of the Black Sea. Ethnically speaking, the Greek historian Herodotus describes the Colchians as "black Egyptians." On the other hand, *The Tempest's* Sycorax, mother of the "uncivilized" Caliban (usually seen as a figure who represents the "savage natives" of the "New World") and, like Medea, a wielder of magic, does not make her appearance in drama until 1611.

8. *Fed Up: A Cannibal's Own Story* premiered at Theater Rhinoceros in San Francisco in the Spring of 1999. It was directed by Reginald MacDonald.

9. "Suzan-Lori Parks and Liz Diamond: Doo-a-Diddly-Dit-Dit," *The Drama Review: A Journal of Performance Studies.* Fall 1995 (39:3), pp. 56-7.

10. *Shadow of a Man* premiered in San Francisco at the Eureka Theater in a co-production with Brava Theater Center in 1990. The play was directed by María Irene Fornes.

11. *Watsonville: Some Place Not Here* premiered at Brava Theater Center on May 25, 1996, directed by Amy Mueller. The play is scheduled to be published in 2001 in a new collection entitled *Some Place Not Here: Five Plays by Cherríe Moraga* (Albuquerque, NM: West End Press). It also appears in *Latino Plays from South Coast Repertory: Hispanic Playwrights Project,* eds. by Juliette Carrillo and José Cruz Gonsalez (New York: Broadway Play Publishing, 2000).

12. Wilson, *American Theater,* p. 74.

13. Passed as an initiative statute in November of 1994 by California voters, Proposition 187 (sponsored primarily by then California Republican governor Pete Wilson) was designed to deny illegal immigrants access to public social services, health care services, and all levels of public school education. As touted in the ballot's official language, the initiative was to be "the first giant stride in ultimately ending the illegal alien invasion." Pandering to a tide of xenophobic hysteria, Prop. 187 argued that undocumented immigrants arrived in the U.S. solely to exploit public social services. It maintained that cutting off public aid and access to education to undocumented immigrants and their families would save California taxpayers millions of dollars. Conveniently, proponents of the proposition ignored the impact immigrants' labor, spending, and taxation have on the overall health of the U.S. economy. Furthermore, the statute required a wide variety of state agencies and local officials, including public school employees, to report persons to the INS who were merely *suspected* of having entered the U.S. illegally, encouraging rampant racial discrimination based solely on appearance or circumstance and converting school teachers, among others, into a kind of unofficial "border patrol." Once passed in 1994, Prop. 187 was quickly diffused by the work of civil rights groups who succeeded in blocking its enactment through four years of lawsuits and litigation. Finally, in 1999, the newly elected California Democratic governor Gray Davis decided not to appeal to the Supreme Court a 1998 federal court ruling that declared much of the proposition unconstitutional, effectively killing the proposition once and for all.

14. *Proposition 209.* Passed in 1996, California Proposition 209 or the "California Civil Rights Initiative," supported (again), by Governor Pete Wilson, negated the crucial links between racial bias, gender bias, poverty and equality and proposed that color-blind and gender-blind measures would ensure equality for all citizens. Defenders of the proposition argued that since 1964 the "playing field" (of business and educational opportunities) for minorities and women had been successfully leveled; therefore, affirmative-action equal-opportunity programs should be

eliminated. In language that flagrantly echoes the Civil Rights Act of 1964, the initiative prohibits "discrimination" or "preferential treatment" in public employment, public education, or public contracting on the basis of race, sex, color, ethnicity, or national origin. In 1997 after a series of legal actions designed to stop the enactment of 209, the Supreme Court cleared the path for 209's enforcement by refusing to hear an appeal filed by the ACLU that offered a broad challenge to 209's constitutionality. Meanwhile, at least 25 other states have proposed or plan to propose laws or initiatives similar to Prop. 209.

Proposition 227. Led by ultra-conservative Ron Unz and passed in November of 1998, California Proposition 227, the "English Language in Public Schools" initiative, proposed to radically reconfigure the teaching of English in the California public school system for bilingual students. Aimed mostly at the children of Latinos (the soon-to-be-majority population in California), the initiative requires all public school instruction to be conducted solely in English. The proposition offered the installation of a 180-day English immersion program, at the end of which students, regardless of English proficiency, would be funneled into English-only classrooms without further aid in language development in either language. The "sink or swim" program refused to recognize the importance of bilingual proficiency, individual learning impediments, or successful bilingual programs already in place at many schools. 227's singular and monolithic model of learning English worked to placate xenophobic fear caused by California's growing immigrant population—a population that actually speaks over 140 languages. The enforcement of English in the effort to acculturate and assimilate children (and in essence wipe away any identification with their ethnic origins) was espoused as the best possible way to guarantee a successful future for bilingual (non-white) children. The truth is that it secures the privileged position of the monolingual Euro-American student, in what has become an increasingly competitive job market. Second-class students will become second-class workers, i.e., working *for* the Euro-American student turned middle-aged capitalist. Ironically, the initiative advocates monolingualism in an era when global markets, along with networks of communications (inherently multilingual), are expanding at an unprecedented rate. In short, English-only speakers (white students) acquiring a second language (Chinese, Japanese, German) in order to compete more effectively in the 21st-century global economy is seen as "good," while children of color, already in possession of a first but "un-American" language, are viewed as deficient and a deterrent to the overall efficacy of California's next generation work-force.

15. The situation for North American Native artists within the art world is distinct from that of Chicano/a artists. Within the plastic arts, there are more opportunities for exhibition and sale for Native American artists than Chicano/as. But the Euro-American interest in contemporary Native American art, traditional work, and Native spirituality often reflects a kind of perverse romantic fascination, which sometimes results in the outright theft of Native imagery, language and religious practices. At such times, invisibility seems preferable. In the mainstream theater world, however, both Chicano and Native American theater artists suffer from virtual disregard by the regional theater community.

16. At the initial writing of this essay, the NEA was being dismantled in Congress. In 1995, the agency's $175 million budget was cut by 39 percent to $99.5 million, causing 89 staffers, nearly half of the agency, to be laid off. In 1997, the Republican House voted to abolish the agency, but the Senate rescued it at the last moment. For a more detailed discussion, see endnote 16 in "Looking for the Insatiable Woman," above.

17. Consider the now-famous case of Cuba's unwitting émigré Elian Gonzáles. In casual conversation among friends, we joke: "Good thing he's white (and cute) or nobody'd give a damn." We aren't exactly kidding. We remember the brutal "welcome" the mostly black and often gay Cuban Marielitos received upon their arrival to "freedom" in the early 80s. We remember the Haitian detention camps, the Senate bill outlawing HIV-infected immigrants entrance into the U.S. We know INS break-ins against undocumented mexicanos occur without warrant or warning and with considerable more violence than we witnessed on CNN in the Miami home of Lázaro Gonzáles this Spring (2000). We know Mexican kids are separated from their parents (just like Elian) daily in Migra raids along the border and there is no public outcry. We know. We aren't kidding.

18. Clinton's acceptance speech at the Democratic National Convention illustrates this perfectly. His "Bridge to the Twenty-first Century Speech" was completely devoid of historical reference. No man, no mention beyond the last four years of his administration.

19. Although many North American Native nations still reside within the same basic geographical area of their pre-conquest ancestors, the harsh socio-economic conditions of most Native communities, on and off the reservation, can certainly be described as a kind of internal "exile" imposed by the U.S. government.

OUT OF OUR REVOLUTIONARY MINDS

1. First presented as the keynote address for the "Chicano Cultural Production: The Third Wave" conference at the University of California, Irvine on April 15, 1999.

2. Robert O'Hara, *Insurrection: Holding History* (New York: Theatre Communications Group, 1999), pp. 38-39.

3. In response to his "master's" admonition, Frederick Douglass writes: "From that moment, I understood the pathway from slavery to freedom.... I set out with high hope, and a fixed purpose, at whatever cost of trouble, to learn how to read." *Narrative of the Life of Frederick Douglass, An American Slave.* First Published in the United States of America by the Anti-slavery Office, in 1845 (New York: Penguin Books, 1982), pp. 78 -79.

4. "The Master's Tools Will Never Dismantle the Master's House" in *This Bridge Called My Back,* p. 99.

5. Hélène Cixous, *Three Steps on the Ladder of Writing* (New York: Columbia University Press, 1993), p. 21.

6. Lorna Dee Cervantes, "Visions of Mexico While at a Writing Symposium in Port Townsend, Washington," *Emplumada* (Pittsburgh: University of Pittsburgh Press, 1981), p. 45-47.

7. Audre Lorde, *This Bridge Called My Back: Writings by Radical Women of Color*, p. 99.

8. Major corporate funding of Ethnic Studies programs, for example, has always supported a liberal assimilationist multiculturalism over more radical "ethnic-centric" projects. See Bob Wing's "'Educate to Liberate': Multiculturalism and the Struggle for Ethnic Studies," in *Colorlines*, 2:2 (Summer 1999).

9. Franz Kafka, *Letters to Friends, Family, and Editors*, tr. Richard and Clara Winston (New York: Schocken, 1978), p. 16.

10. At present I hold a 5-year appointment as Artist-in-Residence at Stanford University. I am forty-seven years old and after 20 years as a nationally published writer, this is the first time I was hired for an extended appointment on the basis of being an *Artist*. Until this appointment I had served as a temporary adjunct in numerous colleges and universities, where I once was allowed to actually teach a Creative Writing and a Teatro course. This was at UC Berkeley. The bulk of my university teaching has involved English Composition, Ethnic Studies, and Women's Studies courses. And I am one of the "better-employed" among us Chicana writers/artists.

11. The conference was sponsored by the Center for Lesbian and Gay Studies of the Graduate School and University Center of the City University of New York in Winter 1999.

12. Ironically, it was feminist activism that initiated consciousness about the female body. This same activism catalyzed the formation of Women's and Feminist Studies programs across the country. As Women Studies began to be replaced with "Gender Studies," however, the focus on the condition of women as living bodies became more theoretical and less politicized. And the activist component (which required students to put their theory into practice) in many Women's/Gender Studies programs began to disappear.

13. Alfred Arteaga, *Chicano Poetics: Heterotexts and Hybridities* (Cambridge: Cambridge University Press, 1997).

14. N. Scott Momaday, "The Arrowmaker," in *The Man Made of Words: Essays, Stories, Passages* (New York: St. Martin's Griffin, 1997), pp. 9-12.

15. Momaday, *The Man Made of Words*.

16. The state of colonialism is, of course, not "post" at all; but appears throughout the globe and our neighborhoods in ever inventive new ("neo") formations.

17. Gloria Anzaldúa, *Borderlands/La Frontera: The New Mestiza* (San Francisco: Aunt Lute Books, 1987), p. 3.

18. Norma Cantú is the author of *Canícula: Snapshots of a Girlhood en la Frontera*. Informal talk presented in Yvonne Yarbro-Bejarano's class at Stanford University in Spring 1999.

19. One of the most vivid examples of the very real oppressive conditions of life on the border can be found in Ciudad Juárez where, since 1993, as many as 200 women and girls have been raped and murdered, and left abandoned in the desert or in the trash. As single females (many of whom are young mothers) working in the maquiladoras, some are forced into prostitution to supplement their miserable wages. As a result, they have generally been regarded as "dispensable" by authorities, and "culpable" for the crimes committed against them.

20. O'Hara, *Insurrection: Holding History*, pp. 14-15.

21. Some debate regarding the potential revolutionary impact of the proliferation of theoretical work being done by Chicanos/as today was generated at the "Third Wave Conference" at UC Irvine in April 1999. Conference materials proffered: ". . . (T)he Chicano Movement has entered into a *third moment* in Chicano/a political and cultural expression."(My emphasis)

22. *Chicano! History of the Mexican-American Civil Rights Movement*, produced by the National Latino Communications Center and Galan Productions, Inc., in association with KCET-Los Angeles.

23. *Proposition 21*, the "Gang Violence and Juvenile Crime Prevention Act of 1998," was passed in March 2000. The California initiative statute created to "deter" juvenile crime significantly changes the legal treatment of youths arrested for crimes, and specifically targets youth of color and the poor. The statute increases punishment for all gang-related felonies. Youth offenders 14 years of age or older charged with murder or certain sex offenses would automatically receive adult trials without judicial review. Informal probation is eliminated for youths committing felonies. Youths would be subjected to longer sentences for serious felonies (85 percent of the sentence given versus the usual 50% as stipulated by the California "Three Strikes" law). Any youth 16 years of age or older convicted in adult court will be sentenced to the California Detention Center instead of the California Youth Authority, without protected separation from the larger adult population.

    Proposition 22 also passed in March of 2000. The "California Defense of Marriage Act," otherwise known as the "Knight Initiative," adds a new provision to the Family Code of California's constitution: "*Only marriage between a man and a woman is valid or recognized in California.*" At the time of the initiative's introduction, the state of California already only recognized marriage between a man and woman as a legal union. However, the inclusion of this clause would in effect cancel out the recognition of same-sex legal unions obtained in other states.

24. Ricardo A. Bracho, in conversation.

25. Calmecacs were Aztec centers of higher education. There the symbolism of Aztec culture was gathered and passed on to future generations. The great poets of the Aztec world were trained in calmecacs, where codices (picture books of the Aztec history and philosophy) were learned by heart and "sung" aloud in Nahuatl.

26. In his introductory essay "Notes on Chicano Theater" for *Actos*, Luis Valdez describes the performance of resistance: "A demonstration with a thousand

Chicanos, all carrying flags and picket signs, shouting CHICANO POWER! is not the revolution. It is theater about the revolution.... The Raza gets excited, simón, but unless the demonstration evolves into a street battle...it is basically a lot of emotion with very little political power, as Chicanos have discovered by demonstrating, picketing, and shouting before school boards, police departments, and stores to no avail.... [The 1966 Huelga march's] emotional impact was irrefutable. Its actual political power was somewhat less." See *Actos* by Luis Valdez y El Teatro Campesino (San Juan Bautista: Cucaracha Publications, 1971), p. 2. See also *Luis Valdez Early Works* (Houston: Arte Publico Press, 1990).

27. In the Foreword to the 1983 edition of *This Bridge Called My Back: Writings by Radical Women of Color,* I wrote: "The *idea* of Third World feminism proved to be much easier in a book than between real live women (of color)." I lamented what was at the time a lack of multicultural organizing among women of color across racial and ethnic differences. Still, *Bridge,* 85,000 copies and twenty years later, thanks to the vision of its multiple contributors, did serve to raise consciousness and provide an ideological base for political activists working in the area of women of color issues.

28. Paulo Freire. *Pedagogy of the Oppressed.* (New York: Continuum, 1993).

29. In 1995, another example of successful student of color organizing occurred. Nine students and one professor conducted a heavily publicized 14-day hunger strike to protest the underfunded state of Chicano Studies at UCLA. The outcome, although a compromise (students had demanded a fully funded Chicano Studies Department), was the establishment of the Cesar Chavez Chicano Studies Center. For more information on the State of Ethnic Studies, see Bob Wing's "Educate to Liberate" in *Colorlines,* 2:2 (Summer 1999).

30. Freire, p.39.

31. Amy Weaver, *Shawano Leader,* 118:56 (Sunday, March 7, 1999). Washinawatok, Freitas and Gay were believed to be have been abducted and murdered by members of the leftist rebel organization, FARC (Revolutionary Armed Forces of Colombia). The motive for the murders remains unclear; but, at the time of the murders, family members suspected a connection between the deaths and a U.S. grant of $230 million to Colombia to fight the drug war and to crackdown on FARC.

32. Associated Press, *Green Bay Press-Gazette,* Sunday, March 7, 1999.

33. "Sovereignty is More Than Just Power," in *Indigenous Woman,* 2:6 (January 1999).

34. Damien Whitworth, *The Washington Times,* March 13, 2000: "The U'wa have threatened to commit mass suicide by hurling themselves of a cliff, should the 'the blood of Mother Earth' be removed. Mass suicide as an act of resistance against colonization was employed by U'wa ancestors as early as the 17th century in opposition to Spanish rule." Republished in the "U'wa Defense Working Group Website" <http://www.alphacdc.com/ien/uwa-2html>. The Web site also offers pertinent information regarding Al Gore's financially motivated complicity in the violation of the U'wa land rights.

35. Momaday, *The Man Made of Words.*

THE DYING ROAD TO A NATION

1. First presented at the Academy of American Religion Conference in Orlando, Florida in November 1998; subsequently presented in a revised version at the National Association for Chicana/Chicano Studies Conference in San Antonio, Texas on April 30, 1999.

2. Although the incursion of Catholicism into the Américas was essential to the project of colonization, i.e., de-indianization, Mexican Catholicism among the poor and working class is less identified with the Church as institution than with rituals, prayer and ceremony that have, over the centuries, maintained a decidedly Native American cultural sensibility.

3. *Shadow of a Man* is published in *Heroes and Saints and Other Plays* (Albuquerque, NM: West End Press, 1994).

4. On March 26, 1997, police found the 39 bodies of the Heaven's Gate religious cult at a mansion in the suburb of Rancho Santa Fe near San Diego, California. Timed with the celestial arrival of the Hale-Bopp comet, the group's leader Marshall Herff Applewhite (whom members believed was Jesus Christ reincarnated) promised his devotees that a UFO—hidden behind the traveling Hale-Bopp comet—would transport the souls of Heaven's Gate members to heaven if the members joined Applewhite in death. When police discovered the mass suicide, all members were found dressed alike (black clothing and new Nike tennis shoes), each with five dollars and several quarters in their pockets; all were neatly laid out upon beds, and a purple cloth had been draped over each member's head and torso. At the side of each bed was a packet of identification papers and a packed suitcase—preparations for their journey aboard the waiting spaceship.

5. The original Portuguese, "conscientização," refers to the awakening of a "critical consciousness."

6. Co-parenting remains a complex and controversial issue among lesbian parents. Being unable to legally marry or reproduce biologically with our same-sex partner impacts politically and emotionally our (and our children's) experience of motherhood. In the effort to protect historically denied lesbian parental rights, lesbian rights advocates generally view the non-biological parent as having *equal* parental rights with the biological mother (with or without co-adoption of the child). I do not share this position, which precludes the integration of a race and class analysis.

    The Euro-American movement for lesbian parental rights has conveniently ignored the history of the institutionalized removal of children of color and poor children from their biological homes through the social "welfare" system, Indian boarding schools, missionary conversions, slavery, and the courts. Such removals have oftentimes come at great cost to the cultural identity and the spiritual welfare of the child; and this history is not forgotten when the issue of mother-right arises among working-class and poor lesbians and other lesbians of color.

    What was once a movement to ensure that lesbian moms retained custody of their children against homophobic ex-husbands and child welfare agencies has evolved into class warfare between middle-class lesbians. The question of custody often ends up being determined by who can hold out the longest financially in a court battle. Lesbian legal rights advocates, for the most part, tend to side with the non-biological mother (regardless of class, race or cultural concerns) since she is perceived as suffering the greatest discrimination as a dyke in the court system. But what of the child's suffering? It is not, in and of itself, homophobic to "privilege" the lesbian birth-mother's relationship to the child. "Blood matters," as I wrote in *Waiting in the Wings: Portrait of a Queer Motherhood* (Ithaca NY: Firebrand Press, 1997), and it matters most in that first primordial identification with the blood mother.

Related to this issue is the rising number of white lesbian and gay adoptions of children of color. Regardless of my personal empathy for, and recognition of, the genuine affection and deep commitment white lesbians bestow upon their children of color, politically I remain confused and alarmed by the growing phenomenon. Where are those kids' birth mothers? We know the answer: *on drugs, in prison, in poverty. What's a white woman to do? There aren't enough women of color adopting colored babies, isn't a good home better than no home?* Still, I believe our work as lesbian activists has failed to really take into account the economic inequities that separate mothers (lesbian and heterosexual) from their children. As we become increasingly middle-class, we believe we should get what middle-class heterosexuals have: babies. But babies at whose expense? There's got to be more about making queer family than just picking up those children that poor women have been forced to discard.

I would hope that lesbians could begin to look at their own class-biased assumptions about mother-right both in terms of child custody issues and adoption. Can we not re-look at "motherhood" between lesbian partners from a perspective that truly recognizes the child's primary biological connection to his or her mother while still respecting the non-biological parent's relationship with the child. And, when applicable, can we connect the history of loss among poor women and women of color to the question of custody? In terms of adoption, can we go the harder road, in the process, and allow our child access to her biological mother (if she is willing), so that the child can know who her people are and where they came from?

I write these words, knowing on some level I have had the "privilege" of being able to birth my own child. Still, I have had to fight for the full mother-right to my son; and, a decade before, my heart was forced to release a boy (rightfully) to his mother, after a handful of years of we three together. In short, I speak from experience.

7. See *This Bridge Called My Back*, xxvi.

8. Ward Churchill's definition: "[An indigenist is] one who not only takes the rights of indigenous peoples as the highest [political] priority. . . , but who draws on the traditions—bodies of knowledge and corresponding codes of value— evolved over many thousands of years by native peoples the world over." *From a Native Son: Selected Essays in Indigenism, 1985-1995* (Boston: South End Press, 1996), p. 509.

INDEX

A

abuela (Moraga's grandmother), ix-x, xiii-xiv, 3, 84, 87

academy. *See* education

activism: Civil Rights Movement, 121-122, 184, 219 n. 14; feminism and, 97, 119, 222 n. 12; El Movimiento, xi-xii, 96-100, 103-104, 149, 179-180, 184, 224 n. 26; reforms accomplished by, 179, 224 n. 29; spirituality and, 120-123; Third World Strike, 173, 187. *See also* feminism; liberation; politics; revolution

affirmative action: dismantling, v, 163, 179, 217 n. 17, 219 n. 14; establishment, 149, 172

African-Americans: in the arts, 152-153, 161, 172, 218 n. 3; Civil Rights Movement, 121-122, 184, 219 n. 14; Combahee River Collective, 99, 123, 128; gender and, 97, 98, 122, 123-124; slavery of, 153, 161, 170-171, 177-178, 221 n. 3. *See also* ethnicity; women of color

AIDS, 175

Alarcón, Norma, 99, 105

Alexander, Jane, 217 n. 16

alienation. *See* outsiderhood

Almanac of the Dead (Silko), 142

American Indian Movement, 121. *See also* indigenous peoples

Anaya, Rudolfo, 145

Angels in America (Kushner), 156-157

Anzaldúa, Gloria, xii, 93, 99, 107, 176-177

Applewhite, Marshall Herff, 225 n. 2

Aristotle, 153, 154, 159, 161

Arteaga, Alfred, 175

arts: in the academy, 174, 175, 186, 222 n. 10; culture and, 148-150, 167-168, 216 n. 15; economics of, 161, 220 n. 15; oppression in, 159, 190, 217 n. 16. *See also* literature; theater

assimilation, 43, 91, 157, 162, 202,

222 n. 8. *See also* visibility

Aztecs: history, vii, 91-93, 102, 223 n. 25; mythology, iii-iv, vi, vii, 146, 147, 207

Aztlán, iv, v, 38, 120, 177, 214 n. 2

B

Baldwin, James, 150

Bambara, Toni Cade, v, 100

Beloved (Morrison), 167

betrayal, 89-95, 103, 104, 204; La Llorona and, 142, 143, 145

bilingual education: economics and, 183; elimination of, v, 163, 179, 217 n. 17, 220 n. 14; establishment of, 172

"Birth of Huitzilopotchli" myth, iii n, 92, 147

"Black Feminist Statement" (Combahee River Collective), 123

Blacks. *See* African-Americans

Boal, Augosto, 154

body: in the academy, 172, 174-175, 222 n. 12; dissociation from, 36, 40-41, 110, 111, 114, 203; feminism and, 119, 148; sexuality and, 115-116, 203; spirituality and, 111-112, 123, 197

Borderlands/La Frontera (Anzaldúa), 176-177

Bowman, Mr., 95-96

Bracho, Ricardo A., 154-155

Brava Theater Center, 159

bravery, 28, 184-185, 189

Brecht, Bertolt, 154

Brown Berets, 179

C

California: Civil Rights Initiative (Proposition 209), v, 163, 179, 217 n. 17, 219 n. 14; Defense of Marriage Act (Proposition 22), 180, 187, 223 n. 23; English Language in

L

The Labyrinth of Solitude (Paz), 109
land: borders of, 163, 164-167,
  176-177, 189; memory and, iv, 162,
  185, 206
language: culture and, 5, 8, 43, 47,
  131-133, 162; outsiderhood and,
  xii-xiii, 157, 182; revolution and,
  176-178, 190. *See also* bilingual education
lesbianism: in the arts, 49, 160, 172,
  217 n. 16; ethnicity and, 30-37,
  103-108, 115-117, 119-125, 130;
  feminism and, 97, 116-120, 121-124
  and gender, 25-26; liberation of, 121,
  179, 207, 209; love and, 23-24,
  127-131; motherhood and, 143-144,
  185, 201, 205, 225 n. 6; oppression
  of, xi, 44, 102-108, 223 n. 23; story
  of, 32-37; visibility of, viii, 107, 123,
  128, 133, 203. *See also* heterosexism;
  homophobia
liberalism, 173, 179, 188, 209
liberation: economics and, 101, 123,
  153, 180, 209; gay and lesbian, 121,
  130, 179, 207, 209; of indigenous
  peoples, 99, 121, 209, 227 n. 8; sexuality and, xi, 100, 120-123, 124. *See
  also* revolution; activism
Limón, José, 145
literacy, 42, 43, 55, 170-171, 172, 221
  n. 3. *See also* education
Literatura chicana texto y contexto (Shular,
  Ybarra-Frausto, and Sommers), 145
literature, 48, 49, 171-174. *See also* arts
Lizarraga, Silvia S., 97
La Llorona (Weeping Woman),
  142-147, 149-150
López, Sonia A., 103
Lorde, Audre, v, 217 n. 16; on oppression, 48, 50, 127, 170, 173
Los Angeles Rebellion of 1992, 179
love: liberation and, 103, 122, 126,
  129, 205-206; Moraga's toward

mother, 85-86, 94-95, 129; for
  women, 13-14, 23-24
Lugones, María, 143, 216 n. 1

M

Malinche, 91-93, 104-105, 108, 109,
  133
Malintzín Tenepal. *See* Malinche
Mapplethorpe, Robert, 217 n. 16
Ma Rainey's Black Bottom (Wilson), 218 n. 3
marriage: colonization and, 164; feminism and, 100, 102, 120; lesbianism
  and, 129, 223 n. 23, 225 n. 6
Marx, Karl, 98, 143
Marxism, 154, 187
materialism. *See* economics
Maya, 92, 167, 178. *See also* indigenous
  peoples
McCullers, Carson, 172
memory: of childhood, 8, 36, 195-196;
  death and, 200, 213; immigration
  and, 162-168, 180; power and, 47,
  207; of stories, vi, 148, 185
Mendieta, Raquel, 180-181
Menominee Nation, 189-190
mestizos: history of, 91-93, 108,
  162-163, 209, 212; identity of, xiii,
  2, 50, 201, 202-204, 206; immigration and, 162-163, 177; love of, 126,
  129, 131
"Mexican Medea" (Moraga), 146, 150,
  216 n. 7, 217 n. 18
Mexico: border with United States, v,
  164, 176-177, 180, 221 n. 17;
  Catholicism in, ix, 12, 110-111, 196,
  225 n. 2; culture of, 102, 115, 204,
  206; emigration from, 43, 162-165;
  history of, vii, 91-93, 204, 207;
  mythology of, 142-147, 149-150;
  women of, 98, 107, 145, 147, 207.
  See also immigration
Milk, Harvey, 57
Miller, Tim, 217 n. 16
Mirandé, Alfredo, 98
Molina, Papusa, 138

Molina, Vivian, 87-88, 90
Momaday, N. Scott, 176, 177, 190
Morrison, Toni, 167-168
mothers: La Llorona and, 143-148; lesbians as, 143-144, 185, 205, 225 n. 6; matricide, 200-201, 207-209; murder by, xv-xx, 142-144, 145-147; sexism by, 93-95. *See also* Elvira (Moraga's mother); Rafael (Moraga's son); reproduction
El Movimiento, 96-100, 103-104, 121-130, 149, 179-180, 184, 187, 224 n. 26
murder: of children, xv-xx, 142-144, 145-147; of martyrs, 57-58, 184, 200-201, 207-209; sacrifice of relationship, 204; of women, 223 n. 19. *See also* genocide
mythology: Aztecs, iii-iv, vi, vii, 146, 147, 207; Aztlán, iv, 38, 120, 177, 214 n. 2; Hungry Woman, 146-147, 149; La Llorona, 142-147, 149-150; Malinche, 91-93, 104-105, 108, 109, 133

N

National Endowment for the Arts, 149, 217 n. 16, 221 n. 16
Native Americans. *See* indigenous peoples

O

Occidental Petroleum Corporation, 189
O'Hara, Robert, 171, 172
oppression: in the arts, 154, 158-162, 190, 217 n. 16; education and, iv, 188, 190; internalization of, 46-50, 109, 125, 143, 158; multiplicity of, 44-46, 99-100, 119, 123-126; sexuality and, 44, 100-102, 123, 126-131. *See also* economics; heterosexism; homophobia; patriarchy; racism; sexism
outsiderhood: education and, ix, xi, 46-47, 173, 175, 180-181; ethnicity and, 87, 206; lesbianism and, xi, 26, 108, 114-116, 172, 204

P

Parks, Suzan-Lori, 156
passing, ethnic, 43, 47, 50, 61-64, 89, 202-204. *See also* visibility
patriarchy: lesbianism and, 49, 104 n, 105; reproduction and, 100-101, 102, 147, 206-207, 208-209; women of color under, 111, 120, 123, 124. *See also* sexism; oppression
Paz, Octavio, 109, 115
Pedagogy of the Oppressed (Freire), 186
pleasure, 5, 109, 110, 113-114, 116, 198
Poblano, Manuel, 90-91
Poetics (Aristotle), 153, 154
politics: in the academy, 180, 186, 188; arts and, 149, 162, 217 n. 16; gender and, 104, 108, 116-117, 119; immigration and, 165; sexuality and, 116-117, 124, 128, 129-130, 158; spirituality and, 120-123. *See also* activism; feminism; liberation; Propositions; revolution
pornography, 119
postmodernism, 176-177, 179, 180, 188
Pratt, Minnie Bruce, 217 n. 16
Proposition 21 (California), 180, 187, 223n. 23
Proposition 22 (California), 180, 187, 223n. 23
Proposition 187 (California), 149, 163, 217n. 17, 219n. 13
Proposition 209 (California), 163, 217 n. 17, 219 n. 14
Proposition 227 (California), 163, 217 n. 17, 220 n. 14

Q

Quetzalcoatl, 92
Quintanales, Mirtha, 117

R

race. *See* African-Americans; ethnicity; indigenous peoples; Jews; racism; whites

© 1993 JEAN WEISINGER

© 1982 BARBARA ADAMS

ABOUT THE AUTHOR

Cherríe Moraga is a poet, playwright and essayist, and the co-editor of the classic feminist anthologies *This Bridge Called My Back: Writings by Radical Women of Color* and *Cuentos: Stories by Latinas*. She is the author of numerous plays including *Shadow of a Man* and *Watsonville: Some Place Not Here* (which won the Fund for New American Plays Award in 1991 and 1995, respectively), and *Heroes and Saints*, which earned the Pen West Award for Drama in 1992. Her two most recent books include a collection of poems and essays entitled *The Last Generation* and a memoir, *Waiting in the Wings: Portrait of a Queer Motherhood*. A collection of her plays, *Some Place Not Here*, will be published in 2001. Ms. Moraga is also a recipient of the National Endowment for the Arts' Theatre Playwrights' Fellowship and is the Artist-in-Residence in the Departments of Drama and Spanish and Portuguese at Stanford University.

Born in the Los Angeles area in 1952, Moraga now lives in Oakland with her lover and their children. To arrange speaking engagements, please contact South End Press.

ABOUT SOUTH END PRESS

South End Press is a nonprofit, collectively run book publisher with over 200 titles in print. Since our founding in 1977, we have tried to meet the needs of readers who are exploring, or are already committed to, the politics of radical social change. Our goal is to publish books that encourage critical thinking and constructive action on the key political, cultural, social, economic, and ecological issues shaping life in the United States and in the world. In this way, we hope to give expression to a wide diversity of democratic social movements and to provide an alternative to the products of corporate publishing.

Through the Institute for Social and Cultural Change, South End Press works with other political media projects—Z Magazine; Speakout, a speakers' bureau; Alternative Radio; and the Publishers Support Project—to expand access to information and critical analysis. If you would like a free catalog of South End Press books, please write to us at: South End Press, 7 Brookline St., Cambridge MA 02139 or visit our website at http://www.southendpress.org.

RELATED TITLES